SUSAN ALIC
MISS CARTER A

SUSAN ALICE KERBY was born Elizabeth Burton, in Cairo, 4 October 1908.

She lived in Canada from 1912 where she eventually married and divorced John Theodore Aitken. In Canada she worked for the *Windsor Star* before returning to England in 1935, living in London and working in advertising, public relations and journalism. During the Second World War she worked part-time as a fire watcher, and published three novels, the last of which was *Miss Carter and the Ifrit*. From 1958 she wrote a number of popular history books under the name Elizabeth Burton.

The author later lived in Witney, Oxfordshire, where she died 30 July 1990.

TITLES BY SUSAN ALICE KERBY
(ELIZABETH BURTON)

Fiction

Cling to Her, Waiting (1939) (as Elizabeth Burton)

Fortnight in Frascati (1940)

Miss Carter and the Ifrit (1945)

Many Strange Birds (1947, aka *Fortune's Gift*)

Gone to Grass (1948, aka *The Roaring Dove*)

Mr Kronion (1949)

Non-Fiction (all as Elizabeth Burton)

The Elizabethans at Home (1958)

The Jacobeans at Home (1962)

Here Is England (1965)

The Georgians at Home, 1714-1830 (1967)

The Early Victorians at Home (1972)

SUSAN ALICE KERBY

MISS CARTER AND THE IFRIT

With an introduction by
Elizabeth Crawford

DEAN STREET PRESS

A Furrowed Middlebrow Book
FM37

Published by Dean Street Press 2019

Published by licence, issued under the UK Orphan Works
Licensing Scheme.

First published in 1945 by Hutchinson & Co.

Cover by DSP

ISBN 978 1 913054 31 1

www.deanstreetpress.co.uk

TO CHARLES

WHO IS SOMETHING OF AN
IFRIT HIMSELF

INTRODUCTION

BY DESCRIBING *Miss Carter and the Ifrit* as 'An Arabian Night of Adventure', the London correspondent of the Lancashire Evening Post (3 October 1945) was promising the reader a novel to transport them from the daily difficulties, such as rationing, that the immediate aftermath of war entailed. For although the eponymous Miss Carter apparently shared their situation she was blessed with an abundance of good things. 'There were pomegranates, glowing like pale garnets in a deep blue bowl. Frilled by green leaves and on a flat yellow dish was a bunch of black grapes, powdered with silver, each grape perfect and the size of a small plum'. How sensuous these images must have seemed in 1945. The delectable fruits had, however, only appeared through the intervention of an Ifrit, a genie inadvertently released by Miss Georgina Carter in her flat in an 'old-fashioned mansion block' in St John's Wood. The author had set her story close to home for through the war, and after, she lived at 23 Abbey Road, St John's Wood.

Susan Alice Kerby was the pen name of [Alice] Elizabeth Burton (1908-1990), who had been born in Cairo, the daughter of Richard Burton (c.1879-c.1908). He was probably English, while his wife Alice (1884-1962 *née* Kerby) was Canadian. The couple had married in Chicago in 1907. It is to be presumed that Richard Burton died around the time of Elizabeth's birth because after returning from Egypt to her home town, Windsor, Ontario, Alice was described as Burton's widow when she remarried in October 1909. To strengthen the 'Arabian Nights' association the *Lancashire Evening Post* reviewer claimed Elizabeth as a descendant of Sir Richard Burton, the Arabist and traveller, an inheritance as improbable as the appearance of the Ifrit. Elizabeth Burton did, however, honour the memory of her father, dedicating her 1949 novel *Mr. Kronion* to him with the phrase *'Arbor viva, tacui; mortua, cano'* (which translates as 'When I was part of a living tree, I was silent. Now dead, I sing'). That she felt entirely happy with the family in which she grew up is evident in the fact she dedicated another novel, *Many Strange Birds* (1947), to 'My Mother and Father A.G.D. and G.M.D.', the initials of her mother and step-father, George Duck.

We first catch a glimpse of Elizabeth Burton in 1926 when, described as a student, she sailed, unaccompanied, from Naples to the USA after spending time in Rome, where she had stayed with an aunt and studied music and history. In 1929, still a student, she again paid a visit to Europe, perhaps visiting English relatives. Back in Canada she launched her career as a journalist and over the next few years worked in radio and in advertising. In 1935 she again spent some time in England, arriving back in Canada in June and then in November, in Windsor, married John Aitken, a fellow journalist. However, the marriage seems to have been short lived; Elizabeth later recorded that in 1936 she decided to move to England. At some point there was a divorce and in 1950 Elizabeth changed her name by deed poll from 'Aitken' back to 'Burton'. However, she maintained her link with Canada, acting as the London correspondent of the *Windsor Star* from 1945-1965.

By 1939 Elizabeth Burton had settled in the Abbey Road flat, working as an advertising copywriter. Also at this address was Désirée Grotrain, with whom Elizabeth lived for the rest of her life. She was clearly devoted to Désirée's family, dedicating her 1948 novel, *Gone to Grass*, to her parents, Sir Herbert and Lady Grotrain, 'Because I am so fond of them and they are both so kind to me', and in her will leaving substantial bequests to Désirée's nephew, Sir Christain Grotrain, and his children. By 1950 she and Désirée also had a country cottage, Grass Ground Farm, at Hailey in Oxfordshire. At least in part, it would have appealed to Elizabeth's appreciation of historic surroundings, for, apart from her six novels, Elizabeth Burton was the author of several works of popular social history. The first was *The Elizabethans at Home*, published in 1958, followed by *The Jacobeans at Home*, *The Georgians at Home*, and *The Early Victorians at Home*. Each book was illustrated by her friend, the artist Felix Kelly, whose aesthetic sense she shared. In her will she left £1000 each to Kelly and his partner, Vernon

Russell-Smith. *The Early Victorians at Home* was published in 1972 and, although new editions of some of the earlier books in the series were issued in the 1970s, this would seem to mark the end of Elizabeth Burton's writing career.

Elizabeth Burton's first novel, *Cling to Her, Waiting*, written under her own name, was published in the autumn of 1939 and her second, *A Fortnight at Frascati*, for which she used the 'Susan Alice Kerby' pen name, appeared in 1940. There was then a five-year gap until the publication of *Miss Carter and the Ifrit* in 1945, suggesting that in the interim she was engaged on wartime business with little time to write novels. Miss Carter worked 'in Censorship' but there is no evidence to tell us how Elizabeth Burton was employed, although it was possibly in some similar capacity. Miss Carter is somewhat older than the author but she does reflect something of Elizabeth Burton's interests. For instance, before the spectacular arrival of Abu Shiháb Miss Carter is looking forward to spending the evening reading a biography of Lady Hester Stanhope, the formidable Middle Eastern traveller 'for whom she had a secret admiration'. The author clearly shared this interest in the region of her birth, with the novel abounding in seductive descriptions and stories of the Orient.

The Ifrit announced himself Miss Carter's slave but she, being Anglo-Saxon, would have none of this, declaring him a friend and naming him 'Joe', for Stalin, then an ally. Joe not only produced delicious meals but on occasion decorated her sitting room with 'a riot of silken hangings, Oriental rugs and piled cushions. The old-fashioned high ceiling was hidden by a billowing canopy of heavy silk, striped in cerulean and white: suspended from the centre was an ornate bowl-shaped lamp of pierced silver, which gave off a soft but slightly smoky light'. Moreover he infiltrated Hitler's Eagle's Nest at Berchtesgaden and, seeing him communing with his own, evil, Ifrit, discovered the secret of the dictator's power. Alas Joe knew this was something he could not withstand and Miss Carter's hope of learning something that might end the war came to naught. However, Joe did reunite Miss Carter with the love of her youth, even wafting her through the skies, protected from the fire of the ack-ack guns, to bring her to him as he lay injured in a North African hospital.

Miss Carter and the Ifrit would appear to have appealed to the reading public, going into a seventh impression by 1947. A little fantasy did not go amiss in the immediate post-war world.

Elizabeth Crawford

CHAPTER I

To LOOK AT Miss Georgina Carter you would never have suspected that a woman of her age and character would have allowed herself to be so wholeheartedly mixed up with an Ifrit. For Georgina Carter was nearing fifty (she was forty-seven to be exact) and there was something about her long, plain face, her long upper lip, her long, thin hands and feet that marked her very nearly irrevocably as a spinster. That she wore her undistinguished clothes well, had a warm, human smile, was fond of the theatre and had never occasioned anyone a moment's trouble or worry, were minor virtues which had never got her very far.

Georgina herself now accepted her state and age without apparent hatred or remorse; in fact she assured herself she was rather glad to be approaching fifty. It was, she felt, a comfortable age, an age past expectation, hope or surprise. Nothing very shattering, nothing very devastating could happen to one after that age. It was a placid, safe harbour. One could indeed then spend the rest of one's life fairly comfortably with a job in the Censorship for the duration, a smallish private income (which, unfortunately, tended to get smaller) and a flat in an old-fashioned block in St. John's Wood, untroubled and untormented by any violent emotion or gross physical change.

Now it is well known that Ifrits are seldom if ever mentioned in connection with people of Miss Georgina Carter's type. In fact, Ifrits prefer young, seductive princesses of beautiful, love-lorn princes. They are the companions of the Bath, or more strictly the Hammam, the ravishers of the harem, the servants of kings and sultans, and rarely have anything to do with anyone of lesser rank than a merchant prince or a Wazir and his family.

One Saturday afternoon, however, during a very cold spell, Miss Carter happened to look out of her window, and there below her in the street was an undistinguished little man with a small cart filled with blocks of wood and crying his wares to the skies. To Miss Carter, who was having trouble with her coal merchant and who had been waiting for weeks for a delivery of coal, the wood blocks looked like a temporary solution of her problem. The problem was how long it would take before she slowly froze to death. Accordingly she rushed down the stairs into the street, stopped the vendor, inquired the price and for fourteen shillings bought one hundred wood blocks. It was impossible to store them in the coal bin, for that had to be kept empty just in case the coal merchant ever did relent and deliver her order. So Miss Carter had the man bring the blocks up to her first floor flat and presently they were stored incongruously but neatly under the wash basin in her immaculate green and white bathroom. The blocks themselves, though small, were liberally soaked with tar; they were, in fact, road blocks.

Miss Carter promised herself a treat that evening. She would have her supper off a tray in front of an open fire. It couldn't be so very wicked and contrary to the fuel economy campaign to have a blazing fire just for once. After all, she'd been without any heat for a fortnight. (The electric heater had been at a shop for three months being repaired.) Miss Carter had had to go to bed every evening at seven for warmth and lie there regretting that the flats she occupied were without either central heating or service Besides, Margaret Mackenzie had given her an egg— and an egg, an honest-to-goodness egg in a shell laid by a kind hen the previous Thursday, called for some sort of celebration!

And afterwards, she promised herself, she would sit in front of her blazing fire and finish the socks she was knitting for her nephew Henry (now finishing his training in Canada); or she might start reading that biography of Lady Hester Stanhope (for whom she had a secret admiration) which she'd got from the Times Book Club that morning.

So, enjoying in anticipation the evening before her, Miss Carter got through what otherwise would have been a dull afternoon of housework, mending stockings and washing and ironing underclothes, in the pleasantest manner possible.

It was somewhere between 8.45 and 9 o'clock that evening that the "Thing" happened. Miss Carter remembered the time afterwards because she had been trying to find out how long two road blocks lasted. She had lit them at a quarter to seven, had enjoyed her egg, washed up the dishes, finished one sock and observed that it was time for another block (noting that two blocks lasted nearly two hours so that one more block would take her to bedtime) and that the news would be on in fifteen minutes. So putting a third block on the fire she settled down to a quarter of an hour of Lady Hester before the news. . . .

The next thing she knew was that there was a loud explosion. The room seemed filled with smoke. The floor rocked. She was hurled from her chair. Her last thought before losing consciousness was: "I didn't hear the warning—"

When she came to she was lying on the sofa, which stood against the wall facing the windows. It took her a moment to realize where she was. Yes, it was her own living room. There on the left was the fireplace, on the right the walnut Queen Anne tallboy inherited from her mother. A strong smell of sulphur pervaded the air, but the wireless was still on and Big Ben was booming its nine deliberate strokes. It seemed very curious that the house should have been struck by a bomb and that the lights and wireless should still function. She thought perhaps she might be unconscious or dreaming, but Frederick Allen announcing himself and reading the news headlines assured her that this was not so. She sat up gingerly. Odd, she seemed to be perfectly all right. The room appeared to be all right too. There was her knitting bag quite undisturbed on the little table beside the fire, the few small ornaments on the mantelpiece were still there unmoved and unshattered, the pictures were straight, their glass unbroken—nothing damaged or out of place! It was all very extraordinary and a trifle unnerving! You couldn't just be blown across a room privately by yourself, an isolated phenom-enon as it were, and have everything else left untouched—or could you? Of course, blast did very curious things sometimes. It couldn't have been a purely self-created effect—a nerve storm in fact—or could it?

Her eyes travelled slowly round the room again noting every reassuring detail until they rested on the tallboy which stood against the wall facing the fireplace. And suddenly she gave a little gasp and sat bolt upright. Her spine prickled, her mouth was suddenly dry. For there on the floor, protruding from the far side of the tallboy, were what appeared to be a pair of slippers. They were large, they were red, they were leather, they were obviously masculine—and they had curiously pointed toes that curled back over what might or might not be an instep, depending upon whether the slippers were occupied or not.

Miss Georgina Carter had never considered herself a brave woman, or even a very clever one, but she had always rather prided herself on her good common sense. Her common sense now told her that the slippers couldn't be there. Her eyes told her that they were. Which could she trust? If she believed her eyes, could she get quietly into the hall where the telephone was and dial 999? No, the door creaked and, furthermore, what would she say? "There is a pair of man's red slippers beside my tallboy." Too absurd! Rather reminiscent of those vulgar stories one unfortunately heard occasionally, about spinsters who hoped for a burglar under the bed.

No, she would have to believe her eyes until her common sense proved them wrong; she would obviously have to confront the slippers herself!

She rose very quietly, reached for her knitting bag, abstracted a long, sharp, steel needle and, thus armed, crossed silently to the tallboy. She stood, back to the wall, right flank protected by the side of the cabinet, knitting needle tightly gripped in her right hand. Then she said in what she hoped was a firm, clear voice: "Come out of there."

Nothing happened. She waited a moment. "Come out of there," she repeated. Still nothing happened.

How perfectly silly, she thought, my common sense was right.

Those slippers are sheer imagination. I must see a doctor. Or perhaps my eyes need examining.

She left her hiding place and walked around to the other side of the tallboy.

Then she knew she was crazy. There, huddled in the angle formed by the wall and the cabinet was a very large, very dark man. His clothes were quite extraordinary. He wore a pair of curious green breeches, full at the top and narrowing down to fit tightly over his calves. His wide cut coat was high buttoned and made of heavy ruby red satin, embroidered with strange designs in gold and silver thread. On his head was an elaborate coral coloured turban ornamented with a bright bejewelled feather.

They stood and gazed at each other for half a minute without moving or speaking. In that half minute Georgina was vividly conscious of all the curious details of his appearance, conscious too that her heart was beating wildly and that her stomach felt as if she had rapidly gone down in a lift. Then she found a voice—it was obviously not hers—and said: "Who are you?"

At this sound the man suddenly fell on his knees at her feet, prostrating himself on the floor and crying a mad jumble of sounds as he beat his turbaned head against the carpet.

At least he seems to be afraid of me, she thought with relief and, as this gave her courage, said in her own voice: "Please speak English. And for goodness sake get up."

The man ceased banging his head, but remained on the floor. "Oh, princess, who is as lovely as the young moon . . ."

"What!" gasped Miss Carter. Poor fellow; he was obviously as mad as a hatter—or was she?

". . . whose skin is white as the camomile flower . . ."

"Don't talk gibberish, my man! . . ."

"Who hath released me from a terrible enchantment . . ." the prostrate figure continued.

Miss Carter bent down and grasped the man's shoulder. "Get up," she ordered.

This had the desired effect; he rose to his feet.

"If you are a parachutist," she told him grimly, "you can't get around me that way, so there's no use your trying." She emphasized the remark by prodding him with the knitting needle. He felt solid enough at any rate. Did figments of the imagination feel solid, she wondered, and how on earth was she ever going to explain this to Dr. Roberts without getting herself locked up in an asylum? "Please move over to that chair," she continued in the deliberate and rather loud voice one reserves for the deaf or foreigners, waving him to a chair by the fire.

The man bowed and touched his breast, his lips, his forehead rapidly with the fingers of his right hand. "To hear is to obey," he said and crossed to the fireplace and sat down.

She seated herself opposite him. "Now," she said, "you'd better confess everything. I am not in the least afraid of you, as you can see. And unless you want to be handed over to the police you'd better tell me quite truthfully all about yourself. Do you understand?"

"Police?" He looked quite blank. "A curious word. What is its meaning, pray?"

The man was obviously and perhaps harmlessly crazy; but, of course, you could never tell with foreigners. Perhaps he was just trying to trick her.

"Police," she enlightened him, "are guardians of the law and they arrest people and cause them to be imprisoned if they break the law—any law. You don't want to be imprisoned, do you?"

A look of horror crept over the man's face. "Not again, O mighty one," he wailed, "it is too much. My punishment has been sufficient unto the day of death."

An escaped convict! she thought. That's it! No doubt stole those curious clothes from a theatrical costumier's. I must inform the police at once. Her thoughts raced wildly, but how can I—he'd never let me out of the room. Perhaps I can keep him talking—make him tea—offer to conceal him—win his confidence—then, when he sleeps, if he ever does, notify the police.

"Well, well," she said, pulling herself together with an effort "We won't talk of prison as I see it distresses you. Tell me, what is your name?"

"Abu Shiháb," he said, leaping up from the chair and bowing deeply. "Abu Shiháb, your slave."

"We don't have slaves in this country," she informed him. "At least, not officially. Oh, do sit down again and tell me who you are . . ."

"I, oh Mistress of the Secrets of Sulayman," he said, "I am an Ifrit."

This meant nothing to Georgina, but she felt it called for some remark. "You speak very good English," she complimented him. "I am sure I couldn't speak—er—er—Ifriti nearly so well, even if I did know the language, which, of course, I don't. We English are really so terribly insular and it's perfectly shocking, of course, but I'm afraid I don't even know where—er—If—is. Do tell me, please." She hoped her interest sounded genuine; she was beginning to be afraid again. The man was undoubtedly a sailor, come to England on a ship from the East, and he had committed some crime and been imprisoned. Horrible! How had he got to her flat? Why?

The man looked at her in wonder. "I do not understand thy words, Oh moon flower," he said. "I am an Ifrit."

"Yes, but what *is* an Ifrit?" she cried, unable to keep up the pretence any longer. "Where did you come from? Why are you here?"

He bent down and picked up one of the wooden blocks from the hearth. "Here," he said, tapping it with a finger, "from a piece of wood like this. Only fire could save me. For centuries, nay, thousands of years, I despaired. Now by your power you have freed me. I am your slave, bound to you until certain conditions shall be fulfilled by an age-old custom. What you command, I perform. Your slightest wish is my law."

Miss Carter gave up trying to understand. The man was a criminal and insane to boot. Unless she herself were insane. Had she established herself sufficiently in his confidence to suggest that she leave the room to make tea (then she could dial 999 or run out of the flat and call for help). Or would he follow her? She'd try it anyway, for so far he appeared to bear her no malice.

"How very interesting it all is," she said in a rather affected social voice, and hoped he believed her. "And I'm sure after all that, you'd like a cup of tea or perhaps coffee . . ."

"Tea—coffee—" he smiled politely, but the words had obviously not penetrated to his brain. "Tea—coffee—" he repeated.

"You are pleased to speak words that your slave cannot comprehend."

"Refreshment," she said, desperately trying to think of a word that would make him understand. "I cannot offer you a glass of milk because of rationing . . ."

"Refreshment!" A genuine smile spread over his face. "Milk," he repeated. "Will the princess put her delicate hands up to conceal her eyes for one moment."

That's done it, Miss Carter thought desperately. That's given him just the opportunity he's been waiting for—what a fool I was to think I could get away with it. He's been playing with me all along. My hands over my eyes! Well, I'd rather not look on at my own murder.

"Please," he said again, "the hands over the eyes."

She obeyed his command with resignation, closing her eyes as well as concealing them. Once more she was conscious of a faint, acrid, sulphurous smell, a warm breeze brushed against her face.

"An it please you to look now," Abu Shiháb requested, most politely for a villain.

Miss Carter dropped her hands, opened her eyes. Then she closed them again quickly. She opened them once more. It was still there—so was Abu Shiháb. He waited smiling and bowing beside a wonderfully wrought silver tray which was placed on the table where her knitting bag had so recently rested. And the tray was burdened with curiously shaped, vividly coloured dishes, and these dishes were filled with strange and wonderful fruits and sweetmeats. There were pomegranates, glowing like pale garnets in a deep blue bowl. Frilled by green leaves and on a flat yellow dish was a bunch of black grapes powdered with silver, each grape perfect and the size of a small plum. Warm, brown dates contrasted with fat bright oranges. Purple figs and smooth-skinned apricots made a pyramid on a base of emerald green glass. Flat sugared cakes and squares of a substance resembling Turkish Delight spilled out of oval shaped turquoise boxes. Small stemmed dishes held in their chalices mounds of sorbet which gave off a faint lemony perfume. There were several long throated flagons of emerald glass set in frames of beaten silver, with goblets to match.

Despite herself Georgina clapped her hands and gave a small cry of delight.

The ballet music from *Rosamunde* suddenly filled the room. She had forgotten that the wireless was on. She had in fact not been conscious of one word of the now finished news. There was something so fantastic, so wonderful about the food—the music—the perfumed warmth of the room that she quite forgot her fear.

Abu Shiháb, however, was on the floor again, beating his head. "Oh, Queen of the Jann," he chanted, "Oh, supreme ruler of the Djinni, Marids and lfrits, your miserable slave prostrates himself at the feet of such superior wisdom and power and begs that you—"

"Oh, *do* get up," she interrupted crossly, "and for heaven's sake stop saying you're my slave. And tell me, please, is all this fruit real, or is it a delusion?" She put out her hand and touched an orange tentatively. It felt as solid as Abu Shiháb.

"Yes, my mistress," he told her, "it is real—real as the music of the heavens which you command with word and gesture." He rose to his feet. "Abu Shiháb, unworthy though he is, will wait upon you. Wine, water and sorbet to cool the palate and delight the senses—milk, honey, fruits and sweetmeats to feed the body and strengthen the soul . . ."

Swiftly and deftly he poured a dark liquid from one of the flagons into a goblet, added water from another flagon and handed her the mixture. She did not even stop to wonder if it were a Borgia cup before lifting it to her lips. It was sweet and tasted of figs and lemon. "Delicious," she murmured, "do have some yourself, Abu—er—"

"Shiháb," he supplied. "It is not meet that the servant sit at the same table as the master . . ."

"But I'm not your master," she said, "you are not my servant. I don't know how these foods got here or where they came from. Certainly not from my larder. Couldn't you just stop fussing and talking in riddles for a moment and sit down and explain everything to me . . ." The drink was beautifully warming; she helped herself to an apricot.

"If you command me to do so . . ." he answered her.

"Very well then, I command you. Does that satisfy you? Just a minute, though, till I turn off the wireless." She crossed the room and switched the button off. "There," she said, "now we can eat and talk comfortably." She was not in the slightest afraid now, not even very surprised any more. Whatever happened next would all be part of this fantastic dream. She only hoped that she would be able to remember it all in the morning. She sat down opposite him again and reached for a sugared cake.

"Yours is a potent magic," he said, and there was admiration and awe in his tone. "You speak and strange music starts. You make a little click and music stops. Who is it that you have ensorcelled in that box yonder in the corner? It must be countless people. First the sound of mighty bells, then the voice of the man, then music from a hundred unknown instruments. My tongue clove to the roof of my mouth when I found myself in your terrible and wonderful presence."

"But this is most extraordinary," she said, "*most* extraordinary. Do you really think I keep people locked up in that box?"

"It is obvious, oh Wise One," the Ifrit answered.

So he thought her a magician—a sorceress. How perfectly ridiculous and amusing. No doubt that was why he hadn't risked murdering her. He was obviously a very primitive type, one who could be kept in order by fear and superstition. So much the better then if he thought her a super Maskelyne and Devant. In the end, she supposed, she'd have to give him up to the police but (here he handed her a peeled orange divided into plump, juicy sections) but for the present . . . She wished she knew, really knew, if it were all a dream or if she had been caught in some violent psychological upheaval. The orange smelled and tasted just as she remembered oranges had tasted. Did one really taste things in a dream? Did one really dream in colour? And what would Freud say!

"So it's obvious," she answered him. "Very well then. Now, Mr. Shiháb, tell me your story—and tell me the truth . . ."

"Hearing and obedience," said Abu Shiháb.

CHAPTER II

"Know then," he said, settling himself back into his chair, ". . . that I was of those unbelieving Ifrits who incurred the wrath of the mighty Sulayman—peace be upon him. For of my tribe there was one who aspired to his throne and to his ring wherein lay his power. And for this and for other crimes against the race of man, Sulayman made war upon us and we, being defeated, he laid upon us various enchantments. Some of us he turned to stone or placed in copper cucurbites. Others he ensorcelled in bottles and jars and sealed them with his great seal. Still others were sealed within caskets and buried in the earth or cast into the sea. There was endless variety to the forms he gave us. I, who was discovered in the garden of his harem, he walled up in a young tree on a lonely hill—only fire could release me—but he put his mark upon the tree so that those who passed might know and would therefore not lay hands upon me . . ."

"Excuse me," Miss Carter put in, for she was feeling slightly confused—possibly the wine—"but do I understand you to say that you were once—er—a tree?"

He nodded. "Yes," he said, "a cedar of Lebanon; walled within it I was, unable to escape. I could, of my essence, flow within the confines of the tree, explore it root and branch, but that was the extent of my freedom."

"And when, may I ask, did all this happen?" Miss Carter reached for a few grapes.

"In the reign of the mighty Sulayman—Sulayman-ibn-Daud—who is truly called the Wonderful . . . to whom the earth gave homage . . ."

"Sulayman!"

"Yes . . . he of the three hundred wives and concubines—of the treasure houses—of the uncounted riches—he who tamed great Sheba's queen."

"King Solomon!" Miss Carter ejaculated and dropped a grape. Somehow she felt that the story was not only incredible, but slightly blasphemous. ". . . but he lived, so far as we know, nearly three thousand years ago!"

"It was written," Abu Shiháb said gravely, "that my years of captivity should number thirty centuries . . . so be it . . ."

"But good Heavens!" she exclaimed, "how old *are* you?"

"I do not know, O princess, perhaps three hundred centuries—perhaps three times three hundred."

For the life of her, Georgina could think of nothing better to say than, "You certainly don't look it."

"I was created with creation," he continued. "We Ifrits of the Jann were of two kinds, the good, the evil; the believing, the unbelieving. My name, Abu Shiháb, means, in your language, 'father of the shooting star' and later . . ." here he hung his head as though in shame and she could see a great pearl the size of a horse-chestnut, ornamenting the top of his turban, ". . . later," he went on in a low voice, "those words came to mean evil spirit, for I was, in those days, evil. I belonged to the darkness like my brethren; we were against all mankind . . ."

"Then you are . . . er . . . really a . . . er . . . spirit."

"Yes, all powerful Queen, a spirit, but no longer evil. My punishment has taught me what Sulayman in his great wisdom knew it would teach me. Now there remains for me the test, but when or how it comes I know not. I, thy slave, Abu Shiháb, am no longer evil. I have forsworn my wicked ways. . . ."

"I'm glad to hear it," Georgina said truthfully. "Now that you're out of pris. . . er . . . confinement, I trust that everything will be all right. That you will be . . . good . . . and happy." She finished lamely. What on earth *did* one say to a reformed evil spirit one met in a dream anyway? "But how did you come to England, of all places?" she asked.

He poured out some milk, mixed in a little honey, and handed it to her. "For centuries," he said, "I was with the tree, standing on that lonely hill top. The tree grew in height and girth. Its roots pushed deep into the earth. It became a giant tree, a landmark. In time the mark that Sulayman had placed upon it became bark covered. Generations came and passed away like mist. Presently the legend of the Ifrit in the tree was forgotten. At one time soldiers with fair skins and bright breast-plates, wearing curious helmets, bearing banners and speaking a strange, harsh tongue, passed me by . . . sometimes resting under my shade. That was a confused period and times were troubled. I never understood what was happening. My tree grew even bigger. I had more space in which to move and to reflect . . . sometimes at night I would utter strange cries and disturb the lovers who dallied beneath my branches. But this was difficult for me, for it was hard to make myself audible.

"Then one day, long afterwards, men came; they came up the hill from the direction of the distant, glittering sea. They laid an axe at the base of the tree. I had to decide swiftly whether to withdraw into the roots or flow into the trunk. I chose the latter course, for at least the trunk would be moved now and I had grown weary of being rooted to one spot. They cut down the tree and with chains and oxen hauled it away and me with it. And so they took us to a town by the edge of a great sea; they worked on the tree with axes and with planes squaring and smoothing so that I was forced to withdraw further and further into its heart. Finally they built us into a great ship. My tree became the strong, solid beam supporting the decks. I went to sea, I changed hands many times, I was rebuilt often. Then people of a country once called Iberia possessed me finally. It was with them I came to England, for I was one of a great fleet dispersed by a mighty tempest. My ship foundered on a rocky coast. The pounding of the sea freed my beam . . . I was cast ashore . . ."

"Incredible," Miss Carter murmured, fascinated. "To think of all the history you've lived through. Of course, lived is hardly the right word, I know. I wonder when all that happened—when you came to England, I mean . . ."

"Not long ago as time is measured," Abu Shiháb told her, "not very long ago when I was discovered on that shore. I must still have been in fine condition and of superior quality for I was soon hauled away again and sold to a man who was delighted with me. He built me into the hall of a great country house. He took great pride in me and would point me out to his guests and roar with laughter and slap his thigh as if at some great joke. The winds howled, the rain came down as if the heavens hated this country; there was little hot sunshine and the language was coarse and strange to my ears. Soon after I had found a place in this house a great Queen came to visit the master. I had not looked upon a queen for centuries. She came and in the rush light I saw her. She was small. Her stiff bejewelled dress seemed to be holding her up. Her hair was the colour with which our women stain their hands and feet. Her heavily ringed hands were beautiful—but dirty. I thought of the queens I had known in my free days and, though this woman was different, I knew that she too was a queen and possessed of greatness. I had seen unveiled women before in this country, but I had never yet looked upon a queen unveiled and I was afraid. Afraid of the punishment that would follow, as it followed after the incident of the harem . . ."

"I do not think Elizabeth would have punished any man for looking upon her face; on the contrary . . ." Miss Carter put in softly.

"No!" Abu Shiháb said, "yet she seemed to wear the look of a woman who punished men—as if to punish herself for some deep-rooted sense of guilt. Or perhaps in hatred of herself—or because she was afraid . . ."

"It's a pity you didn't learn more about her—see more of her," Georgina said with genuine regret. "It would be fascinating to know, besides you could have made a fortune now with such knowledge."

"There were always so many people about," the Ifrit said a trifle peevishly, "that I lost interest. I dozed sometimes for years on end, and always I hoped that the great house would burn down and I should be freed by the ordeal of fire. But my time had not yet been fulfilled. There were still other indignities to come for the great house became neglected; it decayed and in the time of another queen it was torn down. This was several centuries later, of course . . ."

"It can't have been Anne—it must have been Victoria." Georgina spoke half aloud. "Tell me," she said to him, "do you know anything about this other queen . . . ?"

"Only very little. I saw her but once, riding in a carriage preceded and followed by a great throng of people, some in vehicles, others on fine horses. In that throng I saw descendants of those faces I had once known so long before in my own country—the dark skin, the beautiful liquid eyes. Princes on horseback they were—splendid, glittering, beautiful. Whilst I . . ." he swallowed hard, "whilst I was but a support for a great stand whereon many people sat . . ."

"But how could wood last as long as you did!" Miss Carter exclaimed. "Even cedar wood, durable as it is . . ."

"What is written is written," the Ifrit answered. "The tree of Sulayman would last as long as Sulayman ordered it to."

"Well, I suppose if one accepts the story," she admitted, "one must accept that as well. But what happened after that?"

"The stand was torn down. I ended in a place with much other wood. I was still a beam, but much thinner by now. The beam was cut into those blocks." He pointed to the paving blocks beside the fireplace. "As the saw went through I withdrew myself to the farthest end of the beam. Thus I preserved myself—in an agony of despair and discomfort. My prison had grown small again; smaller even than it had been at first. I thought the wheel had turned nearly full circle, my imprisonment must be nearing its end . . ."

"And so it was, you poor thing," Miss Carter said warmly. "How horrible for you."

"Sixty years I spent in a road," the Ifrit said bitterly, "with great things rolling over me. Things I never even saw, except from underneath. When I no longer felt the beat of horses' hooves, I was desolated and all was noise, confusion and bad smells. Lately, though, even that died away . . . but there were other noises and great explosions. After one of these I found myself dislodged from my place. I was sold to the man with the cart . . ."

". . . And I bought you this morning," Miss Carter broke in. "At least I suppose it was this morning," she added dubiously.

". . . and released me by fire," the Ifrit finished. "I apologize for carrying you across the room when I was freed; it was the suddenness, the excitement. I'm sure you understand, oh, gracious one . . ."

"Perfectly," Miss Carter reassured him. "Years of being pent up and repressed—oh, indeed, I *do* understand how you would be carried away . . . or rather I was carried away . . . And it's been such a wonderful story too," she added happily, "much better than Lady Hester and the Arabian Nights, but . . ." she looked at her watch, "goodness, it *is* late; you'd better be getting home or you'll miss the last bus . . ." she broke off puzzled. Where the devil *was* his home? "That is, if you've any place to go to." She looked at him, but found no answer. "You know," she said appalled, "I really don't understand any of this . . ."

"Have no fear, my mistress, my home, an it please you, is— for the present—here."

"But good Lord, man," Georgina jumped to her feet in alarm. "You can't stay *here*! I haven't room . . . besides . . . no it won't do . . . You must go to a hostel, the Y.M.C.A. . . . but you can't go in those clothes. Besides where is your identity card! Oh, what *am* I to do?" she wailed.

"The Princess must not be troubled for even an instant on her slave's behalf," Abu Shiháb soothed her. "She must retire and sleep peacefully."

"But I've already told you, you can't stay here," Miss Carter said desperately. "It's quite impossible."

"Then use your magic, if you so desire, and rid yourself of me," the Ifrit said humbly.

"I'll do nothing of the sort," Georgina snapped. "You use *your* magic."

"As it is your wish," he said and, reaching over to the mantel- piece, picked up from it a small Chinese snuff bottle carved from amethyst quartz. "Am I graciously permitted to use this?" he asked.

"There's no snuff in it." Really the man was impossible. "And it *is* rather precious. My brother sent it to me from the East." She was conscious now that she was not only very upset but very tired as well.

He returned the bottle to the mantel, removing the tiny carved chrysanthemum which was its stopper and placing it carefully beside the bottle. "Have no fear, O Benevolent One," he reassured her again. "I shall not trouble you further this evening for I have already trespassed too long upon your kindness."

Then an extraordinary thing happened; he vanished!

Miss Carter rubbed her eyes and looked round the room. Not a sign of him. She peered behind the wireless, looked under the sofa, examined the thick folds of the curtains; he was not there. There was no sign either of the silver tray or the remains of the food. The room was exactly as it had been. "I'm going to bed," Miss Carter addressed the empty room in a loud voice. "Or am I already in bed?" she asked herself in a lower tone.

She switched off the lights firmly and left the room, banging the door after her. The sound steadied and comforted her.

CHAPTER III

WHEN MISS CARTER awoke next morning she remembered with delight and relief that it was Sunday—her free Sunday at that. She stretched, yawned, looked at her watch; eight o'clock. Then suddenly she remembered the very curious dream she'd had. She chuckled at the memory and muttered to herself, "Perfectly extraordinary!" several times. As she washed, dressed and set about getting her breakfast in the small kitchen, she lived through the dream again. It was simply incredible how vividly she remembered every part of it. Usually she couldn't remember her dreams at all, except in vague disjointed scraps. But this dream she remembered in every absurd and fantastic detail. And the food! What a joy it had been to have a perfect orgy of fruit and sweets. There was a wish fulfilment dream if ever there was one! She'd probably felt hungry in her sleep—or perhaps the egg had proved too rich for her digestion. As for that man! What was his name? . . . Abu . . . something . . . Abu Shiháb, that was it—and his Arabian Nights cum Hester Stanhope story which her subconscious mind had dovetailed quite cleverly, she must admit, into periods of English history! It really was terribly funny . . . proved that the subconscious absorbed absolutely everything seen, heard, spoken or read—and spewed it up at times in new and wonderful pictures while one slept.

She carried her blue breakfast tray into the living room, set it down on the gate-legged table near the window, undid the blackout to let in the grey winter light and settled down to her breakfast and the *Observer*, going through both in a leisurely Sunday fashion. She had nothing to do until the afternoon when Margaret Mackenzie, who worked in the Censorship with her, was coming to tea.

When she had finished her breakfast, she removed the tray, washed the dishes, returned to the living room and set about straightening it up. Not that it required much straightening, for Miss Carter was incurably neat. She pulled a cushion out of the easy chair, plumped it up with her hands and was just going to replace it when she saw something which made her stop suddenly.

There, caught in the crack between the arm and the seat of the chair, was a bright scrap which looked horribly like a piece of orange peel. Miss Carter just stood and stared at it, conscious of a shortness of breath and a feeling of moisture about the palms. Presently she collected herself sufficiently to bend over and pick the thing up. She carried it over to the window and examined it. There was no doubt about it, it *was* orange peel. Thick, shiny peel, oily to the touch—and with a white, pithy underside like peel from Jaffa oranges.

Ridiculously she thought, "A pity it won't do for marmalade . . ." as if her mind would seize and hold on to something perfectly reasonable and sensible for a moment before admitting or realizing that orange peel just didn't materialize out of a dream. She turned stiffly and mechanically from the window and looked at the mantelpiece. Yes, the stopper *was* out of the snuff bottle and the little bottle itself seemed to be gently rocking to and fro on its base.

Georgina suddenly wanted to laugh wildly. The desire was so violent that she checked it only by calling herself an hysterical old fool. Once she started laughing, she felt there was no telling what might happen . . . she might never stop . . . and that was most dangerous. What was the best thing to do in the circumstances? she asked herself, choking down great lumps of laughter. Aspirin? . . . telephone Dr. Roberts? or Margaret Mackenzie? Nonsense. Aspirin would not relieve or dissolve a piece of real orange peel. Margaret Mackenzie would think her suddenly unhinged (which, alas, might prove too true) and Dr. Roberts! . . . he'd probably say that a swaying snuff bottle was a visual disturbance due to a liver disorder and that the odd dream she had had was symptomatic of the same thing—was, in fact, highly developed and vividly coloured spots before the eyes!

With a great effort of will she crossed to the fireplace and forced herself to pick up the snuff bottle. Unthinkingly she held it to her nose as if it were the smelling salts she so needed. A vaguely sulphurous smell tickled her nostrils and it almost seemed as if a thin wisp of blue smoke were lazily curled over the neck. What had he said his name was . . . ? Abu . . . her mind refused the question . . . father of the shooting star . . . which came to mean evil spirit . . . Abu . . . Abu Shiháb, she murmured.

And there he was! Just as he had been in her dream. This must end some time, she thought desperately . . . it can't just go on repeating itself forever . . . what were recurrent dreams a sign of? Something really dreadful, no doubt!

"At your service, O Lady of the Morning," the Ifrit said. "I would have been here before you to arrange your morning repast, yet I felt to do so without your leave might have occasioned anger and envy among your other servants."

"I have no other servants," Miss Carter said stupidly, her mind refusing to function.

"Then who waits upon you? Who speeds your commands? Who executes your wishes?" Abu Shiháb asked in astonishment. "What of those you keep in the box?"

"I look after myself with the help of a charwoman." Her answer was mechanical—"One can't get domestic help these days for love or money, not that I've offered either," she added foolishly.

"But, beautiful mistress," Abu Shiháb's voice was indignant, outraged. "It is not right that you the good, the powerful, should exist in such a manner . . . should fatigue yourself with daily tasks and menial work, and be filled with cark and care. Are you laid under some cruel spell, perhaps? . . . have you been dispossessed of your lawful kingdom?"

Miss Carter collapsed suddenly into the easy chair. A great, tightly wound spring had suddenly unwound somewhere inside her. For no good reason she felt like bursting into tears, a thing she never did no matter how much she felt like it. It wasn't fear, anger, fatigue or bewilderment which had so unnerved her. It was the tone of that absurd, unreal Ifrit's voice—the puzzled look on his face—the gentleness of his words when he asked if she were under a spell—had been dispossessed of her rightful kingdom. That was what made her want to weep—odious tears of self-pity. She *had* been laid under a spell or a curse perhaps. Had been dispossessed, but not in quite the way Abu Shiháb thought. She was nearly fifty—and she was lonely. She had been satisfied with both these states—up to now. No, she had merely accepted them both and forced herself to be satisfied—commonsense had done that for her. But the truth was, and she admitted it openly to herself now, that life had just passed her by without so much even as a casual wave of the hand.

Well, perhaps this was all a dream. Perhaps she was insane. Perhaps even she was dead and wandering in that strange limbo of those half-forgotten things that one had always desired and never achieved. But—and she made up her mind suddenly and firmly—but this present situation she would accept . . . *and* enjoy it, as far as possible. That was perhaps not sensible, but sense be hanged, it was at least interesting! She would look upon it as a private adventure—a high spot. And pay the piper disguised as a mental specialist when he sent in his bill!

Having made up her mind, she turned to him and said, "Please sit down, Mr. Shiháb. There are things I want to ask you."

He obeyed with the remark that it was unseemly for him to sit in her presence.

"First," she said, feeling rather like a kind but firm school-mistress, "you do exist, don't you?" It would be a great relief if she could satisfy herself on this point.

"I am here, Beneficent Lady," he replied.

"But are you really? I suppose you are, for I haven't enough imagination to invent you. You did tell me your story last night. Was all that true?"

"May my tongue be cut out if it weren't."

Miss Carter shuddered slightly—certainly he sounded convincing. "Your language," she said, "is unusual—picturesque is perhaps the better word."

"Your slave apologizes for his thick tongue, his slow brain. Your language I find difficult . . ."

"Where did you learn?" she enquired.

"He who listens learns. I listened for several centuries. I attempted to learn—it helped to pass the time. Though even during that period your language changed and the meanings of words altered. I learned too the language of the men with breast-plates and of the Iberian people as well. I also learned other tongues for often the ship changed hands, but the names of these tongues I know not . . . I have a small genius for languages," he added with becoming modesty.

"You certainly must have," Miss Carter agreed, "we ought to have you in the Censorship," she went on reflectively, "though Latin's not much use these days unless we take to censoring the post of the papal envoy . . ." She addressed the Ifrit again. "And now, what are your plans, if you have any? What do you propose to do? For I'm sure after three thousand years' . . . er . . . captivity you must feel rather at a loose end. I suppose you can't get in touch with—your people?"

Abu Shiháb looked as if about to say something, but he stopped himself and shook his head.

"Come, come," Miss Carter said, "you must do something otherwise you'll brood."

"I am your slave—your servant," he told her obstinately, "and I shall serve you with all the means within my power."

"But, Mr. Shiháb," Georgina felt her patience a little tried, "we've been through all that before. I told you last night we don't have slaves in this country."

The Ifrit looked astonished. "This is a strange thing," he said, "both the great queens had many slaves . . . or so it seemed to my imperfect understanding . . . particularly the first queen . . . many men who called themselves her slaves. I heard them tell her that myself, sweeping the ground with their obeisances as they did so."

"You were grossly mistaken then, Mr. Shiháb. Those men were using merely a flattering figure of speech," Georgina told him firmly, yet feeling rather like a propaganda machine. "Servants, yes—slaves, NO."

"Then whom do you blame, whom do you punish when things go wrong?" he asked.

"I don't really know," Miss Carter confessed and felt that the conversation had got completely out of hand, her hands at any rate, ". . . the Government, I suppose . . ."

"And what is that word—government—if you will forgive my stupidity . . ."

Georgina began to feel slightly dazed and confused again. "Government," she said, "it's a body of men elected by the people to govern or rule the country." She hoped that would stop him. It didn't.

"But have you then no longer a King or Queen, O Princess?" he persisted.

"Good heavens, yes! But they don't really rule . . ."

"Who has dared to depose them?" he cried furiously. "With my aid, O unfortunate, ensorcelled Lady, we shall fight and

restore them to their thrones . . . and they will then, in gratitude, restore to you your rights and elevate you to the highest
in the land . . ."

"Oh, do hush, Mr. Shiháb," Georgina said nervously, for he
had spoken with such emotion and his tone was so loud that
the people next door might hear and wonder—unless they took
it to be a B.B.C. drama. "You don't understand and it's difficult
to explain." She hastily dismissed the idea of trying to explain
the growth of the parliamentary system; she wasn't sure enough
about her facts . . . and then there was that really shocking and
unforgivable business about poor King Charles. He must have
been sleeping in the beam when that happened and perhaps
no Roundheads had ever come to the country house to wake
him with their great clumping boots and voices which professed
piety had not improved. "Can you read and write?" she asked.
"If so I will buy you Trevelyan's History of England. It is most
comprehensive."

The Ifrit bowed his head. "I can do neither, O Mistress,
miserable and ignorant wretch that I am . . . at least, not your
language." The great pearl in his turban shook with his distress.

"Never mind," Georgina said firmly and consolingly, "you
can be taught. I'm sure you're quick to learn and there are plenty
of good night schools and English classes for foreigners . . ." She
broke off, appalled. "But, good Lord, what *am* I to do about you
really. You've no status, no anything . . . you're an illegitimate
alien. I mean you've entered the country illegally. Your story
wouldn't be believed by anyone in their right senses. God alone
knows what will happen to you. Listen, Mr. Shiháb," despair
made her voice high, "what *are* you going to do . . . ?"

"Serve you," he repeated patiently, "if so unworthy a servant
can find favour in your sight."

"But you *can't*," she said desperately. "Single women don't
have men servants in this country, not unless they're frantically
old family retainers. Oh, I know you're *very* old, very old indeed,
but it just won't do . . . it isn't the same thing."

"You are unwed then," he said sadly, "or is your lord and
master away on a journey of many moons? No," he answered

himself, "I can see in your face that you are still virgin—a pearl unpierced . . ."

Georgina hated herself for blushing. "Those are the kind of things one does *not* say in this country," she rebuked him. "I am not narrow-minded and I know that in the East certain . . . er . . . conventions are *quite* different. Here when you make personal remarks like that you give offence."

Abu Shiháb was patently too crushed to reply. He rubbed his feet, shod in those silly red slippers, together. His head was sunk on his breast.

Miss Carter was sorry for him. She hadn't meant to be harsh. Poor, strange creature; the situation must be just as difficult and perplexing for him as it was for her. After all, he was her guest, she supposed—and a foreigner—she ought to be more kind, more thoughtful.

"Come, come, Mr. Shiháb," she said kindly, "there's no harm done really."

The Ifrit looked up. Large, round tears ran down either side of his fine nose. "Oh, unhappiest of all Ifrits am I," he sobbed. "Return me to my tree, my beam, my block of wood. Ensorcell me within that box, for I have offended my rescuer. I have trespassed with clumsy feet upon the feelings of my mistress who will not let me serve her. Oh, woe, woe! Woe to Abu Shiháb, the spurned, the cursed, the homeless. May he seek refuge from Satan the stoned."

The sight of this large, helpless, masculine creature, this spirit of sorts (for she supposed she must accept his word that he was a spirit) in his gaudy, outlandish attire, sitting sobbing in her quiet living room at half past ten of a Sunday morning, was too much for Georgina. She could never bear to see anyone cry, not even in films, and that she had been the cause of his tears filled her with a horrid remorse. "Oh, please, please Mr. Shiháb," she begged, "please don't cry. I am so terribly sorry I hurt your feelings. I didn't mean to. You see it's just because we don't quite understand each other yet that this has happened. We come from different countries; we really speak different languages. Not that your English isn't remarkably good," she added swiftly for fear of hurting him anew. "Indeed, we belong to different centuries—or is it millennia! I'm not quite sure how long a millennium is. But in time, Mr. Shiháb, I'm sure you'll understand our curious and sometimes quite incomprehensible ways, even though you may not approve of them. I shall be glad to teach you myself. In fact, we might start with the alpha. . ." It wasn't the thought of beginning the alphabet that stopped her; it was the realization that she had, by this suggestion, accepted him, had indeed visualized him as becoming part of her household. Well, she'd said it. It was too late to retract now, and, curiously enough, she found she didn't really want to.

Abu Shiháb drew a marvellously patterned silken handkerchief from his coat sleeve, dried his eyes and blew his nose noisily. "Oh, merciful mistress, I am unworthy of such thoughtfulness," he gulped back his sobs, "yet I swear you will never have cause to regret this magnanimous decision . . ."

"Nonsense," Miss Carter said briskly, for she was by now a trifle embarrassed by her impulsiveness, "but the next thing is to decide what I shall do with you—where I can fit you in. For you see, my flat is very small, and I have no spare room—only a wretched collapsible cot that is put up in here. I so seldom have visitors with my nephew gone . . ." she apologized.

He picked up the snuff bottle again. "This shall be my home, O Lady of the gracious countenance. When you wish to be no longer troubled with my presence, a word of command and I shall disappear. For know that we Ifrits have the power to make ourselves small enough to ride on the back of a sand flea, or large enough to fill the whole of this room, nay even this whole dwelling place. Indeed, should you so desire, I can become invisible . . ."

"Oh my goodness, no," Georgina interrupted nervously, "you must never make yourself invisible—at least, not in this flat—and not when I'm about unless I ask you to—it would make me too uncomfortable. You must promise me that . . ."

"Your word is my law . . ." he said.

"Will you be quite comfortable, though, living in that snuff bottle?" she asked.

"I shall be as comfortable as the air within it," he answered. "Pray take no thought for your servant, he is happy only in your happiness and comfort."

"Must you really be my servant?" she enquired uneasily. "Can't you be . . . no, I suppose . . ." her voice trailed off; he might not understand the word friend . . .

"I *must* be your servant," he replied. "It is so written . . ."

"Written? . . . who wrote it . . . ?"

"Sulayman . . . all has been foreordained . . ."

"Do you mean to tell me that King Solo . . . er . . . Sulayman wrote down exactly who would free you, and when . . . and that I was foreordained thousands of years ago for the job?" What had been the use of her worrying and protesting then, she asked herself with amusement, not that she believed in it for a moment.

"Yes, O Luminous Personage," he answered, "it is all written . . ."

"I don't believe it," Miss Carter said stoutly. "Nothing in the world would make me believe it. What has happened is just pure chance, coincidence, that's all."

"One thing may be known by many names," he said softly, "the snail, the man, the bird see but different aspects of the same field."

Miss Carter felt that further argument would be worse than useless; it might even be dangerous to her reason, or, rather, what reason she had left, if any. "All right, Mr. Shiháb," she said, giving in as graciously as possible in the predestined circumstances. "I think we can't argue about that now for we each have our own opinion on the subject. But there is one other thing that you can do for me—if you will . . ."

The Ifrit jumped to his feet. "Yours to command," he said in an almost military voice.

"Sit down," she smiled, "it's nothing very much, really quite simple, in fact. It's about that exaggerated form of address you use. Oh, I know it is usual in your country, but here it sounds very strange and it makes me feel decidedly uncomfortable . . ."

"But I do not understand your meaning, O lovely one."

"That's it," she pointed out. "Lovely one, you always call me by many . . . er . . . names or titles. I am not a princess or a queen or a wise one or a pearl or a luminous personage . . ."

"But you are a sorceress—your magic . . ." the Ifrit started in astonishment.

She interrupted. "I know *no* magic," she told him emphatically. "No magic at all. Nearly everyone in this country has a box like mine," she waved a hand in the direction of the radio. "It's called a wireless . . ."

"Everyone!" the Ifrit said in amazement, "this is a country of sorcerers then . . ."

"No, indeed it isn't, quite the contrary," she denied impatiently. "There's no magic, nothing supernatural about a radio or wireless. It's quite common, quite usual . . . completely ordinary, in fact."

"But, Queen of the Universe . . ." the Ifrit rolled his large eyes in bewilderment. . . . "if it is not magic, what is it? How do the voices and the songs of the instruments come from it?"

Georgina was stumped and ashamed of herself for she hadn't the remotest idea how a wireless worked. And here was an Ifrit, a real magician, or whatever it was, humbled before a mechanical contrivance for which she, in her apathy and ignorance, could give no explanation. It flashed across her mind that a good many of the things in everyday use which she had always taken for granted and as a matter of course, even when first invented, would look like magic to the Ifrit—or even to a person living in the last century. "I shall have to get you a book which will explain it all to you as soon as you can read, for I am ashamed to say that I do not know how a wireless works, or how it is constructed," she confessed. "But, Mr. Shiháb, we have wandered a long way from our original subject." How extremely difficult it was not to digress, like talking to an intelligent and enquiring child; one got involved in countless questions and explanations. "I started to ask you," she recalled to him, "if you would please not call me anything but Miss Carter, for that is really my name, Miss Georgina Carter . . ."

"Miss Georgina Carter," he repeated after her. "Pray tell me what does it mean?"

"What does it mean!"

"Yes, what do the words stand for . . . like my name Abu Shiháb . . . father of the shooting star . . ."

Miss Carter laughed. "We're not very poetic about names in this country, I'm afraid . . . my name doesn't mean a thing."

"But you cannot have a name that is just meaningless," the Ifrit spoke indignantly. "Are you not named for beautiful things in nature? Are you not called by words which signify some characteristic of mind or body?"

"No," Georgina said, "we're not. My name Georgina is the feminine form of the name George. George perhaps may mean something, in fact it probably does, but all I know is that it was the name of a legendary hero who slew a dragon. It is also the name of our King."

The Ifrit was delighted. "To bear the King's name is an honour," he said happily, "oh Prin. . ."

"Now, now, Mr. Shiháb," she admonished. "Miss Carter, please."

"And what is the meaning of Carter?" the indefatigable Ifrit asked.

"I don't know that either." How stupid he made her feel, she must try to do better really. "Perhaps it belonged originally to a man who owned or drove a cart—like the man I bought the road blocks from—and he carted things from one place to another—wool most probably for I believe Carter is a Lancashire name—until finally the family who engaged in this trade became known as Carter . . ." she hoped she wasn't giving erroneous information.

"Then your names do have meanings," the Ifrit beamed. "I was sure they must. Now please, what is Miss?"

"Why Miss is just a title, a common form of address. Unmarried women have Miss before their names. Married women are called Mrs. And men are called Mister . . ."

"So . . . and what do they call unmarried men . . . ?"

"Why, just Mr. That's all."

"But there are different names for married and unmarried women," the Ifrit shook his head, "it seems a strange, nay, even an unwise thing," he commented.

"Well, I suppose it is odd. I'd never thought about it. Odd and a trifle unfair. But what shall I call you," she drew her eyebrows together. "Mr. Shiháb sounds equally odd, while Abu Shiháb makes me feel silly. I suppose that's very English of me. I think I shall just call you Abu, that would be simplest."

"But, Queen of . . . Miss Carter . . ." the Ifrit stopped her hastily, "it is not seemly that you call me that for I am neither venerable nor a priest. Nor have I the honour to be your father." Georgina laughed. "So that's what Abu means. How stupid of me not to guess. No, Abu won't do at all, that's obvious. I must give you a new name. What shall it be?"

The Ifrit looked anxious. "Perhaps George," he said tentatively. "I would then be part of your name, as if I belonged to . . ." he broke off wistfully.

But Miss Carter shook her head. "No, not George, for that *was* my father's name; but your last name can be Carter, if you like." She coloured slightly as she said this. "What about William?" She eyed him narrowly. "You're not a bit like a William really, nor like a Thomas . . ."

"Francis?" he suggested, "would that do? There was a man with the great queen called Francis . . ."

"No, somehow that doesn't suit you either." She was silent for a moment; then, "I have it," she cried, "Joe. You shall be called Joe. Do you mind?"

"Not at all." He bowed graciously. "I am honoured to be called Joe. What does it mean?"

Miss Carter saw herself answering questions for the rest of her life. Having an Ifrit around the house was not going to be all fruit and wine. "I don't think it means anything," she explained patiently, "but it is a good name. It is the name of a very wonderful man, a great, strong man who is . . . er . . . almost a magician, like yourself. Besides it's a short, solid, matter-of-fact, real name. I think," she concluded, "that this whole situation is so terribly unreal that we must somehow inject a note of practicality, or everydayness, into it. Even if it's only in your name."

She could see that the Ifrit had not understood any of this, wasn't even listening, for he just sat and repeated, Joe Carter . . . Joe Carter . . . with almost childish delight.

"Oh, well, it doesn't matter," she told herself. Then she spoke to him. "By the way, aren't you hungry?" she asked. "I shall start getting lunch. Perhaps you'd like to watch me, and then, if you really *are* going to help about the house, you'll know where things are kept!"

CHAPTER IV

MISS MARGARET MACKENZIE had left. She had not stayed with Georgina so long as usual. Normally, Sunday afternoon tea with Georgina was a leisurely affair, lasting well into the evening and sometimes embracing a lateish light supper as well; but not to-day! For undoubtedly there had been something wrong with Georgina. No, not exactly wrong, but different, unusual, perhaps described it better. Georgina hadn't been herself at all. She had seemed diffident, abstracted, even nervous—as if she expected or was afraid that something was going to happen. Margaret couldn't quite put her finger on it, but it was as if Georgina weren't really interested in tea, or any topic of conversation which she, Margaret, suggested, and only went through hostess-like and friendly motions from force of habit or for the sake of being polite. Indeed, Margaret was forced to confess reluctantly to herself, indeed it had almost seemed as if Georgina hadn't wanted her there at all! Margaret Mackenzie had known Georgina for twenty-five years—since the last war. A friendship which could last through two wars and two jobs in the Censorship could survive almost anything. She considered that she knew Georgina pretty well, and vagueness was certainly *not* one of Georgina's characteristics, neither was a certain inability to concentrate, or a jumpiness of manner. And those peculiar, almost secretive, remarks about the cakes!

At the thought of the cakes—two of which she now carried wrapped in a bit of tissue paper in her handbag—Margaret felt again nonplussed—and hungry. For they were like no other cakes she had ever eaten—granted that war-time cake had almost made one forget what a real cake had once tasted like. Still, Margaret felt that even in pre-war days these cakes would have been in a class apart. They were made of layer upon layer of pastry rolled transparently thin, and between each layer there was a filling of finely-ground almonds mixed with honey and faintly flavoured with lemon. Each cake was then dusted with sugar. They were golden, melting, delicious . . .

"These are simply too marvellous, Georgina," she had observed. "Where on earth did you get them—and in war-time too!" For it was obvious that Georgina, who was a good, plain cook, hadn't made them herself.

Georgina had looked a little confused by the question. Then she had answered briefly "That's a secret."

"But Georgina!" Margaret had cried, "do be an angel and tell me. I should so love to get some myself, and you know that I wouldn't tell a living soul . . ."

"I'm terribly sorry, my dear," Georgina had really seemed embarrassed—"I'm afraid I just can't tell you."

Margaret was hurt—it seemed rather small of Georgina— Then she was struck by a horrid thought, and put it bravely into words. "Georgina," she said very gently, "they're not—not off the—I mean they're not Black Market, are they? I shall, of course, never, never breathe it to anyone. But knowing you as I do—I'm just a little surprised—Do say they're not . . ."

It was then that Georgina's behaviour became *really* peculiar.

For she suddenly started to giggle like—yes, like a silly schoolgirl. The giggles grew to uncontrollable laughter—her shoulders shook and she turned quite red. "Oh . . . oh!" she gasped, "I suppose you could call it *that*." She struggled, and regained composure. "I'm so sorry, Margaret," she apologized, and Margaret felt it wasn't quite sincere. "You must think me dreadfully rude—but your remark about a Black Market—well, it was *so* funny. . . . Do forgive me, won't you? Some day perhaps I'll be able to explain why . . ."

Yes, Margaret thought, as she descended into the Underground, Georgina's manner had been altogether most peculiar. War-strain? Nonsense. Perhaps it was living by oneself for too long. Margaret had often felt—as she bore with the demands of an extremely ancient mother and the idiosyncrasies of a brother with an alarmingly scientific mind—that it would be wonderful to live alone. This afternoon had made her doubt that—living alone was obviously dangerous—it certainly seemed to make some people a little queer!

Georgina, however, was far from living alone. That evening as soon as Margaret had left she summoned the Ifrit from the bottle. The two hours Margaret had stayed had seemed interminable. Georgina found herself wishing a dozen times that Margaret would go. She was mortally afraid that she might betray her secret to Margaret and it was obvious that had she confessed all to Margaret, Margaret would have refused to believe it. Even had she gone as far as summoning the Ifrit she was afraid that he might have been invisible to Margaret's eyes—for she wasn't quite sure that one didn't need rather special vision to spot an Ifrit—rather like the highly developed sight of those people who claimed to be able to see auras. Even had Margaret accepted him as more or less real, she would have been sure to designate him as an evil spirit, despite the fact that she had a taste for theosophy. So, Georgina argued with herself—knowing in her heart that she just didn't want to share the knowledge of Joe with Margaret Mackenzie or anyone else for that matter. She wanted to be utterly selfish about him—for his good and her own!

It had, of course, been sheer madness to let the Ifrit produce those cakes, but he had been so desperately eager to please, had wanted to conjure up such fabulous things, that she had had great difficulty in restraining him, and the cakes had emerged as a sort of compromise.

However, all that was past now, and tomorrow she would see Margaret again and within the dull framework of the routine job of scanning letters from America and Canada, the rather horrid implication of the cakes and the Black Market would be, she trusted, quite forgotten.

At the moment she sat comfortably in front of a small fire with Joe, and she was trying to explain to him a number of things about masculine dress with the aid of a number of magazines and newspapers. She felt it would be so much safer if Joe adopted Western attire for his materializations. Then, if by any chance anyone spotted him in her flat, he wouldn't look quite so suspicious and out of place. Besides, after dark she would be able to take him out for a walk—for he couldn't remain cooped up all day without fresh air, particularly after his long captivity. In the blackout they would be comparatively safe, and provided they didn't infringe any laws or find themselves in a situation which called for the production of an identity card, Joe would be all right. Of course in any really sticky circumstance Joe could just vanish, but that would be bound to leave her in a mess, and if she were unable to satisfy any of the questions which might be asked on such an occasion goodness alone knew what might happen . . . plain clothes men shadowing her . . . or keeping watch on her flat . . . simply no privacy at all . . . or even 18b invoked and the Isle of Wight—or was it Brixton?—for the duration! Miss Carter was just a trifle hazy as to the powers of the police these days—or was it parliament? But she believed more firmly than ever that the appearance of evil, or even irregularity, should be avoided, thus saving oneself and everyone else a vast amount of time and trouble. Of course if Sulayman really *had* foreordained everything, as that ridiculous Ifrit suggested, then there was just nothing she could do to prevent whatever peculiar fate he had thought up from overtaking her—but quite naturally she didn't believe that poppycock.

"You see, Joe," she said, "you must really adopt Western dress. You will be less conspicuous and besides you will be warmer. This climate is really very damp and dressed as you are you're bound to catch cold or get rheumatism . . ." It was a great pity that most illustrations of men in magazines showed them in various uniforms. For it was difficult to explain to Joe that uniform wasn't the kind of dress which he could wear, and indeed if he did wear it he would be liable to severe penalties, for Joe had been particularly impressed and excited by an illustration of a guardsman in full colour, which advertised a well known brand of cigarette.

"Dress like that," he said, "though it strikes oddly upon my eyes is yet pleasant and colourful. The other pictures you show to me seem to reflect sadly the taste and feelings of the men in this country. How dull it must be for the female that the male does not display himself like the peacock or bird of paradise in gorgeous raiment. Is he then ashamed of his body that he hides and covers it with the dress of mourning and poverty?"

Miss Carter reflected quietly that there was little point or purpose in entering into a discussion on that subject. Why tell him that men had once dressed with gorgeous impracticability . . . how to explain that to-day their dress was nearly as impractical, and a great deal less beautiful . . . No, she would just have to be firm with Joe, point out the garments that he could wear and insist that he wear them.

There was no use showing him the most recent news photograph of Mr. Churchill, for in that the Prime Minister was clad in his siren suit and wore a funnier hat than ever. The Archbishop of Canterbury was no use either, nor was the Speaker of the House of Commons in full regalia—there just didn't seem to be a normally dressed man in the whole country—not according to the press. There was, of course, the cabinet photograph of her father, but that had been taken in 1910—and there were various snaps of Robert in a blazer or cricket pads, and some of Henry in an Eton jacket or rugger shorts—none of them very helpful. She decided that the position at the moment was hopeless. She would just have to wait until morning and point out to him ordinary men walking down the street.

"How I'm going to provide you with clothes, though, I really don't know," she told him. "Even if I dared to take you shopping—you haven't any coupons and I just can't spare mine . . ."

"Are coupons your word for money?" he asked, "for if that is all that is required you but have to speak and all the long hidden treasures of the East are yours."

She smiled indulgently at his extravagant language. "No, coupons aren't money," she explained, "they're little bits of stamped paper given us by the government. Each person receives a number of these—we all receive exactly the same number—and they must last us for a certain period. We give up a specified number of these coupons for every article of clothing we buy, and when we have no coupons left, we can't have any more clothes."

"Then money is not necessary," he cried. "What a wonderful, what a kind country is this . . . the poor can be clothed as well as the rich . . . Everything is quite clear to me now . . . I understand the curious costume of the men . . . it is done so that all may be clothed equally well, none set above another by the gorgeousness or richness of his raiment . . ."

Miss Carter disliked having to disillusion him, nevertheless, she did so, for it was no use having an Ifrit with false ideas around the place. "No," she said, "that is, I'm sorry to say, not at all the case. We must give up money as well as our coupons. But it wasn't always like this," she went on, for she suddenly realized that quite probably the Ifrit knew nothing whatever about the war . . . how odd to find someone like that! "You see," she explained, "this country is at war and we have to have those bits of paper—or coupons—for nearly everything. They are really good because they make sure that everyone gets his fair share of food and clothing . . ."

But the Ifrit was not really interested in the latter part of her explanation. "War!" he exclaimed, and his face lighted up for an instant, "Your country at war, Miss Carter! Tell me who are her enemies!—I will defeat them; I will summon up five thousand—nay, ten thousand—horsemen whose might will be as the winds of heaven, whose banners will petrify the heart, and whose terrible battle cry will melt the bowels of the enemy into terror . . . Alas," his voice dropped and the light faded from his eyes, "Alas," he repeated, "I was forgetting . . ."

"Forgetting what, Joe?" Miss Carter enquired, glad that she didn't have to disillusion him a second time within so few minutes by explaining the pitiful futility of ten thousand horsemen.

"Forgetting what I have learned," he told her sadly, "forgetting the lesson of three thousand years—that I must not raise my hand against mankind—that I must have in me peace, amity and goodwill for all the sons of men—that I have forsworn for ever any magic that may do evil or hurt to any mortal, no matter who he be . . . and that I have no general power as yet to do good even, not until I have passed the great test whose nature, even, is hidden from me. My only remaining magic now is personal stuff—child's play . . ."

Miss Carter was both fascinated and relieved by this statement. "I think, Joe," she said, "that it's probably just as well your power is curtailed a bit . . . you'll probably be happier this way. Less likely to get into . . . I mean to be tempted into trouble. I suppose, though, that's the punishment you and your tribe had to suffer for making war on Sulayman."

He nodded, "And those before him," he confessed, "for you must know we were created of fire and stand only below the angels—but we were given great power and because we used this power only for ourselves and used it evilly, we in time became evil, though not all of us, for some remained good and were of the hosts of Sulayman himself—at least that is what I concluded when I was imprisoned, for I had enough time to think and repent—and perhaps my brother Ifrits have discovered this to be true also. But I know that I myself have no longer the same power within me—nor the old desire for wickedness. Now that I have learned to want to use my gift for good, it is, perhaps, too late . . ." he said sadly.

"You're not alone in that," Miss Carter comforted him. "More or less the same thing has happened to your ancient enemy, man, the only difference is that you seem more advanced in your attitude than he does . . ." she sighed.

"Ah, but we had power," the Ifrit cried, "power that man had not. We could transport ourselves through the air in the twinkling of an eye . . . we could follow the great monsters of the deep under water . . . we knew where lay the hidden treasures within fee earth . . . we could become invisible . . . all material things were within our reach . . . we were more gifted than any creature on the earth. . . ."

"But man does all these things now," Miss Carter interrupted—"with the exception of making himself invisible—and I daresay that will come—though there's always camouflage—and what's more, he wasn't born knowing how to do them, he had to learn these things for himself. But"—her voice trailed away. She felt unaccountably sad. The evening had become tinged with melancholy. She thought of Henry learning to fly in Canada—of Henry's father missing since Singapore because of a submarine. She thought of the air charged now, not with Ifrits, but with planes, and it seemed to her that man had progressed right back to where the evil Ifrits had been 3,000 years ago and hadn't really learned a thing. It was all very strange and confusing.

"But you are melancholy . . . my beaut. . . Miss Carter!" the Ifrit broke in on her thoughts. "I see the worm of sadness eating at the petals of your heart. Pray do not be sad on my account, for I am reconciled to my loss—besides you belong to a race created for happiness and joy. Shall I summon dancing girls and those proficient on the lute to cheer you and enliven your spirit!"

Miss Carter shook her head and smiled. "No thanks," she said, "dancing girls are hardly in my line. I'm not really a ballet fan—dreadfully un-English of me I know—but there it is. And we still haven't solved the problem of your clothes, Joe. But never mind, we'll think of that tomorrow. Perhaps I can find you a suit in a second-hand shop. By the way, what size do you take?"

"But I take any size," the Ifrit said; "Look," he rapidly expanded and contracted himself several times.

"Of course, I'd forgotten that! What a useful accomplishment," Georgina laughed. "I've always wanted to do that ever since I read *Alice in Wonderland* when I was a little girl . . ." She sighed. "Joe, I'm really very tired. I think I'll go to bed now. Are you quite sure you'll be comfortable in that!" She waved a hand in the direction of the snuff bottle.

"But quite, quite comfortable," he answered. "A quiet sleep and may your dreams be pleasant. At what hour will you break your fast in the morning?"

"Half past seven," she told him. "But don't you bother about it. I'm quite accustomed to preparing my own breakfast."

The Ifrit smiled. "Good night, Miss Carter," he said, and on the last syllable, vanished.

CHAPTER V

GEORGINA FOUND it very difficult to keep her mind on her work next day. As a matter of fact, the censoring of letters which had always before seemed interesting and vaguely romantic (for one might really be the means of uncovering a spy ring), now appeared extraordinarily flat and devoid of all meaning. In fact she found herself wishing that a law would be enforced to compel people to use either a typewriter or block capitals. No longer did the sight of a tortured and indecipherable calligraphy fill her with the peculiar zest and delight commonly known to crossword puzzle fiends. And how could so many people write so much about so little!

To be truthful, on this winter Monday morning, Miss Carter found the censorship just downright dull! She realized as she slashed out a gossipy reference to a bomb—that her job was no longer the major part of her life. It was a minor but unfortunately a nagging one and each hour was far too long. Her real life, she thought, as she tried to decipher what a "billiser tack" was—the new, intensely secret and strangely dream-like, yet vivid life, had nothing to do with the way she had existed before a quarter to nine last Saturday evening.

Yet, being in the office, carrying out the routine, talking to her co-workers, lunching with Margaret Mackenzie, did prove two things. The first was that she wasn't dead—for even Hell itself couldn't be as dismal as the Censorship. The second was that she wasn't dreaming—for when one dreamed about the office it was always quite a different place from the real thing—or one was sitting at one's desk inadequately clothed. But the office was the same as always—only worse—and she wore her old, but well cut tweed costume. Of course, the thing that *wasn't* proved was whether or not she was mad! But she didn't give a damn about that any longer (she snipped out a perfectly innocent but slightly pornographic sentence). If this were madness it was at least interesting, pleasant and exciting—and intensely prefera-ble to the so called sanity of the past four years—or even her whole adult life. Georgina felt decidedly reckless—she almost wished that fate had made her an adventuress.

Margaret Mackenzie, who had resolved to ignore the curi-ous happenings of the previous day and who had also resolved to take dear Georgina out of herself by taking her to a theatre (dutch treat) one evening soon, was rebuffed and even a little hurt by the new Georgina.

"No thank you, dear," Georgina said as they finished their lunch. "I don't go out in the evenings any more, I'm rather busy just now—besides I don't really think there's anything on that would interest me very much."

"Oh, but Georgina," Margaret protested, "that can't be—you were always so . . . I mean what has hap. . ." the words fell in a descending scale, her voice died away leaving the sentence unfinished for she saw that Georgina really was *not* interested. Georgina, she was aware, though present in body was just not there. She wore an other-world look as if her eyes and mind beheld some secret place where none could trespass. It gave Margaret a queer feeling, that look; it was as if Georgina, whom she knew so well, had suddenly become someone whom she did not know at all. She wanted to ask "Georgina, what is it? . . . something is troubling you . . . can I help . . ." But Georgina's look was definitely not that of one who was bothered by some wearing misfortune, such as a debt or a drunken relative.

So she said in a faint voice after looking at her watch, "We'd better be getting back now, Georgina, I've left a tip," and she drew on her carefully mended gloves and wondered suddenly, "Is she . . . can she be in love!"

Georgina turned her key in the lock that evening with a feeling of expectation and fear. Expectation because she looked forward to the evening with Joe. Fear that he might not be there—in fact never had been there.

"But this is sheer nonsense," she told herself, going straight to her bedroom and taking off her hat and coat, "for I certainly did not get my own breakfast this morning—and I distinctly remember eating some fresh pineapple that would have put Fortnum & Mason's to shame even before the war." She remembered, too, as she cleaned her face and did her hair, the curious porridge that had been set before her. It was made from some kind of ground grain and liberally seasoned with pepper—once you got over the first shock it wasn't at all unpleasant. "And I couldn't have invented that, even in delirium," she told herself.

She opened the door of the living room, noted that the fire was lit and that the scent of some incense—faintly reminiscent of the smell of St. Peter's in Rome, hung in the air. She switched on the light and called, "Joe—I'm home."

But there was no need to call for he was there, sitting cross-legged in a corner, looking at her with great, sad eyes.

"Joe!" she gasped, "what on earth—"

"I trust it meets with your approval," he rose stiffly to his feet and made obeisance so that she could see him in his full glory.

He wore a morning coat over a brilliantly red and yellow checked flannel shirt, a pair of plaid trousers tucked into wellingtons, and on his head a bowler hat two sizes too small.

"Joe!" She sat down weakly and felt herself turning quite purple with the effort not to laugh. "Oh Joe! . . . your clothes. . . . But where in the world . . ."

"Then you do *not* approve, Miss Carter," he broke in. "I am glad for they are indeed not comfortable and I have to remain quite still to keep this curiously fashioned and ill-fitting turban on my head."

"For goodness sake take it off," she gasped. "Men don't wear their heads covered in the house in this country . . ."

Was there nothing she could think of, no depressing circumstance, or sad event that would dissolve the lump of laughter knotted in her throat. She struggled wildly—and exploded. She lay back in her chair and laughed till her ribs ached and her eyes streamed. She laughed until her breath was exhausted. She, who had never laughed much in her life, made up for it now. The thought that the people in the flats about here might hear and wonder, the thought that Joe might be mortally wounded, had not the power to stop her. It was only when she realized that Joe was no longer there that she stopped and sat up filled with sudden remorse and realizing that she had done the unforgivable thing. One must never laugh at a child who has done something to please one, no matter how ridiculous, she thought—and one should never, never laugh at an Ifrit, even if he were several thousand years older than oneself.

"Joe!" she called, now quite collected and very distressed, "Joe, where are you?"

"One moment, please," a small thin voice replied and she realized that it came from the snuff bottle.

And in a moment he appeared again, clad in his own clothes, while on the floor lay those garments which he had discarded. "Forgive me," he apologized, and stooping to pick them up ". . . but your laughter gave me the permission I required and I took the opportunity to change."

"Oh Joe," she told him. "I'm sorry I laughed . . . it was very rude and thoughtless of me . . . I just couldn't help it. I do like you much better in your own clothes and I'm truly sorry you can't wear them in this country. Tomorrow, however, I'll go to a second-hand clothes dealer and try to get you a plain lounge suit—even if it does mean coupons . . ."

"I had hoped to surprise you," he said, "and to save you the trouble of clothing your unworthy servant. But it appears difficult to know in this country what is worn . . ." he shook his head, puzzled.

"Well," Georgina comforted him, "you certainly did surprise me . . . and I'm sure laughing so much was good for me. But Joe," a thought suddenly struck her—"Where did you get those clothes?" she enquired curiously.

Joe smiled. "It was so excessively simple, Miss Carter, you would have indeed laughed again and distractedly, I assure you. Many times I wished you were there to see."

"See what?" Georgina asked in a flat voice, feeling a little chill run up her spine. "Look here—you really must tell me *where* you got those clothes . . ." She might as well know the worst, even though she preferred not to; 'Face up to things' had been a phrase drilled into her in childhood—she couldn't forget it even though she wanted to.

"I took them," he told her gaily. "It was quite simple."

Georgina groaned. "Oh, my goodness gracious," she said, "I was afraid of that . . . it's all my fault . . . you're my responsibility." She spoke more to herself than to him. Then squaring her shoulders she said, "From what shop, Joe?—you'll have to take them back, you know. For what you have done is called stealing and it isn't right—we might get into fearful trouble by your action if anyone saw you do it. And anyway, even if you weren't observed, it doesn't make any difference for it was a very wrong thing to do. I'm not really blaming you—I'm blaming myself. But I must ask you to return those clothes," she pointed to where he'd placed them neatly folded on a chair.

Joe drew himself up and she suspected that he made himself several inches taller as well.

"It is not to steal when one leaves payment for more than the value of the garment;" he said with great dignity. "Furthermore, I became invisible, so the maggot of fear need not eat your brain over that—for I was unobserved. And as I could not find the bazaar I therefore entered no shop."

"But I don't understand," she cried, somewhat relieved by the news. "What do you mean, you paid for them and yet you didn't buy them in a shop!"

Joe for an answer dropped a handful of coins into her lap. She picked one up and looked at it. It was thick, irregularly round, and made of very yellow gold. On one side a man seemed to be engaged in fighting a ram, on the other side a curiously branched tree flourished.

"I paid with these," he said, "nor do I think the weather was cold enough to occasion the people much harm—besides, I took but one garment from each person." He looked at her as if begging her forgiveness.

Georgina didn't know whether to laugh or cry; so he'd just gone about stripping unsuspecting and respectable citizens, and pressing antique gold coins (no doubt of great value) into their hands! She felt it was wiser to carry her questions no further—it was obvious now that the less she knew about the details the better, cowardly as that might be, for such questions might prove embarrassing. Joe seemed so uninhibited! Besides, he had really not been dishonest in himself—his methods were a little peculiar, conditioned by circumstances, but they had not been wrong or evil. Obviously now she couldn't get him to return the varied garments to their various owners—or could she!

She made up her mind quickly. "Joe," she said, "I want you to do something for me late tonight." She rummaged in a book case until she found a sectional map of London. Turning to the page which gave her Piccadilly Circus and environs she pointed out to him the exact position of Vine Street Police Station. "When I have gone to bed," she said, "will you please transport all those clothes to this place? It is a place, I imagine, of many rooms; leave the clothes in one of the rooms and return quickly. And whatever you do," she charged him, "make sure that you are not seen."

"As you command," Joe said, and bowed. "And now, after all this care on my behalf, you must be feeling the pangs of hunger, and dinner awaits your word. Tonight we have a fowl stuffed with plump raisins and pistachio nuts—and young lamb prepared with wine and savoury herbs, and bread as white as the snow that lies on mountains where no dust is, to be eaten with ghee—and fruits not unworthy of a queen to follow . . ."

Miss Carter did not bring up the subject of clothes again that evening. And next morning, when she read in her paper that a spate of curious incidents connected with clothing had taken place, she merely laughed. The major of a Highland Regiment, who had been de-bagged behind some bushes in St. James's Park. . . . The elderly barrister who had been stripped of his coat as he entered his club in Pall Mall. . . . The labourer who had lost his shirt without putting it on a horse (the bowler and the boots were not mentioned); well, it all seemed very amusing and remote now. Her conscience was reasonably clear.

It was also terribly funny to see that Joe had not been able to resist changing his turban for a policeman's helmet. She hadn't the heart to scold him. But she did buy him a quiet lounge suit that very day, in a shop near Berwick Market. As she handed out six pounds and a frightening number of coupons she reflected sadly that the wonderful antique gold coins could not be used as real money.

CHAPTER VI

NOW THAT Joe had come, apparently, to stay, Georgina found that her own life, though complicated to a certain extent by his presence, was materially much more simple, much more pleasant. She had always kept very much to herself, not from habit or design but from shyness and diffidence, and as she grew older there were fewer and fewer people with whom one could be on intimate terms. Her early friends had married or moved away or gradually, almost without her realizing it, they had dropped from sight. She had never been a joiner of organizations or active in church or social work. Such activities slightly repelled her. Her main object in life had been to give as little trouble as possible, to live quietly and sensibly. The war had added to her loneliness too; her few friends were out of London, and week-end travelling was impossible and unpatriotic as well!

Of course there had been, in the old days, Robert and his son Henry—and although Robert and his wife, Ellen, had lived for many years in India, Henry had been sent to England to be educated and she had had him during holidays, and there had been theatres and concerts and trips to France with Henry—and she was very attached to him—but now he was twenty, nearly twenty-one, and three thousand miles or more away, and that was that.

She did not know any of her neighbours in the old-fashioned flats in which she lived. She didn't particularly want to, for she had lived there for nearly fifteen years and had seen them come and go . . . those who stayed any length of time—say five years—were too much like herself either to be interesting or to seek companionship. Then there was Margaret Mackenzie . . . she was *such* a dear, but . . . Georgina didn't quite know what she meant by that qualifying 'but.' It conveyed, perhaps, a vague feeling of impatience . . . one knew Margaret *so* very well . . . or was it—horrid thought—boredom? She was terribly fond of Margaret, but . . .

Georgina knew really that she, Georgina, just didn't belong anywhere. No one needed her. That was it, no one *needed* her. Robert, Henry, Margaret . . . it really made no particular difference to them that she existed . . . "I a stranger and afraid . . . in a world I never made. . . ." or words to that effect. It was odd she had never admitted these things to herself before . . . at least not for a good many years. And it didn't help to realize that it was entirely her own fault . . . she hadn't known how to go about making herself necessary to people . . . she had been afraid . . . afraid of appearing foolish—emotional. She supposed she really was repressed, frustrated, but to be otherwise, at her age! Well, it seemed just slightly indecent.

Nevertheless, she was glad Joe had happened—crazy, abnormal (or should it be supernormal?)—as it was. For Joe had certainly given her a new interest, had stirred things up. Joe, by making things pleasanter, simpler, had left her free to think. For Joe did all the housework. She didn't even have to have Mrs. 'Oward, the char, once a week. She didn't have to prepare meals or wash dishes or dust behind the wireless. She could stay in bed later in the mornings—and of course there was a great saving on food bills! And it was so pleasant to have someone who was there only when you wanted him to be there! Someone who would appear or disappear at a word, with no hurt feelings. Miss Carter felt that all human relationships would be far happier—would, in all probability, endure for ever—if you could conjure people up only when you wanted them and dissolve them at the first sign of weariness and strain.

"A thoroughly selfish attitude," she scolded herself, "and frightfully bad for the character." But she was nevertheless convinced that it would be an ideally happy arrangement.

She and Joe now occasionally went for walks in the evening. She had great pleasure in trying to explain London to him (she had kept her promise and was teaching him the alphabet too). Trying to explain things simply and clearly to Joe was forcing her to learn about things for herself. There were certain aspects of modern life that she just couldn't explain; such things as the internal combustion engine—the telephone—how electric lights worked—these he would have to find out for himself when he learned to read; and although she did her best to make him understand why people lived in vast cities, why they were forced to spend their lives in offices, shops and factories, he seemed to think it an absurd and monstrously stupid way of life.

"When people have all these wonderful things—music from a box . . . light from a button . . . transport without horses, why do they live lives so dull, so colourless, so lacking in joy and imagination?" he asked.

And although she tried to make him understand, she found her heart wasn't in it. "Why on earth did they?"

One morning, several weeks after Joe's arrival, Georgina, at breakfast, expressed a desire for grapefruit.

"Grape fruit—you mean the fruit of the grape vine . . . nothing simpler," Joe said, and with a slight 'swoosh' a large bunch of white grapes appeared on the table.

"I *do* wish you wouldn't do tricks like that, without warning me first, Joe," Georgina said, a trifle crossly. "It always startles me—and on a practically empty stomach, too. Besides, that's not what I meant. . . ."

"I am extremely sorry," Joe said penitently. "I had no desire to startle you . . . but only the wish to give you pleasure—"

"I know it, Joe," Georgina smiled and patted his hand as if he were a precocious child—really, she had become very fond of Joe—"and you do spoil me abominably. Really I believe that all this pandering to my whims is bad for me—ruining my character. But it *is* so pleasant." She sighed, detached a few grapes and put them dreamily into her mouth.

"Yes, but what *is* a grapefruit then? What is the country of its origin?" Joe persisted.

"Why, Joe!" Georgina said in mock surprise, "you amaze me. I thought your knowledge of fruit rivalled that of Luther Burbank."

"It is a name I do not know," Joe said humbly. "I pray you relieve me of the burden of my ignorance."

It was really a shame to tease him so, particularly when he took it so seriously. "A grapefruit," she explained—"I don't really know quite how to describe it, but it's a large fruit," she made the thumb and third finger of each hand come into a circle, "about that size. The skin is yellow like a lemon, but not so coarse. The meat is pale yellow too, and grained like an orange—but the flavour is most difficult to describe—both bitter and sweet at the same time—and very juicy and refreshing."

"A most amazing fruit," Joe said politely. "Strange I never heard of it. In what country and in what manner does it grow?"

"Oh, on trees, in a number of places," Georgina told him, pushing her chair back. "California—Florida—I believe the best ones come from there." She looked at her watch. "Good Lord! I'll be late. I must dash! Goodbye, Joe, have a pleasant day."

It was raining when Miss Carter left the office that evening; therefore it was more than ever pleasant to get home to a fire already lit, a dinner already prepared—and a dozen or more grapefruit, glowing like small, pale Belisha beacons—decoratively arranged on a low table by the fire. Joe sat cross-legged beside them. He hated chairs and found them vastly uncomfortable, he had confided to her.

"Joe dear!" Miss Carter exclaimed. "What a delightful surprise. How very nice of you! How did you manage to conjure those up?"

"I didn't," Joe replied. "My powers do not extend to the things I do not know, therefore I cannot produce them. I must seek them out for myself. Though, had you explained that these," he touched a fruit with his finger, "were but an improved variety of Pompelmoose, which indeed I used to be familiar with, I need not then have gone to Florida for them—not but that I didn't enjoy the journey," he added hastily.

"You—went all the way to Florida for these?" Miss Carter exclaimed. "Oh Joe"—disbelief smote her—"Are you *sure*? Florida is so *very* far away."

"It is nothing—merely a matter of a few minutes," he reassured her. "And I picked the fruit myself—fresh from a great orchard—leaving a coin at the base of the tree as you would have wished me to, I know. I thought of you, Miss Carter, and desired that you were with me. The weather was so wonderful, not like this. It was so warm, so sunny—it would have done you good to feel the heat and the sunshine—"

Miss Carter looked at him with curiosity. "Could you take me to Florida?" she asked, a little nervously.

"But easily, my dear Miss Carter!" the Ifrit cried. "Come, put on a warm coat, for the high air is cold—and we will set out at once. You would enjoy the sea-bathing as I did this afternoon—and the women are so gaily dressed, and all colours there are so bright and beautiful."

"No—oh no, Joe," Miss Carter cried, in sudden panic that he might be carried away by his words and carry her with him—"at least not now—I can't leave right now"—her tone was more normal. "I haven't had any dinner. Besides, I'm not sure that I want to go to Florida really. I'm . . . I'm frightened," she admitted, ashamed of her craven heart—her lack of adventurous spirit.

"Frightened! When you are with me!" Joe jumped to his feet. "Oh Miss Carter, how could you be—I, your devoted servant, and,

I had hoped, friend—who lives only to repay the debt he owes you." His voice choked with emotion and he stopped speaking.

Georgina felt a worm. Ifrits were *so* sensitive, and she had not meant to wound him. "Dear Joe," she said, "please forgive me. Of course I'm not frightened of you—or with you—it's just the idea of going through the air such a long way, for the first time. Why, I've never even been up in a plane! That's what frightens me. I must get accustomed to the idea before I do anything so rash. I think I'd like to do a few short trial—er—flights first."

CHAPTER VII

THAT WAS HOW it came about that the following Saturday afternoon Georgina Carter might have been observed sipping tea in a shop in Brighton. In place of a railway ticket she carried in her handbag a snuff-bottle carved of amethyst quartz.

As a matter of fact she *was* observed, (as she drank her tea and ate a bit of cake which looked and tasted like compressed sawdust), very closely observed, by a gentleman dressed in an American major's uniform, who might have been fifty or perhaps a bit less. The major just sat and stared at Georgina—in fact, had his stare been less fixed, had Georgina been twenty-five years younger, his look might have been interpreted as an ogle.

Georgina, though not of an age to be ogled, was in truth looking quite charming. She wore a soft brown tweed suit with a coral pullover, and over that a brown travelling coat flecked faintly with sage-green. Her small brown hat was plain and becoming—not the usual middle-aged spinster's hat, for it was neither too young nor too old for her. Her cheeks were faintly pink, and her eyes sparkled. There was a definite poise and confidence about her, as if she possessed some inner virtue, some secret well of strength or knowledge, some hidden store of security, which gave her the look of one who was master of her own destiny and of herself. This was, of course, due solely to the fact that she was probably the only woman in England who had just travelled sixty miles (in as many seconds) through the air without visible means of support or locomotion.

The major, having stared for fully three minutes, could bear it no longer. He rose from his chair and crossed over to Georgina's table. "Excuse me," he apologized, and Georgina, who had not noticed his coming, looked up, startled.

"I trust you will not think me rude," he continued, "but are you . . . could you be Miss Georgina Carter?"

Georgina stared—and then suddenly she saw this man, not as an American major, but as a young lieutenant in British uniform. His hair was black, his eyes very blue, he was tall and slim and "Richard!" she exclaimed, and went quite white. "Richard Taylor! What on earth! . . . I just don't believe it . . . oh, *do* sit down . . ."

The major sat down rather heavily. "Of all the incredible things, Georgina . . . I kept staring at you, hardly believing that it could be you—yet I knew it must be—"

"If you tell me I haven't changed a bit," she said, "I shall hate you."

The major laughed. "We've both changed. . . . It took you nearly a minute to recognize me . . . twenty-odd years is a pretty long time . . ."

"And yet," Georgina said, with pardonable sentimentality, "it might be yesterday." She pulled herself up suddenly. Seeing him, after all these years, was bringing back memories which had once been painful. There were so many things she wanted to ask him—most of them couldn't be asked—at least not now. So she said: "What are you doing in Brighton?" and added: "What a stupid question—I haven't seen you for so long I just don't know where one should begin . . . but it does seem odd to find you here, of all places—"

"I find it more than a little odd myself," he told her. "I was in Washington only a week ago to-day. Sheer sentimentality brought me here—to Brighton, I mean. My parents used to live in Hove—I still own some property there. I haven't been in England since just after the last war, you know."

"Yes, I knew you'd gone away," Georgina said, a little stiffly. "Robert told me—"

"Good old Robert!" the major cried. "Gad, I'd like to see him again. How is he? Is he here or still in India?"

"Neither," Georgina told him. "He was at Singapore . . ."

"Oh Lord, I *am* sorry to hear that." The major's voice was warm with sympathy. "I suppose he's—I mean . . ."

"Reported missing . . . believed to be a prisoner of war. I haven't heard . . ."

"How terribly difficult for you," the major said. "Is there anything I can do to help? I know how agonizing it is, waiting for news. My son was posted as missing in the Philippines."

"Oh," said Georgina. "Oh, I am sorry," and she wondered swiftly what his wife was like. "Did you hear finally? Is he alright?"

"Oh yes, I heard eventually, and he *says* he's alright . . . but you never know . . . he's so young, only twenty-two . . ."

"Robert has a son too," Georgina told him. "Probably you knew that, though. He's in Canada now, finishing his R.A.F. training."

"Yes, I did know about the son. Robert sent me an announcement at the time he was born. Tell me, Georgina, how's his wife, Ellen? Is she over here with you?"

Georgina shook her head. "You hadn't heard, then, Ellen died ten years ago," she said. "It was a dreadful blow to Robert; they were absolutely devoted."

The major sighed. "I'm certainly sorry to hear that," he said. "I can feel for Robert. My wife died shortly after our boy was born." Georgina was horrified and ashamed to find that her sympathy was not unmixed with relief. I'm a wicked, foolish woman, she told herself sternly. Still—it was rather hard to deal with a situation in which you found yourself suddenly confronted, after nearly a quarter of a century, by a man for whom you had once cherished a desperate and hopeless affection! It was bound to be a trifle embarrassing emotionally. "And so you had to bring up your son yourself," she said. "How dreadfully difficult for you," and realized, with scorn for herself, that she was really asking "Did you marry again?"

"Yes," he said, "it was difficult in a great many ways. But he's a grand boy despite the faults of his upbringing for which I'm afraid I'm alone responsible. You'd love Simon, Georgina—everyone does." He laughed. "Funny my having an American son, isn't it? Simon's certainly that all right."

"Does he speak like one too?" she asked, smiling.

"Lord, yes! Even chews gum in the reckless American manner."

"*You* don't—I don't mean chew gum—there's only a trace of American in your voice. Did you become an American too? But how silly of me—of course you did, or you wouldn't be in that uniform."

"Don't be misled by this uniform," he told her. "It's just a form of fancy dress. I'm an American citizen alright, but not an active soldier. Too old for that—besides, as you may have noticed, the last war left me with a stiff ankle. No, I'm here purely as an observer in a way—doing a sort of liaison propaganda job. Anglo-American co-operation you might call it. Interesting, but maddening at times—but Georgina, tell me about yourself. We've done nothing but talk about me!"

Georgina was struck with sudden panic. What was there to tell? Nothing had happened to her in the interval. She had not married, produced children, become famous or infamous. There was just a space—twenty-five years—flat like that. Nothing had happened; she had just stood and watched nothing happen. She doubted if there were anyone on earth duller, less interesting, than herself. But . . . but . . . there was Joe! Good heavens, she's completely forgotten about Joe. She gripped her handbag. He must be so bored, cooped up in that bottle. But she couldn't tell Richard about Joe . . . couldn't possibly explain. He'd think that time past had affected her not only physically, but mentally as well.

But she had to say something; already too long an interval had passed since his question. She sighed. "There's nothing to tell, Richard," she said, wishing in a way she were unscrupulous, or had sufficient imagination to invent a few lurid details. "I've done nothing, really; haven't married or taken to chicken farming, or even good works. Have a small income from my father's estate, and am now working in the Censorship—exactly as I did in the last war if you remember. I'm afraid it's all very dull."

"I'm sure it's not really," the Major said gallantly. "You're just being modest as usual, or terribly English. Georgina, forgive the rudeness and curiosity of an old friend—why didn't you marry? There were a number of young men—friends of Robert—who were in constant attendance. I remember one—John . . . John Evans. I thought—thought . . ."

"John Evans?" she cried, "goodness, no—there was nothing in that." How very tactless this question had been; really, sometimes men were as sensitive as cabbages. "But as to why I didn't marry—well, there are many women like myself in England," she admitted frankly. "The men who might have married us were killed in the last war." She did not add "or left the country, if they could, to find jobs."

"There used to be a lot of morbid talk about the 'lost generation' back in the 'twenties," she went on, "but we are really the lost generation, only we didn't rush around screaming about it— too inhibited or ashamed to, perhaps . . ."

She was thankful to be interrupted by a waitress who begged that if they were finished they would remove themselves, as there were others waiting for tables.

The major said "Sure," and asked for a bill. He also asked Georgina what she was going to do next.

"Go home," she told him.

"Then you live in Brighton? No," he corrected himself, "of course you don't if you're in the Censorship. You're going back to London—what train?"

This staggered Georgina for a moment—she'd forgotten the usual mode of travel. "Oh . . . about sixish," she lied. "I'm not quite sure of the exact minute."

"Seven minutes past six," he told her authoritatively. "I know it's the one I planned to go back on. How lucky—we can travel up together. Here you are." He handed the waitress a note and rose to assist Georgina with her coat.

Georgina was thinking fast. It was simply appalling how quickly one lie could involve you in another, and how dreadfully enmeshed you got. She wasn't a good liar, and she knew it, but what on earth could she say to excuse herself from travelling on the same train with Richard? What about Joe? He'd be so disappointed. What about having no ticket? She could pretend she'd lost it, of course, but that would make her look so stupid and inefficient. Besides, she really didn't want to return to London on a train, even with Richard. She preferred to go by air. She hadn't realized how wonderfully exhilarating air travel could be. Joe had carefully deposited her in an empty field between Rottingdean and Brighton, and she had caught a 'bus into the town. She had planned to go back the same way, and now what could she do? Having said she was going by train and at about six, she must stick by it. There seemed no alternative, unless she wished to appear either scatter-witted or just plain rude—and she didn't want Richard to think her either of those. But how would she let Joe know of the enforced change of plans? She must try to find some opportunity of telling him—but how, or where? The ladies' lavatory was the only refuge left, but somehow she felt it was hardly the place for an Ifrit.

The major got his change, left a tip, looked at his watch. "Ready?" he asked.

Georgina nodded.

"It's twenty to six," he said. "Plenty of time—we can stroll along to the station."

They walked slowly to the station. At the barrier Georgina admitted, with genuine confusion, that she couldn't find the return half of her ticket. It was true in a way, she consoled herself, for you couldn't find what you'd never had.

But this apparent carelessness put the major in an even better humour. He laughed heartily and remarked "How like a woman!" Georgina privately wanted to hit him—he might have spared her that—but of course, she had *put* herself in a position to be more or less insulted—she, who had always prided herself on her efficiency and neatness of mind!

He redeemed himself, however, by remarking further how pleasant it was to find a thoroughly human woman for a change, and not a monster of efficiency and self-sufficiency masquerading in feminine attire. Although she deplored his attitude to herself, she nevertheless made a careful note of it—women had changed, perhaps, but men obviously hadn't.

He bought her a ticket and a 'Lilliput,' found two corner seats, asked if she minded a pipe, was assured that she not only didn't mind but actually liked it, offered her a cigarette, which she accepted (though she rarely smoked), and they settled down for a comfortable journey.

When they arrived at Victoria they knew very little more about each other, for the carriage had been too crowded for much intimate conversation or questioning. But he had invited her to dine with him the following Wednesday. She had, however, refused, insisting instead that he came to tea the following Sunday. For she preferred to meet him next time on her own ground.

They said good-bye at the Underground. She went home and released Joe immediately, explaining—for he was somewhat confused to find that they were back in the flat—what had happened, in great detail.

"And a very good thing," Joe said sagely as she finished her story. "I quite understand why you could not avail yourself of my services."

"But wasn't it really the strangest coincidence," Georgina said happily, "that I should pick to-day of all days to go to Brighton, of all places!"

Joe smiled and raised an enquiring eyebrow. "Coincidence?" he said.

CHAPTER VIII

IN THE WEEK that elapsed between her meeting with Richard Taylor and her Sunday tea party Georgina had plenty of things to think about but little inclination to think them. Sometimes she almost regretted the chance which had been responsible for their meeting in Brighton. The past was, after all, the past— not even owning an Ifrit could alter that—and it should be left decently dead and buried, not resurrected suddenly to hit one in the face. And surely it was true that the ghost of a slim young man whom she had once found infinitely attractive was, equally infinitely, preferable to a solid, middle-aged major, a widower with one son! She wondered if the meeting with her had made Richard feel the same way. Probably not. Men were more practical than women about such ghosts. Men were inclined to be sentimental about the past, while women were downright romantic. It was all very foolish—Richard had never really cared a farthing for her—and now he was only pleased to see her as one would be glad to see any old acquaintance when one was far from home. It was a little—well, indecent was almost the word she wanted—that she should make such a 'thing' about it. She was Georgina Carter, forty-seven years old, presumably adult— not Georgina Carter aged twenty-one, sitting between Robert and Richard at His Majesty's Theatre and being enormously diverted by 'Chu Chin Chow.'

Strange how the music of that show had remained for ever evocative of that first meeting. Strange, too, that she found herself mesmerised into making an appointment to have her face, hair, and finger-nails done the following Saturday morning.

But, despite all her mental and emotional indecision, she did not neglect Joe. Indeed, she threw herself into the job of educating him with more zeal than ever . . . it was such a relief to have something useful and practical to do. He had by this time mastered the alphabet, and she now set herself the task of teaching him to read. He learned very quickly, and in a very few days had mastered such intricacies as "The cat sat on the mat" and "The rat is in the trap"—although, as he pointed out, such sentences seemed to be of no particular beauty or utility.

But Joe was eager to learn. He had all the insatiable curiosity of a child, combined with an adult, or apparently adult, mind. His theme was still "Why?" She found it comparatively simple to tell him who Hitler and Mussolini were, for example—she found it less simple to explain why they were. She could tell him how cities vast and sprawling came about; she found it difficult to explain why people lived on top of one another in great structures built like a book-case.

Oddly enough, his questions did not exasperate or tire her. She enjoyed trying to answer them, though she felt herself to be hopelessly inadequate to the task. Still, having Joe about forced her to think for herself to explore new lines of thought. Living alone, she admitted to herself, had certainly tended to make her lazy-minded, self-centred perhaps. Learning, or at least keeping alive to new things, simply for one's own sake, with no one to share one's thoughts or even to argue with, was a bore and hardly worth the trouble. And so one let things slide, one's mind functioned on the surface only, one accepted the obvious, slipped into easy grooves—well, the only difference between a groove and a grave was one of dimension! She saw that now. Joe was therefore good for her. He had become a mental stimulant, and she did her careful and conscientious best not to misinform him on any subject about which he asked a question. For she determined he should not become a pale reflection of her own opinions, for what opinions she held were, at worst, wrong or superficial, or at best, a little out of date. Therefore she did her utmost to be scrupulously objective, and found that the most difficult problem of all.

When Sunday finally caught up with her Joe took the afternoon off. She realized after he had gone that he was merely being tactful—for all week long he had expressed a rather embarrassing desire to know more about the major. Yes, it was tact that had taken him away from the flat—for he couldn't be really interested in the Zoo! Wherever he came from—and Georgina had only the vaguest idea of where that was, for all middle-Eastern

countries seemed so terribly similar and so difficult to iden-
tify, particularly as they changed their names so often—she was
sure he must have seen a greater variety of strange and interesting animals than were housed at Regent's Park in war-time.
She warned him, however, to remain invisible, and, as an added
precaution, insisted that he wear his Western clothes—the neat,
inconspicuous lounge suit she had bought him—and she was
firm about not letting him wear the policeman's helmet.

Still, she was grateful for his tact, for it really was better to
have him right out of the house. It was a trifle inhibiting to keep
an eavesdropping wraith in a snuff bottle when entertaining
one's friends, and a little unfair to the friends as well; faintly
reminiscent of the Gestapo and dictaphones concealed in various unsuspected places.

The flat, she thought, looked charming, thanks to Joe, for he
had produced great bowls of roses and lilies and she knew that,
if questioned, she could say they were given her by a friend—
unseasonable though they were—they could have been raised
in a greenhouse. Joe had also provided cakes, similar to those
which had nearly led to disaster with Margaret Mackenzie. She
herself had made sandwiches, and as a special concession to
Joe—and to herself as well—had permitted him to conjure up a
lapis lazuli box filled with sugared plums.

Yet in the hour that passed between Joe's departure and
Richard's arrival she found herself wishing nervously that she
had not asked him to tea. She told herself acidly that she was
an old fool, and was behaving like any addle-pated girl. She
excused herself on the grounds that it was so long since she'd
entertained anyone—Margaret Mackenzie didn't count—let
alone a major of the opposite sex, that it was bound to be a little
unsettling and to make one nervous. Besides, what one earth
would they find to talk about?

Richard arrived with a box of chocolates. "These," he said,
"came all the way from America with me. I've been saving them
for a special occasion. And these," he pulled a small tissue-pa-
per-wrapped package from his tunic pocket—"also came with
me. I brought them for any distant female cousin I might happen

to run into. . . . Hope they're the right size—I'd much rather you had them."

Georgina opened the packet and found three pairs of silk stockings. Real silk—so fine that they looked like a breath. She looked down at her legs, clad in good, sensible lisle. "Richard," she said, "you may think I'm insane, but I just don't care. I'm going to put on a pair of these right now. Oh, I know it's madly impractical of me . . . I *should* save them, but . . ."

He laughed. "You go right ahead," he said. "I believe in enjoying things as they come. Glad you like them."

"You sit here and smoke," she said, passing him a cigarette box. "I shan't be two minutes . . ."

And she wasn't. She returned on legs sheathed in silk, bringing the tea-tray with her and thinking with wry amusement how much more she appreciated stockings given her by Richard than any of Joe's presents.

As they had tea they talked of the past. They remembered the last war. They told each other what had happened since, in greater detail. She found conversation wasn't difficult at all. Of course, Richard did most of the talking, but she was glad of that—besides, what he said was interesting. She discovered that he'd invested his small capital in America in something with the weird name of the 'Tuskalee Gazette'—had, in fact, become a co-editor. The journal had originally been a weekly, and employed four people. He became the fifth. But the 'Tuskalee Gazette' refreshed by new capital and new blood, had grown, had improved, had set out to be an independent paper with independent views—had eventually become a daily, and had in the end made its owners independent. For the 'Tuskalee Gazette' was now known all over America for its sound views and honest reportage. The 'Tuskalee Gazette' had, moreover, gained the reputation of being as prophetic as Old Moore's Almanac, and considerably more accurate. At first this had gone against it, for it had foreseen the depression, the ultimate result of appeasement, and other disasters, and people hadn't liked that. It had prophesied Japan's attack and was violently anti-isolationist as well, but it had never pompously said "I told you so," and so in the end it became popular. It had the reputation now of almost unprecedented integrity. It could be bought by neither politics nor advertisers.

Richard was in England because of his paper and its reputation, and he was on his way to "somewhere else" soon. "I'll be leaving England in about ten days," he told her. "It's a pity, because I have a sentimental desire to see spring once again in England . . . but maybe next year . . ." he sighed.

"Oh, I *am* sorry to hear you're going," she said.

"So am I. But it's an interesting job I'm going on. I'll let you know about it when I get there—if I can. I say, Georgina, I must have a party before I go. How about a theatre Friday night, and supper afterwards?"

"I'd love it—I haven't been to a theatre for ages." Her mind darted through her wardrobe and came out dejected—fortunately no one dressed these days.

"What would you like to see?" he asked. "Got a paper?"

"I've hardly seen anything," she told him, handing him 'the Observer'.

He scanned the theatre column rapidly. "Um," he grunted. "There seem to be a good number of American plays running. Shall we try one of those? Interesting to see if they've suffered a sea change. How about 'Arsenic and Old Lace'—it wowed them in New York . . ."

"I should adore it," she said.

"Good! I'll pick you up here at five and we can have a drink beforehand. How will that do?"

She laughed. "You forget I'm a working woman, Richard, and I'll have to meet you at the theatre. What time does it begin?"

"Six o'clock—an unholy hour," he commented.

"All right—I can just do it if I sneak out a bit early. I'll meet you there at ten to six—will that do?"

"I suppose it will have to," he told her. "You know, Georgina, America hasn't really changed me very much essentially. I'm still pretty conservative and English at heart—or perhaps I mean old-fashioned. I liked the days when things were done with a certain amount of grace and leisure—when we made going to the theatre an event. One called for the lady in the correct manner. She wore white kid gloves, of course, and a bunch of violets pinned to the fur collar of her velvet evening cloak. . . . Silly, isn't it?"

"No," she said, "not silly . . . a pretty picture, but quite false. That picture belonged to our mothers and fathers more than it belongs to us. We're really post-last-war, Richard, not post-Boer-war . . . and even then leisure and elegance were mannerisms of the past and appeared as ridiculous to the young. . . ."

"You're right, you know," he laughed, "but as one grows older one regrets . . ."

"The charm and grace one never had," she broke in. "Oh, I know the feeling, Richard . . . it's terribly nostalgic, but it's really part of the remembrance of one's childhood—and a late Victorian and Edwardian childhood at that, and the eyes through which we saw our parents. It's just our bad luck that our youth fell in a period of transition—it makes one romanticize one's childhood so."

"Our youth," he said, and sighed. "Would you like to be young again, Georgina?" he asked.

"Only if one could be young . . . and different. No, on the whole I don't think I would."

"Most women would have resented that question," he said. "American women have a fetish about keeping young, you know—it's very tiring, really—particularly if they remain adolescent all their lives."

"Good heavens, Richard!" Georgina said. "You must be living in another era. I hope women have learned to be sensible instead of sensitive about age. It's no good minding about age these days, not in this country at any rate—we have to fill it in on so many official forms . . ."

"Dear Georgina," Richard said, in a fond, elder-brother voice. "What I like about you is that you're feminine without being either silly or aggressive."

She didn't quite know what to do with that remark. Its flattery made her uncomfortable, and it was certainly not the remark of a typical Englishman. But Richard could be counted now more

American than English. Besides, she knew how unworthy she was of this tribute, for not two hours ago she'd been indulging in the silliest thoughts. Aggressive—no; silly—yes. So she just smiled and said "Well, well—it's nice to be thought sensible. But about the theatre—it's agreed, then, that I meet you in the foyer at about ten to six." The sentence, she thought, sounded both ungracious and greedy, but he seemed not to notice.

"That's the programme," he said, "and be prepared for a large evening. Golly, Georgina, do you remember the last show we saw together? . . ."

To pretend not to know would be worse than silly, it would be downright coy. "Of course I do!" she answered enthusiastically, "'Chu Chin Chow!'"

"Well, fancy your remembering!" he said, delighted, and hummed, slightly off key, the first bars of the Cobbler's Song. "I've often recalled it myself—a sort of nostalgic hair-shirt—but I didn't think *you'd* remember. You, Robert and I. Poor old Robert—I certainly would like to see him. We'll plan a post-war reunion, shall we?"

She smiled but didn't answer, because she couldn't. "How awkward I am," she thought. "I never know what to do with my mental hands and feet."

He looked at his watch, remarked a dinner engagement, and was off, repeating earnestly as he left the date, the time, the place of their next meeting.

She wondered, as the door closed behind him, if all men didn't at heart regard all women as congenital idiots and incapable of following out the simplest routine or remembering the most elementary instructions. Still, it was rather more pleasant than annoying to be regarded as such, for a change. Perhaps she'd always been too independent. But she'd never had much choice—independence was so often the sole refuge of a woman who was shy and plain.

"Now what on earth shall I wear?" she murmured aloud to herself as she returned to the living room and observed without surprise that Joe had returned.

What did surprise her, though, was that he had obviously brought a parakeet back with him, for it perched on his shoulder—a splash of vivid, varied colours.

"Joe," she said wearily, "you'll have to take that bird back—"

"But they have others," he said, "—I thought it would bring brightness into this room . . ."

She shook her head. "I'm sorry, Joe," she said. "It was very thoughtful of you, but we can't keep it. Now run along and return it, there's a dear."

The parakeet, obviously stung by this reception, opened its beak. "Dirty old b. . . ." it said, in a raucous, mechanical voice. "Dirty old b. . . ."

Georgina covered her ears. "Take that bird out of here at once," she said firmly. "And Joe, don't you ever let me catch you using that word . . ."

"B. . . ." said Joe—"a word I do not know. What does it mean, Miss Carter?"

But Georgina did not hear him—her hands were still clapped to her ears—though she guessed his question.

"Be off," she said firmly, "and stay invisible." Really, sometimes even a well-intentioned Ifrit was a strain.

CHAPTER IX

IT WAS UNFORTUNATE that on Wednesday of that week Margaret Mackenzie should invite Georgina to accompany her to a lecture on Friday evening, for Georgina was forced to refuse.

"I'm so sorry, my dear," she said rather unconvincingly as she removed the top of her soap-dish, for the invitation had been issued in the wash-room as they prepared to go home—"but I'm going to the theatre on Friday."

"Oh," said Margaret, "Oh, I see . . ." But she didn't see at all, for wasn't it only a few weeks ago that Georgina had refused to go to the theatre, saying quite definitely that there was nothing on which interested her? "You'd have enjoyed this lecture, then," she continued, with slight bitterness. "It's on Drama through the Ages—given by an English mistress from Roedean, and illustrated by readings from the greatest dramatists."

Georgina thought privately that she wouldn't have enjoyed it at all. She soaped her hands, thankful to have escaped. Margaret was an inveterate lecture-goer, and she, Georgina, had attended several of these functions with her. They were uniformly dreadful. For one thing, they never began on time. The collapsible chairs were hard, and not infrequently lived up to their name. The audience looked dreary and coughed incessantly, while the lecturer seldom, if ever, had anything of sufficient interest to say to overcome the external discomforts of a lecture hall. Still, in a way she admired Margaret's dogged pursuit of—she supposed it was culture. . . . Margaret at least made an effort to keep herself mentally alert. She dried her hands, conscious that by her refusal the unacknowledged breach between Margaret and herself had widened. She attempted to bridge it by saying "Oh dear, I *am* sorry to miss it. It sounds most interesting—but you know how it is I've made another engagement and I just can't break it."

"Of course not," Margaret agreed, a little stiffly. "I quite understand." She wanted to ask "Who are you going with? What are you going to see?" But . . . well, the wash-room was crowded, and as Georgina hadn't vouchsafed the information of her own free will and accord, Margaret felt she couldn't very well ask.

They finished washing and went to get their coats and hats in silence, Margaret thinking that Georgina certainly *had* changed recently; Georgina feeling, with a certain amount of impatient guilt, that she was treating Margaret badly.

As they put on their coats and adjusted their hats, Georgina made an effort at reconciliation. "Let's go and have a drink before going home," she said, suddenly.

"A what?" Margaret's voice was shrill with surprise.

"A drink, dear—a sherry or something. I'm sure it would do us both good. It's been a thoroughly exasperating day. I'm tired, and I'm sure you must be too."

In all the years Margaret had known Georgina, she had never known her to make such a suggestion—not a drink just for the sake of a drink! When they had gone out to dinner before the war, or had dined together at Margaret's house or Georgina's flat, they had indulged in a glass of sherry or perhaps a mild, sweet cocktail of grapefruit juice and a salt-spoon full of gin. Could it be . . . could it be . . . that Georgina was drinking secretly? Margaret shuddered with horror at the thought . . . impossible, of course, but she remembered, too, the wife of the organist of the Church of St. Eulalia in the village where she had lived as a child—a most competent and capable woman who had gradually become queerer and queerer and more and more irresponsible. Everyone in the village had put it down to pressure on the brain or high blood pressure, and had been sympathetic and kind and had ignored it, until one day the lady had been discovered dead drunk and naked in the choir loft by old Dunaway, the sexton— and, of course, it leaked out—the whisper went round that she drank! Gossip had it that the organ itself had been used as a cache for spirituous liquors, which no doubt accounted for some of the extraordinary wheezes from the instrument itself. Naturally, such gossip could not be kept from the tender ears of the young Margaret and the hushed and scandalized voices in which the sad tale had been unfolded had made a deep impression on her . . . and to think no one in the village had ever suspected that the poor woman drank. . . .

"Well, what about it?" Georgina's voice snapped her out of her contemplation of the past.

Margaret made a rapid decision. She would accept! She must accept. If Georgina stopped at one drink, that would be alright. If, however, she asked for another . . . ! "I'd like a drink, Georgina," she said. "I do feel a trifle over-tired—where shall we go?"

"Oh, there are dozens of places," Georgina said airily, and Margaret felt that her worst fears were confirmed. "There's that little bar, the Green something or other, not far from here. How about that?" They walked down the corridor together.

"Isn't that rather too near the office, dear?" Margaret asked timidly, terrified lest Georgina's 'weakness' be discovered by any other member of the staff.

But Georgina was quite brazen. "What earthly difference does that make?" she laughed. "Just because we happen to be employed in the Censorship is no reason why we should allow it to inhibit our actions out of office hours." She essayed a pun—"We may be censors, but we needn't be censured."

Margaret felt slightly sick. One always read that these unfortunates who were addicted to drink or drugs would go to any length to get them—would toss decency and discretion to the winds. "Just as you like," she agreed, in a barely audible voice.

They came out of the building and turned a corner. "There," Georgina said, pointing to a small doorway—"there's the place I mean—'The Green Bay Tree.'"

Margaret, murmuring mentally "and the evil shall flourish," followed her in. Thank God the place was almost deserted. She sank gratefully into a shabby, green-covered chair near the entrance. A Methuselah of a waiter crept up to their table.

"Two light sherries, please," said Georgina.

"Eh?" the waiter queried, cupping a thin hand behind his ear.

Georgina repeated the order in a louder tone.

"No sherry, madam," he said, shaking his head.

"Oh dear," said Georgina—"What will you have instead, Margaret?"

"I don't know," Margaret answered, wishing she had the courage to say "nothing" and walk firmly out of the place.

"Whisky?" the waiter suggested helpfully, "or a gin and something . . . ?"

The bar was filling up rapidly. The waiter looked round at his potential customers. "Have a pink gin," he advised.

Margaret nodded. Georgina shook her head. "Not for me," she said. "I'll have a whisky and a small bottle of soda water, please."

"Eh?" the waiter enquired.

"Whisky," Georgina raised her voice, and to Margaret it seemed as if she bellowed, and that everyone in the room paused and turned to look.

Georgina was not in the slightest perturbed. "You know, Margaret," she said, as the waiter left them, "it seems to me that our lives need a little brightening—the same old routine breeds a habit of mind as well as of body."

Margaret could only nod. She had been brought up in the school which believed that no lady drank whisky, except for medicinal purposes. Gin was only just permitted, for use in cocktails—was a pink gin a cocktail? It sounded as if it might be one—she'd chosen it because pink was such a nice safe colour.

Georgina was quite oblivious to Margaret's unhappiness. She felt as if she'd struck a blow, if not for freedom, at least for sophistication. "My trouble has always been," she confided, as she tasted the whisky and only just saved herself from making a face—"that I've never allowed myself to do any of the things I've really wanted to do."

Margaret closed her eyes. This was dreadful. God knew what shattering revelations Georgina was about to make! Drink did away with all reticences. She hoped Georgina would remember that she, Margaret, was not deaf like the waiter, and would therefore keep her voice pitched low.

"I don't think," Georgina went on, "that I've ever been gay enough . . . spontaneous enough, if you know what I mean. Perhaps I've always been too concerned with what people might say or think about me. It's the penalty of a Victorian upbringing, I suppose. But you know, Margaret, I think after all it's a mistake. One misses a lot—one becomes isolated—self-centred." She looked at Margaret and observed her closed eyes. "Oh, my dear," she said, "what *is* the matter—have you got a headache? I *am* so sorry. . . ."

Margaret clutched at the straw. "A dreadful headache," she admitted, untruthfully. "It's been coming on all day. Do you mind if we just finish our drinks rather quickly and go home?"

"Not at all." Georgina was genuinely sympathetic. "I shouldn't have dragged you out."

She felt suddenly flat and disappointed. Her first attempt at more or less unpremeditated and footloose gaiety had not been a success. Margaret had not entered into the spirit of the thing at all! Perhaps Margaret was right, and she only ridiculous.

She paid the bill, left a tip and they went outside in silence. "Are you sure you can get home all right?" Georgina asked.

"Of course I can"—Margaret's voice was emphatic with relief.

"Good night, then. Take some aspirin and go straight to bed. See you to-morrow."

They turned in opposite directions, Margaret wondering whether Georgina would really go home; Georgina consoling herself with the thought that perhaps it was better this way—for she might, in an unwise moment, have told Margaret about Joe. And Margaret—she saw it quite clearly now—was just not the person who could understand or appreciate Joe, even though she were confronted by him in the flesh. . . . In fact, Georgina doubted if Margaret would even acknowledge his existence, other than as a hoax!

CHAPTER X

GEORGINA WAS STILL feeling vexed and depressed when she got home. It was futile to try to be gay unless there was some-one to be gay with. She wondered if that were typically English of her. The English were never just gay by themselves out of sheer exuberance of spirit. They seldom laughed or sang in the streets unless harmlessly potty or 'under the influence.' Or didn't she really know anything about it. Had she become so out of touch with people and events that she no longer knew (if she ever had known) what was fact and what was fancy! Why! the whole national character of the race might have changed in the past twenty years without her being aware of it. Anyway, wasn't it just slightly idiotic to attempt even the mildest gaiety in the middle of the war and at her age!

How had she ever reached forty-seven, she suddenly asked herself, almost without knowing it or anything else for that matter—sleep-walking her way through all those years! It was dreadful. She had lived, she told herself as she let herself into the flat, with about as much imagination and awareness as a stuffed owl under a glass dome in an empty house—and now there was next to nothing she could do about it.

But her depression lifted a bit as she removed her hat and coat and remembered Joe! She might have missed much but *there* was an experience no one else had had—at least not for thousands of years and so it might be claimed as being original and peculiar to herself. Even though Joe could be accounted responsible for her sudden dissatisfaction with herself, it was at least interesting to have him around. Or was Joe really responsible—wasn't it perhaps the sight of Richard Taylor which had suddenly made her feel how empty and wasted her life had been. "A bit of both," she said, "and you're a dreadful fool, Georgina Carter, to start such a fuss about living now. There's nothing to be done but accept the situation as gracefully as you used to do—and be glad that"— she stopped impatiently—"but I'm a different person," she told herself, "I don't feel a bit like myself—at least half the time I do and half the time I don't . . . it's all *so* unsettling and difficult. Then be firm with yourself, you idiot—an elderly spinster who attempts a first and last fling is a ridiculous and even pitiable object." It always made her feel better to scold herself.

So she felt almost cheerful as she opened the living room door and stepped into, not her own living room, but what appeared to be a technicolour version of the interior of a sultan's tent!

For the room, her room, no longer existed. Gone were the comfortable, plain covered easy chairs, gone was the dark green carpet. Vanished the tables and the inherited tallboy, the few well-chosen water colours and grandmother's sampler (*quite* good enough for a museum). The place was a riot of silken hangings, Oriental rugs and piled cushions. The old-fashioned high ceiling was hidden by a billowing canopy of heavy silk, striped in cerulean and white: suspended from the centre was an ornate bowl-shaped lamp of pierced silver, which gave off a soft but slightly smoky light. The walls were clothed in salmon pink and turquoise damask patterned with flowers worked in gold. Where the couch had stood against the wall, there was now a luxurious divan, soft with rugs and cushions. Low tables, laden with fruits and all manner of sweetmeats, stood dotted about the room. Only the fireplace remained as it had been and standing before it was Joe, newly dressed for the occasion—or rather undressed, for he wore nothing but an olive green loin cloth fringed with silver, and two hammered silver bracelets about his upper arms. Moreover, he stood there like a newly cast bronze statue, unsmiling and holding a silver scimitar unsheathed in his right hand.

"This," Miss Carter said to herself with unnatural calm, "is the end. Sooner or later it was bound to come. That I should be beheaded in a silk tent in mid-London by an Ifrit is a fantastic enough ending to any life, no matter how dull or how vivid that life might have been . . ."

She wondered for a moment if, perhaps, unused to whisky as she was, the whole scene might not be a rather rare form of delirium tremens. She thought rapidly of what Richard's feelings might be when she failed to meet him in the foyer on Friday evening. Her mind flew to Henry, to Robert, and passed to the revolting headlines sure to appear in the gutter-press despite the paper shortage—hints of a secret cult—implications of obscene rites—a mad recluse—a woman of curious tastes and habits. She shuddered, the fatalistic calm dissolving; the publicity horrified her more than the thought of the crime about to be committed. She put her hands up to her eyes. How awful! she was going to faint . . . still it was better far to die unconscious . . . she swayed and a strong arm steadied her.

"Why, Miss Carter," Joe's voice was as gentle as it was astonished. "You are unwell. I am indeed sorry. I have no doubt stunned you with my little surprise. Come, lie down and rest—a cooling drink—for I perceive you are fevered . . ."

"Delirious," she murmured as he led her carefully to the divan and, arranging cushions and rugs, seated her there. It was all much too much—she felt as limp as a rag. What a weak person she was, scaring herself to death.

"There," Joe soothed, holding a goblet to her lips, "drink this, it will do you good."

She sipped it. The room was so hot, so stuffy, with all those beautiful but she was sure insanitary hangings. The liquid was so cool and refreshing, she went on sipping slowly.

"But Joe, where are all my things?" she asked faintly, "my furniture, my books, my pictures . . ."

"Oh those paltry and unsuitable furnishings," Joe said with faint contempt, "they are well concealed on the roof behind the parapet. Have no fear, I will dispose of them to-night—I shall drop them into the sea. This setting," he encompassed the room with an airy wave of the hand, "is infinitely more worthy of your quality, Miss Carter . . . it is not unworthy of a queen. Here you may entertain your friend the Major in a manner which will make his senses swoon with delight. He will be ravished by such splendour and magnificence. He will sue for your hand and heart," he finished happily.

Miss Carter didn't know whether she felt more like Sarah Crewe or a—houri (she had some difficulty in remembering the word), probably the latter. Divans—or rather an oriental divan—*looked* so abandoned! She felt uncomfortable. Joe had, as usual, with childlike directness and total lack of embarrassment, planned all this for her sake—or for the sake of ensnaring Richard Taylor . . .

He broke in on her silence. "As for myself," he said, "I am now clothed in a manner befitting your slave. What you and your lover wish it will be my duty and indeed my pleasure to perform."

"Joe," Georgina interrupted. "You have a wrong idea about the Major and myself. We are friends—good friends—we have known each other for years. You must not refer to him as my lover—for that word has a narrow meaning in our language."

"Oh, my mistress, . . ." he cried, "What . . ."

"And don't call me your mistress either," she said testily. "It's an old-fashioned word. We do not use it either . . ." How delicate the conversation, how difficult—perhaps she was super-sensitive. She took another sip of her drink.

"Then all this is unavailing, of no use, you do not like it," Joe's voice wailed with despair and frustration.

Georgina was sorry for him, but what could she do! She couldn't live in a room like this! She hadn't the temperament for it. And besides, she'd never be able to entertain anyone in the place. They simply wouldn't understand—and where would she have been able to get such silk, satins, damasks, without coupons!—or money. It was no use—though she regretted the dullness of her life, she couldn't change now, couldn't plunge slap into such flamboyance—it just wasn't in her nature. She couldn't live up—Or down—as the case might be to such a setting.

So she said, "Joe dear—you are the kindest, most thoughtful person I know. But you must believe me when I tell you that this beautiful room does not suit me. I am neither young, nor beautiful. Nor are my friends, and if they saw me here, they would not understand . . . and I couldn't explain about you and your gifts . . . they'd think me mad. Besides . . . besides . . . Major Taylor likes me—if at all—because I remind him a little of things as they used to be in his youth. If I changed . . . if the setting were changed, it would terrify him. He would probably stop being my friend. I can't afford to lose friends, Joe, I have so few . . ." she finished her drink. How tired, how sleepy she was—she hoped he understood; she hoped she hadn't hurt him. She could hardly keep her eyes open . . . strange . . . emotion of any sort was no doubt exhausting. Her head fell back among the cushions, her body relaxed. "Don't please destroy my furniture . . . bring it back, Joe, you may not think much of it but I do," she murmured and was asleep.

Joe sighed and smiled with satisfaction as he looked at her. Then, pulling a tape measure out from under a cushion, he carefully measured her, length, breadth, width and circumference. "Ah-h," he said softly as he finished, and smiling with delight he rolled up the tape measure, muttered something unintelligible—and vanished.

CHAPTER XI

GEORGINA WAS PUZZLED when she wakened next morning. Half asleep, she lay and pondered where she was . . . it wasn't her neat grey and blue bedroom—furthermore, she seemed to be fully clothed. Then, as her mind stepped clear of sleep, she remembered. Good heavens! She was still lying on that over-luxurious and slightly depraved divan, covered to the chin with a tiger-skin rug. In the semi-darkness she could just make out the striped ceiling and the bulbous hanging lamp. She put out a hand and felt the heavy silk of the walls. She sat up. Impossible to find the light switch beneath all this unfamiliar fabric. . . .

"Joe!" she called sharply—and he was beside her in an instant.

"Yours to command," he said.

"You might let a little light into this tent," she snapped. Her head ached slightly, and she remembered she'd had the most wild and fantastic dreams.

He crossed the room and pulled back the hangings, disclosing the original windows and curtains underneath. It seemed almost as if the good, grey English daylight hesitated to penetrate this gaudy hide-out. Yes—in the morning it looked even more impossible than it had looked last night, she thought, as she pushed back the rug and swung her feet over the edge of the divan. Like some Hollywood set—the Goldwyn touch— or a coloured illustration from an expurgated edition of Scheherezade. It was definitely *not* the kind of room one wanted to wake up in—and what the devil was she doing waking up in it fully clothed?

"Your bath is ready, Miss Carter." Joe's voice was smooth as cream. ". . . and so is your breakfast."

Thank: heaven he had put on his sober western attire again. That loin cloth! That scimitar!

She stood up. "If you've put any of that vile lotus perfume in my bath water this morning," she remarked ungraciously, "I just won't take a bath at all! I reeked of the stuff all yesterday.

I'm sure I affronted the nostrils of the whole office . . . it's too heavy . . ."

"Mountain pine this morning," he reassured her, "very cool, very fragrant, very refreshing. Did you not sleep well?"

"I suppose I must have, as I slept fully clothed and without any dinner. I must have been terribly tired—but you should have wakened me Joe—it always makes me cross and disgruntled to sleep with my clothes on . . . my disposition was simply foul during the blitz."

"But I had not the heart to waken you," he said gently, "you looked so peaceful . . ."

Georgina looked at her watch and let out a yelp. "Good lord, it's ten o'clock! Oh Joe—how could you? I'm hours late!" Her voice was panicky. "And I've never been late in my life!" She made for the door.

"Miss Carter," Joe caught her hand. "Pray take a holiday to-day—it will do you good."

"You just don't understand," Georgina shook herself free. "I can't just stay away from my office unless I'm ill or something."

"But couldn't you pretend to be?" Joe asked, blandly.

Georgina halted in her tracks. "Joe," she started, "that's not the sort of conduct . . ." She stopped. She had been about to read him a little moral lecture about one's responsibility to one's employer and to oneself—about the wrongness of telling a deliberate falsehood to cover a fault. But, lord, lord, she'd break his spirit if she went on at this rate—provided a spirit's spirit could be broken. How insufferable she was! How smug—how pompous—Joe was certainly teaching her as much, if not more, than she taught him—only the things he taught came near to being unpalatable truths!

"And you know," Joe was continuing sweetly, ignoring the interruption, "and you know, Miss Carter, I have arranged for you to-day the most pleasant surprise imaginable."

"Not another!" Georgina wailed. "Oh, not another surprise, Joe—I simply couldn't bear it. I can't bear to have the familiar externals of my life so violently changed or disarranged—the internal changes are difficult enough, as it is."

"Come—take the day off," Joe tempted. "It is already late. The work—oh horrid word—will now be well started, and though you will no doubt be missed for yourself, your work could be done by someone else—just once. Furthermore what would you say if you went in late? What reason would you give?"

"That I overslept." But that sounded absurd—not even absurd—just careless and disinterested—weren't people fined for oversleeping, these days? Besides, she'd never overslept in her life . . . well, better late than never—no, better never late. How confusing the simple things became when one thought about them! And only last evening she had said to Margaret Mackenzie, "I don't think I've ever done what I really wanted to."

"Perhaps I'll think it over," she said weakly, making for the refuge of the bathroom. It was dreadful, wasn't it, the way she was letting Joe corrupt her (how fortunate she hadn't lectured him), for it was corrupt and dishonest to stay away from the office if one hadn't a really valid reason.

She stepped into the bath. Still, she did have a slight headache, and it was her week-end on! The very thought of working at the week-end tired her. No, it was no good looking for an excuse. She ought to be ashamed of herself. If she stayed away it would be deliberately wrong, and she would have to face up to her own conscience.

"Joe," she called, as she soaped herself thoroughly.

"Yes, Miss Carter." His voice only came through the keyhole.

"You didn't destroy my furniture, did you?"

"No, Miss Carter—everything is all right."

"Good. I shan't be long."

She finished her bath, dressed, did her face and returned to the living room. It was as it had always been (Joe was certainly a wizard at getting things done quickly). Dull, perhaps—but home! Her breakfast was waiting on a tray on the table. She rang her office—explained, with only a faint scruple, that she had a sick headache, and that she hoped to be in early in the afternoon.

As she finished her breakfast Joe came back into the room, staggering under the burden of pasteboard boxes of various shapes and sizes piled one on top of another. He placed them as carefully as he could on the sofa. "There," he said, and his voice was triumphant.

"What in the name of Allah—" Miss Carter was amazed to find herself using the word "Allah"—"are those?"

"The surprise, Miss Carter, an it please you to examine it when you are ready. For this time your servant lives in hope that his judgment has been right, that he has erred in no respect, and that this will really please you."

Miss Carter pushed back her chair and crossed to the sofa. "I trust they don't contain zoological specimens," she said, looking down at the boxes. She saw with some misgiving that several seemed to be labelled 'New York.'

"Now what have you been up to this time?" she asked, undoing the top box and removing from it numerous soft folds of white tissue paper. "Oh!" she cried. "Oh, Joe!" and lifted out a frock. But such a frock! Even if the label hadn't told her, the look of it simply cried a famous dressmaker.

It was a very fine, soft wool-georgette, long-sleeved, and the colour was a magic blue. It was perfectly plain, depending only upon line and fabric for its effect. She looked at it—she felt it—she held it up to herself. She put it down, speechless, and opened the next box. Here was a coat of the same marvellous blue, only just a tone darker, and trimmed with a collar and pockets of mink. She slipped into it. It fitted perfectly. She knew she ought to stop opening boxes—knew that she should enquire sternly of Joe just *where* such clothes had come from, but she couldn't. She had to go on—to see—to feel—and then . . .

She opened another box. It contained a pouchy suède handbag in deep wine red, with a great blob of a clasp in gold. There were fine suède gloves to match. Still another box held shoes in the same colour, while another box contained a hat, small, neat, fur-trimmed. Smaller boxes revealed plain, tailored satin underwear, silk stockings and handkerchiefs; while a very small box held a wonderful brooch—a single gigantic sapphire clawed in gold. Held to the light, deep within it she could see the points of a star. She put it down.

"Joe," she said, and her voice shook, "where did all this come from—and how? I don't really want to know for fear I will have to make you take it back, and I confess—immoral as it sounds—I don't think I ever wanted to keep anything quite so much in my whole life . . ."

Joe smiled. "Fear nothing—all is well this time. They are bought and paid for, and couponless."

Georgina's relief was evident in her smile and voice, "you'll have to tell me before I'll believe it," she said.

"Would it not be better if you first tried them on to see if they fit? If they don't there is still time to complete alterations before to-morrow night."

"Oh, Joe," Georgina was near tears. "How *did* you know—how did you guess—I've been longing for something new to wear."

"Do you remember the Sunday the major came to tea?" Joe asked, "the Sunday when I brought home that pretty parakeet for you, but you made me take it back? Well, as you came into the room you were saying quite aloud but to yourself 'What on earth shall I wear?'—and then, later on, you told me that the major had asked you to go to the theatre, so then I knew why you were so rightly troubled about your apparel."

"But Joe, you couldn't have known! I mean . . ." she stopped, remembering an earlier conversation she'd had with him. "Is that why you were asking me what sort of things women wore when they went out to dine publicly in this country? Oh, I know—and you asked me my favourite colour, too. How very clever of you—but . . ."

"But do go and try them on," he interrupted. "One must be sure that they are right in every detail."

Georgina forgot about the office; forgot lectures and scruples. She picked up coat, hat and frock and disappeared into the bedroom with them. She dressed eagerly, and surveyed herself in the long mirror fixed to the back of the door. The clothes were perfect; they fitted almost miraculously—perhaps half an inch more in the length of the skirt—that was all that was necessary. Georgina had always loved clothes—good clothes, and she knew perfectly well, as she reviewed herself in the mirror, that in this new outfit she looked a really handsome woman. Joe's taste was really remarkable—and remembering his love of colour and display, she found it even more incredible that he should have chosen so well—she could not have done better herself.

She returned to the living room, smiling with satisfaction. "There," she addressed Joe, who was doing a little sleight-of-hand with what appeared to a hookah. "How do I look?"

"Splendid, Miss Carter," he cried, making the hookah vanish. "Even I, prejudiced as I am against Western dress—for I much prefer bag trousers for women—think you look as ravishing as—" he stopped. "I almost forgot that *you* have a prejudice against my phraseology. But none the less, I am glad that you are pleased with my surprise—and indeed, Miss Carter, it becomes you wonderfully well. I am sure that the American Major will be astonished and enchanted when he sees you. He will . . ."

"Now, now," Georgina held up an admonitory forefinger. Sometimes she wished that Joe were not quite so uninhibited. "I must let the hem down a bit," she said, changing the subject, "but I can do that to-night—there's plenty of time."

"Indeed! And that I can do for you so do you not trouble yourself," Joe told her. "I find sewing soothing; a pity your costume couldn't have been quite perfect—but you are tall, Miss Carter."

"Don't rub it in, Joe—it's a curse really."

"But fortunately the Major is even taller"—Joe's voice oozed satisfaction.

"You're incurably romantic, Joe; all I'm concerned about is this hem. If I let it down and marked it, do you really think you could do it? Mind you, it has to be done perfectly."

"Nothing simpler," Joe reassured her. "Tell me, do the shoes fit too? They were most difficult to procure. American sizes, I discovered, are quite different from English sizes. In fact, I had to come all the way back here and fetch a pair of your shoes to make sure."

Georgina, who was just leaving the room, was stopped by her conscience. All this was very well, but he hadn't *really* told her *how* he'd got the clothes. He had merely assured her that they were bought and paid for . . . and, of course, he might have been lying.

No matter how good his motives, a lie was still a lie—and no euphemism could really disguise theft as anything but theft. How *had* he managed it—and to get her measurements too? She asked him.

He shifted his weight uneasily from one foot to another, but did not reply.

She came back into the room and sat down. "Tell me all about it, Joe." Her voice was a sigh. She hoped that when he had told her she'd have the courage to make him return the clothes. It was all very difficult . . . but she might have known if was too good to last. The fault was hers—she should have gone straight to the office, should never have allowed herself to try on the clothes without first finding out all about them. "Come, Joe, tell me," she repeated.

"—I do not know what to say," he said, refusing to meet her eye, "for you will be angry with me and perhaps not trust me any more. Yet I could think of no other way of achieving my purpose, for I knew you would argue, object and protest . . ."

"Then if you knew, Joe, it was very, very wrong of you to do it. If you know a thing's wrong, and do it, it's much worse than if you didn't know it was wrong." How terribly moral-reformer she sounded . . . how unbearably priggish—it was dreadful to have to be scolding him continuously for the generous things he did for her—yet it had to be done. She was, after all, responsible for him—and for herself.

"But you felt no ill-effects," he cried. "Oh, Miss Carter, pray reassure me on this point, I took such care that you shouldn't—"

This was a bit of a *non sequitur*. Was it done deliberately to throw her off the scent? "Ill-effects!" she asked.

"Yes," he said, appearing most agitated, "from your sleep."

A great light nearly split Georgina's skull. "Do you mean to tell me you drugged me?" She was very angry—she remembered the cool, refreshing drink—how sleepy she had felt. Obviously he had created that room solely to disguise his *real* purpose.

Joe nodded. "How else could I have taken your measure-ments?" His voice was plaintive. "You would never have allowed me to. Nor would you have allowed me to bring you those lovely clothes. I had to find your exact size so that I would know what size to make myself so that I could try them on—even then it wasn't easy, certain physical characteristics are—but let us not discuss that. I do apologize most sincerely for making you become unconscious and for dissolving in your drink a little bhang."

"A little *what*?"

"Bhang."

"Bang?"

"Yes—if not taken in quantity or habitually it does no harm. Indeed, in some countries it is a form of relaxation and amuse-ment."

"So is wife-beating," Georgina said, a little stiffly, "if you have taste for that sort of thing. Personally I find the whole idea horrifying. Oh Joe—*do* get up," for Joe, in agony of distress or remorse, had fallen to his knees and was now beating his head on the carpeted floor, "Joe!" Her voice was sharp, but it had no effect. Heavens, how difficult it was, and wasn't it all slightly idiotic too? All right, he'd drugged her, and she objected to drugs other than medicinally, on principle. She had the average woman's horror of surrendering her consciousness to anything but natural sleep—why, anything might happen to one in such a condition—but wasn't this case just slightly different? Joe had meant no harm, and provided he promised faithfully never to do it again . . .

She leaned down and said as much in his ear.

"Oh, I *do* promise." He leaped to his feet. "It shall never happen again. I swear by the ring of Sulayman. I meant in no wise to offend you."

Now was the time to show confidence. Although Joe wasn't English, surely he could be trusted. "I'm sure it won't happen again," she said, smiling, "now that you know how I feel about it. Now Joe, tell me all the rest, about the clothes, for you see, I'm not going to be put off the track."

"You have a singleness of purpose worthy of a wazir who aspires to the throne," he commented, "but the clothes are paid for in gold—for gold is good anywhere, you told me that yourself, extraordinary as it seems to me. And do you remember telling me when I asked you—in fact, you troubled to look it up— what gold was worth per ounce in both American and English currency?"

"So that's why you were so interested!" Georgina exclaimed. "I nearly rang up the London School of Economics to see if they had a correspondence course on the subject, for I thought you had decided to become a banker—though how that was to come about I didn't see."

Joe bowed. "A simple ruse," he admitted, "and you will, I trust, pardon the deception for I meant you no harm. And it will soothe you to know that your clothes, though not bought in the sense that I handed out money in a bazaar, are none the less paid for."

"I see . . ." Georgina said, and hoped that this faint acquiescence was not damning her immortal soul.

"Of course, I went to New York for them because of the coupons," he went on. "I knew that, had I attempted to procure such clothing here without coupons you would have scolded me and forced me to return the clothes, as you did the garments I first obtained for myself. You see, I gave the whole problem my most serious consideration, for there were many difficulties to be overcome."

Georgina agreed that he had thought it out in minute detail, and for that she was thankful; but she demurred that the whole affair was just a little irregular, if not illegal.

"But I violated no law," he exclaimed. "I paid in gold—ounces of pure gold, since my coins were worthless as currency—and I paid double the value of the clothes, just to be safe . . ."

"Nevertheless," Georgina broke in, "I don't think that is, strictly speaking, right. I don't know the law, but I don't think you can just go into a shop, after hours, and take things, no matter how much money you leave for them."

"I do not understand why not," Joe answered stubbornly. "It saves much time and fuss. Must we have permission to buy, then, as well as having money?"

"I don't really know," Georgina said helplessly, "but you could probably be charged with breaking and entering . . ."

"But I didn't break anything to get in!" he said indignantly. "Even I know better than to do that. Besides, for me such a foolish course is unnecessary, as you know. I leaked in through the crack underneath the door—if I may use such a phrase. No, Miss Carter, I will not have it that I transgressed the law. You are as afraid of the law as if you had some great guilt to hide—"

Georgina was so startled by his sudden—it wasn't impudence—nor indignation—that she couldn't protest or even be very angry—for what he said was unfortunately true. "Perhaps you're right," she said, a trifle sadly, "but Joe—you force me to say it—it's you I feel guilty about, not myself. It's you I have to hide. You are an alien—you entered this country illegally, according to our law—you're not registered—you have no identity card, and no one in this hard-headed or hard-hearted age would believe your story. No, not if you performed all your tricks before their very eyes—they'd certify themselves first, and I'd be blamed. If you were discovered I'd get into the most frightful trouble, for I should have reported you to the police the minute you—er—arrived. In other words, Joe, I am an accessory."

"Oh, Miss Carter," Joe cried, "you must not suffer on my account. I would rather submit to centuries of imprisonment again rather than that you should be made unhappy. Tell me what to do, and I will do it gladly."

"I suppose," Georgina brooded, "I should give you to the National Trust or allow you to be tracked down by the Society for Psychical Research—they'd no doubt solve the problem—but I can't allow you to become just a rather superior bit of ectoplasm—you're far too intelligent."

"Banish me," he cried, "but do not give me away. Have pity, O merciful mistress, have pity . . ."

"Oh, hush," she said. "I wouldn't give you away for all the world, either literally or figuratively. Other women keep pets—

why shouldn't I?" Still, one has to have a license even for a dog . . . but not for a cat, she thought.

"I am deeply grateful," he said humbly, "and now—do I have to take the clothes back?"

"No." Georgina rose from her chair and went towards the door. "No—you don't. Though I suppose . . ." she broke off, her hand on the door-knob. "Oh Joe," she cried, "be thankful that you haven't a non-conformist conscience. It's hell to live with."

CHAPTER XII

As SHE DRESSED herself carefully next morning for the entertainment of the evening, Georgina felt slightly uneasy. It wasn't that she was dissatisfied with her appearance. Far from it! She knew she'd never looked better in her life. She looked and, what was even more important, felt quite distinguée. But the thing that nagged her was the comment she would cause by appearing in the office in her new finery. To burst suddenly into a drab office, no longer one's drab self, was bound to excite a certain amount of interest—and the thought of it made her feel sharply uncomfortable, even silly. Although she loved clothes, she had a hatred of wearing anything new for the first time . . . it made one feel *so* conspicuous.

Then there was Margaret Mackenzie! She at any rate would be sure to ask perfectly natural but nevertheless *most* awkward questions. Indeed, yesterday afternoon Margaret had interrogated her a little too closely, even for a friend, as to the reason for her absence that morning. Remembering the cross-examination now, it seemed to her that Margaret's attitude had been one of disbelief, even suspicion, despite the fact that she, Georgina, had confessed freely to her that the real reason for her absence had been oversleeping. That was a partial truth, to be sure, but it should have satisfied Margaret, for how could she have told her that it was a drugged slumber induced by an Ifrit who was her servant! No, Margaret certainly wouldn't have believed the real truth and who could blame her! Nevertheless, she was puzzled by Margaret's attitude these days. It was almost as if Margaret were . . . well, perhaps 'spying' was too strong a word.

Georgina thereupon proceeded to her office self-conscious but defiant.

It was as she expected. Questions *were* asked. A little group gathered about her in the wash room at lunchtime, chattering and curious—Really it was simply too girls' school for words. "Where had she got such lovely clothes? . . . and what a beautiful hat. Could someone try it on" . . . and of course she had to say yes . . . and like a fool remembered too late the New York label inside. How lucky she had said 'Harrods' when questioned about the frock. But how to explain a New York hat and coat! Why hadn't she thought of that before . . . or removed the labels and sewn "Swan & Edgar' or something equally respectable and unsuspicious in their place . . . it was too late now . . . she was caught.

But surely hadn't she heard of English people with relatives or friends in the States, who had received gifts of clothing. Why couldn't she invent . . . then she remembered with a wave of relief, Henry! What more natural than that Henry, perturbed by what he'd read and heard about the coupon situation in England, should send his dear Aunt Georgina a warm coat and a hat, with a frock tossed in as a magnificent gesture . . .

Oh dear, oh dear, what terrible untruths one descended to at times!

And though the incredible story of Henry's superb generosity and taste satisfied the office generally and drew forth many undeserved compliments on Henry's nature, a quick look at Margaret as she related the 'facts' showed that her tale hadn't gone down in that quarter. Margaret knew Henry too well. Henry would be too broke, apart from being too young and thoughtless ever to have picked out an outfit like the one she wore.

". . . and . . . and . . . a ferry pilot brought it over to me," she ended, stuttering a little with relief and nervousness. The stutter was, of course, misunderstood to be the result of excitement.

Thank goodness, she thought, I'm not wearing that brooch. That could never be explained by a nephew. The brooch was tucked away in her handbag and she hoped to be able to pin it on, unobserved, before going to the theatre. Really being forced into a life of deceit and deception was too exhausting. She was not, she felt, well cast for such a rôle.

But all this irritation vanished as she walked into the foyer of the theatre that evening. Richard was already there waiting for her. She spotted him at once, despite the crowd.

He took both her gloved hands in his. "Georgina," he said, "you look simply stunning. I've always said you have to go a long way to beat a really well-dressed English woman . . ."

"Now, that's very nice of you, Richard," she said, feeling warm and happy. Running the gauntlet at the office had after all been worth it for this.

". . . and very un-English of me I suppose. Englishmen never do tell women how nice they look. Americans always do . . ."

"Even if they don't?"

"Even if they don't," he repeated. "Good Lord," he exclaimed, realizing what he'd said. "I've spoiled it all by that remark, haven't I? What a clumsy oaf I am . . . comes of being unused to the company of women. Georgina! You look wonderful. I mean it. Come on, it's only about a minute until the curtain goes up."

They came out of the theatre some two hours later still laughing. "I've a car waiting for us," he said as he piloted her down a side street.

"A car! Good lord. I haven't ridden in a car for years. I shan't know how to behave."

"Taxis I find are difficult, so are taxi-drivers. And one can't take a lady out in the evening, particularly such an elegant creature as Miss Carter, and expect her to ride in a common public conveyance, such as a bus—so, I hired a car . . ."

"Really, Richard, you spoil me as much as . . ." she stopped, she had nearly mentioned Joe.

"As who?" he took her up quickly.

". . . as much as you probably spoil that son of yours . . ." she added lamely and was aware that he knew quite well that she had switched the meaning of the sentence. She was thankful that he did not pursue his questioning further.

As he handed her into the car and climbed in beside her, they were both too engrossed to notice a woman hurrying by. It was unfortunate that the woman should be Margaret Mackenzie, just released from the lecture hall nearby. It was unfortunate, too, that just at that moment Richard should light a cigarette, for Margaret saw them both in the instant flame of the match—cameo clear—and by a simple process of addition arrived with a horrid shock at quite the wrong answer.

They dined at Manetta's, and Georgina was persuaded, with some little difficulty, to waltz. For, as Richard pointed out, even if Georgina hadn't danced for years (and he didn't *really* believe that) she had once been very good at it . . . and in any case it didn't much matter what she did with her feet, as the floor was so crowded no one would notice.

Richard, she thought amused, should not attempt gallantry for he always ended on a supremely untactful note. Not that she minded really, in fact in a way it was most reassuring. He waltzed very well, despite his stiff ankle, she thought.

There was also a great deal of satisfaction to be had in looking around the room at the other women. They were for the most part younger and prettier than she was . . . but none was better dressed.

The knowledge that this was so gave her a sweet feeling of power and self-confidence. It was curious, she reflected, that she had started the day in a perfect agony of self-consciousness. She had positively shrunk from appearing in her office in her new clothes and here she was ending the day self-possessed, assured, able to hold her own against a whole roomful of people! It was probably easier to put on a new personality with new clothes, provided one chose strangers to experiment on rather than one's friends and acquaintances. Anyway, it was all very pleasant and exhilarating. It was so nice to be someone else for a change, even though it were only for a few hours.

They left the restaurant at a reasonable hour and as the car arrived at her door she invited Richard in for coffee. "Can't offer you a drink, I'm afraid," she said.

"What, not even a glass of elderberry wine!"

"No, nor even the arsenic" . . . she laughed, remembering the play. "Though I expect you find English coffee poison enough anyway."

"It is pretty frightful," he admitted. "I don't know what they do to it over here—though, as I haven't tasted your coffee, I can't really judge."

"If you mean by that that you expect it to be even worse than the coffee you usually drink, then I'd better give you tea . . ." She led the way up the stairs and he followed.

She wondered a trifle nervously how she would manage to get rid of Joe without Richard knowing it. Joe might be anywhere in the flat, although he usually stayed in the living room. She wished she'd thought to ask him to disappear when he heard her key—but she hadn't really expected to bring Richard home with her.

She opened the door into the small hall. "Can you put your things there?" She pointed to a small chair. "I'll just go ahead into the living room and see if the black-out's done. My char is sometimes forgetful," she lied.

"I'll help," he said, dropping his overcoat on the chair.

"Oh, no—please don't," she begged. Perhaps Joe had heard their voices and had had sense enough to vanish.

"But I'm sure I'm very good at black-outs," he said. "Though you may not believe it, I'm really very handy about the house . . ."

She took him by the hand and led him into the kitchen. "If you're as good as you say you are," she said, handing him a tin of coffee, a spoon, and a coffee pot, "you can prove it by making the coffee." Really she was becoming quite practised in handling a delicate situation.

"Well, I'll be darned," he said, "making me prove my words like this. Georgina you're . . ." but Georgina had vanished into the living room.

"Joe," she hissed, for he was sitting there beside the reading lamp deep in a book called 'The Wonders of Modern Science.' "Joe," she put a finger to her lips, "disappear quickly."

For once Joe obeyed without argument.

"Were you speaking to me, Georgina?" Richard's voice came from the doorway.

She whirled around and saw him standing there. "Oh . . . no," she said. "Oh no . . . I wasn't."

"I could have sworn I heard your voice," he looked slightly puzzled.

Georgina laughed but felt with a mixture of anger and shame that she looked dreadfully guilty. "The black-out *was* done," she exclaimed. "I . . . I . . . just commented on the fact to myself. Living alone, you know, one gets into the way of talking to oneself—a bad habit . . ."

"You know," his voice was serious, "you shouldn't live alone, Georgina . . . it's not good for you. I think I must do som. . ." He stopped suddenly and sniffed. "The coffee!" he cried. "Holy Moses! It's boiling over! . . ." He vanished almost as swiftly as Joe had done.

"Damn the coffee," Georgina swore to herself, jerking off the new hat and flinging it violently on the settee . . . "Damn everything" the coat followed the hat.

The conversation was not resumed when he returned. They talked instead of the play, his work, the war, the past. He was leaving England the early part of next week, he told her, for 'parts unknown'—or rather parts 'unspoken.' He wouldn't be able to see her before he left—he was all tied up with various people unfortunately—but he'd drop her a line when he got to where he was going . . . and, of course, he'd be back . . . sometime.

CHAPTER XIII

BY THE FOLLOWING Tuesday night Georgina knew and admitted that the case was hopeless. No hour had passed since the previous Friday evening that hadn't found her thinking of, or wondering about, Richard.

"This," said Georgina to herself, as she lay awake in the darkness of her bedroom, "is love. And it is," said Georgina, turning over on her side, "most unfortunate and even ridiculous. But," she switched on the bedside light and looked at her watch—3 a.m.—"I dare say I shall get over it. Besides," she reached for a book on the bedside table, "it's all too adolescent of me and I am surprised at myself . . . it's rather like coming down with chicken-pox at seventy. Unexpected and uncalled for. Funny to the outsider—but most unpleasant for oneself."

She put the book back, having discovered that it was 'Little Lessons in Grammar for Beginners.' "Still," she consoled herself, "it's a state—a disease, if you like—that can't last long. I got over it before and I can do it again. It should be simpler the second time—besides perhaps things die more easily as one grows older. One has learned not to want the things one can't have." She turned her pillow. "Oh bother," she cried mentally, "this is all so stupid! And would I really want to marry Richard Taylor? He's nice and comfortable, but he must be as set in his ways as I am in mine. His way of living is totally different. He has a son. Would I want to uproot myself and go to America? A country which has always terrified me!" She sat up in bed. "The answer, equally unfortunate, is yes . . . if he asked me."

She got out of bed and slipped into a woollen dressing-gown and fleece-lined slippers. "I'll make myself a cup of tea," she said. "There's really nothing like tea in a crisis—it got me through the blitz. But I wonder *why* he never married again—too wrapped up in his job and in his son, perhaps."

She went into the kitchen and put the kettle on. "Still, if he were going to marry again, it wouldn't be me, just for old times' sake—it would be someone younger, surely. Men of that age usually do. Well, I hope it's someone nice and stable, someone who won't fling her youth in his face and make him unsure of himself and unhappy. . . . Shut up, you old fool," she said, biting the end of a burned match viciously. "You're getting positively maudlin—holding a little renunciation scene all by yourself—and renouncing something you haven't got."

She took a cup, a saucer and a teapot down from the glass-enclosed cupboard, rattling them noisily against the table as she set them down. She really wanted to fling them on the floor and smash them to pieces, but . . . china was so hard to get these days—besides, they were part of her set of Royal Doulton.

"Miss Carter," Joe's voice came to her from the hall, "Miss Carter! Are you up—are you unwell—is there anything I can do to assist?"

Drat the man, Georgina thought, why couldn't he leave her alone? "I'm only making myself a cup of tea," she called. "I can't get to sleep."

He came into the kitchen. "I will do it for you," he said. "Oh, Miss Carter, you should have called me in the first place. You go and sit down, and I will make you a cup to soothe the liver and cheer the heart. For I perceive, Miss Carter, that you are much agitated and distressed."

"But I *like* to do it myself!" she said, with a touch of irritation, "and I am *not* distressed. You go back to bed, Joe. I'm quite alright, really." It was all very well to tell him to go back to bed, she thought, but how would she like to sleep in a snuff-bottle? She had a moment's vision of the inside of the snuff-bottle filled with minute pieces of furniture, like the tiny ivory carvings that fitted into a walnut shell. An uncle had brought her one when, she was a child, and it had fascinated her. Still, it might be pretty uncomfortable to live in. "You don't have to go to bed, Joe, if you don't want to," she said, repenting a little.

But Joe had gone.

I suppose I've hurt his feelings again, she brooded, as she finished making the tea. Really, men were the devil. So were women for that matter, as she thought of Margaret Mackenzie, who had in the past few days adopted an infuriating, sorrowful attitude towards her. She must really ask Margaret to tea or dinner, or something, and try to clear things up. After all, Margaret was an old friend—whilst Joe was merely an old fiend.

This abominable little joke made her laugh. "I am essentially simple-minded," she thought, and carried the tray—with an extra cup—into the living room.

"Have a cup of tea, Joe," she said, for he had not returned to the snuff-bottle, but was sitting on the floor poring over the latest issue of 'The Young Mechanic,' a paper to which she had recently subscribed for his benefit.

"I now know how to fix fuse plugs and mend faucets and kettles," he told her proudly. "The parts of a boiler are no longer a mystery to me, they stand revealed! Soon I shall be a really useful servant."

"That sort of domestic repair work doesn't come in your bag of tricks, then—mending things, I mean . . ." She set the tray on the table and poured out a cup of tea for each of them. How fantastic it was that his magic couldn't meet the requirements of modern civilization. She supposed it was because it was given to him when the world was young and when food, clothing and jewels seemed to be, from his account, the only material requirements—while flight was still a strange, miraculous secret known only to birds—and Ifrits.

"I'm only beginning to realize now," Joe told her chattily, "how very old-fashioned and out of date my power is." He shook his head slowly and sadly. "It makes me feel very old and a trifle confused at times, and somehow useless. When I remember those early days, when people marvelled, and feared the things I could do—and desired to possess—But there, Miss Carter, I must not add to your sorrow with my foolish regrets for time past. Would indeed that I could cure your sickness of heart."

Georgina started to say "don't be absurd"—she started to deny his accusation, to protest that—but why should she? Surely Joe, so private, so personal to herself, was the ideal confidant. Joe wasn't human, so there was no need to put up a wall between them.

So she said, "I'm just upset, Joe. Don't worry about me. It will pass away in time. Everything does—fortunately."

"Forgive my indelicacy," Joe said softly, "for it is not meant as such, and arises only because I do not yet understand the English and their fear of showing any emotion or feeling whatsoever—but is it not perhaps, Miss Carter, that you are upset because your friend the Major has gone away?"

"Yes." She was surprised that she admitted it so frankly. "Yes—it is. Isn't it silly?"

"No—not at all silly. And we can put that right in the twinkling of an eye. For I will go and fetch him for you."

"You'll do no such thing, Joe Shiháb, I mean Joe Carter," she cried, so violently that the tea spilled over into the saucer.

"And why not, pray? His absence makes you unhappy; it is therefore abundantly plain that his presence will make you happy again."

"I wish I'd *made* you go to bed." Georgina's voice was grim. "No, Joe, this is ONE THING you can NOT interfere in. For the whole truth is that the Major himself is *not* unhappy to be away from me."

"Fiddle-de-dee," exclaimed Joe airily—then explained rather anxiously, "I found that word in the dictionary. Did I use it correctly?"

"Yes—no—Oh, I don't know." Georgina was impatient. "What did you mean by it, anyway?"

"I meant—what nonsense! For it is a fact that I, Abu Shiháb—I mean Joe Carter, for indeed it is an honour to bear your name, should be unhappy away from you. Why not the Major, who is far less self-sufficient than I am?"

"The whole situation is quite, quite different. And you don't understand it in the least. Now, let's not discuss the subject any further . . . I almost wish I hadn't told you about it at all."

Joe was not to be put off so lightly. "But where *is* the Major now?" he persisted.

"I haven't the foggiest idea—off on a mission, or some business connected with the war. He wasn't allowed to tell me where he was going."

"By the great father of all the Ifrits!" Joe cried. "He may be, then, in frightful danger?"

"He may be—but I doubt it." Georgina's tone held a calmness which she did not feel. "His is a non-combatant job."

"That makes no difference," Joe said darkly. "If what I read in the papers is true, no one is safe these days."

"Well, as safe as possible, then. Oh Joe, why *did* you bring that up? You've made me start worrying again, and I was getting along so nicely. He said he'd write me when he arrived. Oh dear—oh dear . . ."

"If he arrives," Joe remarked, with none too delicate emphasis on the word 'if.'

"Stop it!" Georgina commanded. "It really is horrid of you, Joe, to torment me like this. There's nothing I can do about it, anyway—"

Joe nodded his agreement. "You can't but *I* can," he said, sagely.

"You? Don't be silly."

"I can keep an eye on him—an invisible eye, of course—and help should it be necessary."

"Too like a private detective," Georgina murmured to herself. Then, aloud, "How can you if you don't know where he is?"

"Has he left the country yet?"

"I don't even know that," she wailed.

"Where was he staying?"

"At the Savoy."

"Can you not telephone them and ascertain whether or not he is still there?"

Georgina shook her head. "I could . . . but I wouldn't—not at this hour. Besides, it would . . ." she did not finish the sentence.

"Ah well, it is of no matter really; I'll just fly along there myself and see what can be found out as to his whereabouts."

"Joe!" she caught him in the act of vanishing. "Don't! You'll get into trouble."

"Oh, but indeed I won't." He had returned, complete, but a little vague in outline. "I understand about things now. I comprehend your rules and regulations—and your fears—and so I am in truth most careful never to be perceived in a compromising situation—for you have made abundantly clear the necessity for avoiding the appearance of evil. So you need not be afraid for me, Miss Carter; I assure you no harm will come of it . . . and furthermore, do you not be alarmed should I fail to return immediately."

"Oh, but I shall be most dreadfully alarmed." Georgina's agitation was very real now. To lose both Richard *and* Joe—life would be unbearable.

"Very well, then," Joe said, settling down and looking slightly martyred. "Since you refuse my aid in this direction, and since you cannot rest or sleep—which is, I tell you, recognizable as the fourth state of your disease. . . ."

"Disease!" Georgina interrupted, "don't be so absurd, Joe. I'm not ill and," she added, refusing to remember that she herself had likened her state to a disease, "you're not to prescribe for me." Quite without her bidding she found a tune running through her head. She recognized it as 'I attempt from love's sickness to fly.' She stopped in the middle of the rather involved 'fly,' furious with herself. Really one's mind did play one some rather mean tricks at times.

Joe, however, serenely ignoring the interruption, proceeded to elaborate his argument. "Yes," he said, "the fourth stage. It is indeed serious enough, but the fifth!" He beat his clenched right hand against the open palm of his left to emphasize his despair, "the fifth is even worse—you must be preserved from that and the succeeding stages at all costs."

"Good heavens, Joe," Georgina sipped her tea. "Don't rant so. And what's all this nonsense about stages, you sound like a postillion!"

"I do assure you, Miss Carter," Joe said earnestly, "it is as removed from nonsense as—er—you are! It is well known in my world that there are ten stages of love sickness, they are catalogued and set down."

"Pooh," Georgina said, "really, Joe, you lay far too much stress on the romantic. I don't like it, in fact I find it just a little nauseating."

"That," remarked Joe, "is no more than I expected, for you are rapidly passing into the fifth stage which is Loss of Flesh, occasioned by sickness of the stomach and lack of appetite."

"I suppose," Georgina murmured, "nothing will prevent you from outlining for me these ten stages in detail." Anyway, she thought, it might be interesting to see just what the Eastern people thought of the matter. They were, she felt, bound to be very thorough about such things.

"All right," she said to him, "get on with it. Tell me what they are."

"The first," Joe said, settling himself more comfortably on the floor, "is Love of the Eyes. Even I perceived that the Major has extraordinarily fine eyes, judged by your standards, though for us they are too light and not sufficiently liquid and melting in their glances. Though that, of course, is not the point."

"Oh," said Georgina, but didn't disagree for it was true Richard had fine eyes, "and pray why tell me all that if it's beside the point?" Joe smiled but did not answer; instead he continued: "The point is—you see with the eye, so the eye is the first contact with the beloved. The second is more subtle, it is the Attraction of the Mind—a thing you Westerners seldom consider—"

"Tell me where is fancy bred," Georgina thought; had Joe been reading Shakespeare on the quiet and paraphrasing it for his own purpose?

"The third stage," Joe said, dropping his eyes modestly, "is the Birth of Desire. Indeed of this stage it is quoted 'desire my food, and my drink sleeplessness.' Now it is easy for me to see that you . . ."

"Yes, yes," Georgina put in hastily, "and the fourth you've already told me, is loss of sleep, from which you seem to think I suffer, whilst the fifth is Loss of Flesh. Is that right?"

"Quite correct," Joe said. "Now you must know that the sixth comprises the Indifference of the Senses to sight, taste, touch or smell, to heat and cold."

"A useful state," Georgina said, "particularly in winter in wartime."

"Ah, but that does not last and the seventh stage you would not like, Miss Carter. Indeed it would horrify you being, as it is, so contrary to your nature. I speak of the Loss of Shame."

Georgina said nothing. She wondered, rather dismally, if she weren't just a little affected by the seventh stage already. Oh; not in the perfervid Oriental manner. After all she was Anglo-Saxon, yet even in admitting to herself and partially admitting to Joe her feeling for Richard Taylor was a thing which ravaged one's pride considerably. But perhaps pride and shame weren't quite the same thing.

". . . while the ninth is Loss of Consciousness. The long swoon wherein one's agony is forgotten."

"But what about the eighth, Joe?" she asked, "you left that one out."

He looked at her. "Indeed I did not," he said sadly, "I spoke it quite clearly and distinctly. You did not hear?"

She shook her head.

"The eighth," he told her, "is Distraction of Thought."

Georgina burst out laughing. "Oh, Joe," she said, "I did fall into that trap, didn't I? I suppose you regard it as another sign supporting your silly contentions."

Joe did not trouble to argue. "The tenth," he remarked gloomily, "is Death! Death the Destroyer of Delights, the Severer of Societies."

"Heavens," she mocked him gently, for from his voice and manner there was no doubt but that he firmly believed all he had told her. "You're nearly as bad as a lugubrious Victorian novel. Never mind, Joe. I found it very interesting. Though I do assure you not true—for me at any rate. So you're not to worry about me. I am perfectly all right, truly I am, I'm just not sleepy, that's all."

"You require diversion then, Miss Carter," he told her, "would that—since—since you prevent me from transporting the object of your affection to you—would that I were allowed to divert you with music and dancing, with the innocent magic taught by Harút and Marút. Speak the word of command and I will summon slave girls and musicians and singers whose voices will make your senses swoon. Or I can show you how to make a fortress from a grain of sand or a palace from a single coriander seed. Or do you wish a bathing pool with warm and perfumed waters? Or I could, if such unworthy entertainment would suffice, relate to you a tale of long ago, a story of the time when Sulayman—peace be upon him—was King."

Georgina smiled at the extravagance of his language. She only half believed that he could do these things. Still, better to take no chances. The flat was rather small for a troupe of dancing girls and musicians in whom she felt not the slightest interest. As for the singer—well, the Arab singing one heard on the wireless sometimes nearly set her teeth on edge. As for fortresses, palaces, bathing pools and conjuring tricks, it might be unenterprising of her but she'd no taste for such things at this hour of the morning. Yet there was poor Joe waiting so eagerly to be allowed to help—and here she was as wide awake as if she'd never sleep again—and it might be fun to know a little of his supposed background. So . . .

"I think I should like to hear the story better than anything else, Joe," she said.

He was so delighted at this unexpected flattery that for a moment he could not reply. Then he gulped, rose to his feet, made her a ceremonious bow and said in a very loud voice: "The Tale of Akh-al Jahálah and Sitt-al-Milah."

". . . but tell me softly, Joe," she begged.

CHAPTER XIV

"ONCE LONG AGO in Al-Yaman there lived a lady whose name was Sitt-al-Milah, which on being translated means Fair of Countenance. And in truth she was fair for her eyes were beautiful enough to steal the senses from any man, her thighs were like twin gazelles, so graceful were they in movement and her mouth was the beginning of all delight. But she was not happy for all she was the daughter of a King living in sumptuous splendour in a palace whose gardens were the wonder of the world. And though many a prince had sought her yet she would have none of them, for no man pleased her until—"

"This is going to be a love story, then," Miss Carter said. "I had thought it would be one of adventure—knowing you."

"Surely there is no greater adventure than that of love," Joe said rather pompously, "and there are only two stories in the world anyway—love and war."

"Yes, yes," Georgina agreed hastily, sorry that she had interrupted him for although she had often lectured Joe she realized that he just as often admonished her by means of various devices, and this she felt was going to be one of his lectures not too thinly disguised.

"To continue," Joe said politely, "no man pleased her until a curious circumstance befell her. It happened in this wise. One night when she lay sleeping beneath the silken coverlets of her divan it seemed that she had a dream and in her dream an Ifrit stood beside her bed. In his hand he held a bejewelled box which he opened and commanded her to look inside. This she did and beheld the likeness of a young man whose countenance was as the full moon and as she looked upon his beauty the shaft of love pierced her breast and she cried out and swooned away.

"Her ladies, startled from their slumber by her cry, came running to her swiftly and when they found her lying there, the coverlets in disarray, and she as pale as death and bereft of her senses, they feared that some man had penetrated into the harem and used her after the manner of such things. Then they said, 'This is surely a strange thing,' for upon closer examination they perceived that no man had been there and they sprinkled her with rose water and restored her, asking her all manner of questions. But she answered them no word but seemed as if to be about to die and she continued in this fashion for upwards of three days.

"Then seeing that they could do nothing to relieve their mistress they sent and apprised the King, her father, of these happenings and he came to his daughter himself and addressed her thus, 'O, my daughter, it has been brought to my notice that you are sore troubled in your heart and indeed your countenance speaks of this in plainest fashion. Tell me, then, what it is that has caused this change in you so that I may seek with all my power to put it right.'

"But Sitt-al-Milah made him no answer and fell to weeping until she lay back upon the divan insensible."

"What a way to carry on," Miss Carter put in. "I must say your young heroine seems to me to have had very little common sense—or pride."

"That may be," Joe said, "and indeed as you know now the ten stages of love sickness you should not be surprised at that. Nevertheless I do assure you, Miss Carter, that I am relating this tale to you exactly as it happened."

"I see," Georgina said and looked at him curiously but refrained from remarking what she had in her mind. "Well, then, what happened next?"

"Then the King, her father, went away troubled in his mind about this and bethought himself of the girl's mother who had been a favourite slave girl. So he went to her and told her of the condition of their daughter and said, 'Do you try to ascertain what the cause of this may be, for in truth it puzzles me.'

"So the mother went to the girl and stayed with her some little time and questioned her ladies as well, but could discover nothing. So she returned to the King and craving private audience with him said, 'O my Lord I know not what aileth our daughter in fact, but my senses tell me that either she is in love or has been ensorcelled by an Ifrit.'

"Then the King was very wroth with this, for he feared it might be love and that as his daughter had refused all the suitors he thought meet for her, this love would be for someone beneath her; so he cried out 'By my life it shall not be and I charge you to find out which of these conditions be the true one.'

"So the mother then thought of the girl's old nurse who was skilled in such matters and who was gifted with the sight, and summoning her she begged her to use all means to discover the girl's secret. 'For,' she said, 'in truth she is in sad case and I fear both the wrath of the King and that she may die of this disease.'

"Then the nurse went away and sat by the girl and presently by examining her closely and by diverse means, according to the lore she had, she perceived and ascertained the cause of her malady and she went and apprised the girl's mother of this, saying: 'O, my lady, in truth it is love which hath afflicted your child. For it has been revealed to me that whilst she slept an Ifrit came to her, as if in a dream, and showed her the features of a youth painted on silk and she was instantly stricken with love for him, as indeed the Ifrit knew she would be. For this Ifrit bears a grudge against the King, who at one time defeated him in combat. And indeed the likeness of the young man he shewed your daughter, is that of a prince of Al-Aksa who was spirited away when young by the same evil Ifrit and ensorcelled so that he knows neither his name nor his rank.'

"Then the mother was sorely troubled and asked, 'What can be done in this affair for I see no hope of a happy ending to it?'

"The nurse answered her, 'Do you ask the King, your lord, to allow your child and I to go upon a journey saying that her affliction is of the spirit and that the only hope lies in changing the air she breathes. We shall go by caravan of camels and horses and you must beg him to furnish us for this journey for I can see no help for this thing unless it be done.'

"So the mother besought the King and happily all was granted as requested and Sitt-al-Milah and the nurse, taking with them only a few ladies and servants, set out on the route that leads to the sea."

This is an extraordinarily long and rather child-like story, Georgina thought, still he's giving it the authentic flavour of such stories . . . but I wonder just why Joe picked out this particular one to tell me . . . so far it's not preaching at me. She was in fact beginning to feel sleepy but she didn't like to tell Joe this for fear he would be hurt.

"Until the night of the third day their journey was passed in uneventfulness," Joe continued, "and indeed the princess Sitt-al-Milah was hardly conscious of the passage of time. But at sunset of this day they rested for the night in a small Wadi and the princess, dismissing from the tent her ladies, fell upon the divan and fell to lamenting her fate. Whilst she lay there full of cark and care she heard in the distance the distressful crying of a bird, and so she left off lamenting to set out and discover from whence the pitiful noise came, for she was by nature kind of heart and tenderly disposed toward all the little living creatures fashioned by Allah.

"Having proceeded then a little distance from the Wadi, taking her direction by the cries which had in no wise abated, she soon found a Katá—or sand grouse, entangled in a fowler's snare. 'Poor creature,' she addressed it, 'you are in similar case to mine,' and stooping she loosed the snare and set it free.

"No sooner had she done this, however, when appeared to her an Ifrit of the Jann who, bowing low, thanked her. 'For know,' he said, 'that bird is my soul transformed thus into the swift winged Katá—so that no one should discover and destroy it and thus destroy me. But it fell into the hands of mine enemy who was about to wring its neck, when it escaped only to be here entrapped. O, lady, you may soon have need of me and when that time comes depend upon it that I shall attend you.'

"So saying he vanished and the bird with him. And Sitt-al-Milah returned to her tent, her heart relieved somewhat of its burden and fell into a deep sleep. Waking at dawn, refreshed, she called her nurse to her and related the events which had befallen the previous evening.

"'That, my lady,' the nurse said, 'is in truth a sign that this journey will not be long or fruitless, for that Ifrit was of the believing tribe and good must come of it.' At which the princess cried out with delight so that her ladies came running in happiness to rejoice with her.

"Now on the seventh day they reached a city near to the sea and passing through it they passed through the bazaar. And the lady Sitt-al-Milah looked about with interest on everything she saw, until suddenly her heart smote her and she swooned away in her litter and continued in this wise for some hours. When she recovered herself she ordered a halt and the tents pitched for they were now beyond the town, and summoning her nurse confessed in agitation and despair that in the shop of a cloth merchant in the bazaar she had glimpsed the visage of her beloved 'an there is no help for it but we return,' she said, 'so that I may quench my thirst by sight of him, else I die.'

"Then said the nurse, 'Be easy in your heart, my child, for it shall be done. But it must be done in seemly fashion so that no smirch of shame attaches to you. And for that you must go in disguise of a youth and I will attend you.'

"So Sitt-al-Milah hastily doffed her bag trousers and apparelled herself as a youth and ordering swift horses to be saddled she and the nurse returned to the bazaar.

"When they had discovered the shop of the cloth merchant, they engaged him in conversation of this and that and ordering various lengths of damask and fine silks, peered about but could see no sign of the loved one Then presently at a sign from the nurse Sitt-al-Milah fell to the ground.

"Then the nurse feigned alarm and cried to the merchant, 'O, sir, have you any place where we can lay this poor youth, my master, for he is afflicted with the falling sickness and should not be exposed to the curious gaze of passers by, but should be left quiet somewhere till he recovers.'

"Then the merchant assisting the nurse they brought Sitt-al-Milah into the shop and transported her to the private room at the back, and laid her on some rugs which a youth there made ready for them.

"'Akh-al-Jahálah,' the merchant addressed the youth, 'do you run and fetch rose-water, for this poor youth is in dreadful case and indeed has now become pale as death so that I fear his soul will depart his body.'

"And in truth Sitt-al-Milah, who had hitherto feigned illness, upon observing the youth Akh-al-Jahálah to be none other than her beloved had been seized with such an agitation of delight as to be well-nigh witless.

"The youth then departed and returning at once with the rose-water Sitt-al-Milah was restored sufficiently to sit up trembling, not daring to look about her.

"'Come, my master,' said the nurse, 'we needs must return to our caravan,' and speaking to the cloth merchant she thanked him for his kindness and requested that he send the stuffs they had chosen to them that evening by the boy Akh-al-Jahálah, 'for,' as she said, 'he must be rewarded for his attention by some small token and as we have nothing by us at the moment, direct him to bring these lengths of cloth this evening and he shall gain his reward.'

"The merchant looked somewhat astonished at this request and that so much attention should be paid to the youth Akh-al-Jahálah, nevertheless he speedily agreed to it 'for,' as he thought to himself, 'there is more in this thing than the eye perceiveth and for aught I know this handsome though sickly youth may be a prince in disguise or indeed he may be none other than Zu'l baysun, son of Shaytán himself and that old crone may indeed be Awwá his mother, so that if I do not obey this injunction they will make mischief for me in the bazaar. . . .'"

"Forgive me interrupting, Joe," Miss Carter stopped him, "but I don't quite follow the story. Who did the merchant think would make mischief for him?"

"Zu'l baysun—one of the nine sons of Shaytán—or, as you call him, Satan," Joe explained, "he was the one whose sphere of influence was solely the bazaars, causing men to cheat and be cheated, to quarrel and berate each other, causing goods to disappear and bewitching certain articles. For as I have said Shaytán had nine sons by his wife Awwá."

"Goodness!" Miss Carter exclaimed, "what a curious belief. You must tell me about the other sons, Joe."

"That I will and gladly," Joe said, "but, by your leave, I will save that for another time, for in truth our story now proceeds at vigorous pace to its appointed climax."[1]

Just as well, Miss Carter thought, nodding a little. How odd the Oriental mind was, really. How odd to realize that England was an Oriental Empire . . . and had anyone troubled to study the Oriental mind!

"Then the nurse and Sitt-al-Milah returned to their encampment where Sitt-al-Milah doffed her boy's clothes and donned her own. And the nurse gave her certain instructions which, in due time, she obeyed.

"Presently to the caravan came Akh-al-Jahálah and being relieved of his burden of damask and silk was shown into the tent of Sitt-al-Milah, where he found the lady gorgeously apparelled and seated upon the divan. And though she gave him many languishing glances, yet the sight of her awakened nothing in his heart, and this she perceived and it was painful to her. 'How is it,' she meditated, 'that such a thing can be, that I can love him to distraction and yet he returneth not so much as a glance of mine!'

1 The substance of what Joe later told Miss Carter about the sons of Satan was as follows: Each of the sons has his own special field of endeavour or sphere of influence: Wassin is the dark lord of times of trouble; Zu'l baysun's workshop is the bazaars and he is no doubt engaged in business to-day; Awan who was the evil counsellor of kings—and as in those days kings were virtual dictators—he is undoubtedly still going strong. Marrah presides over musicians and dancers, while Haffan looks after wine shops and drinkers. Masbut, who was at the elbow of news spreaders, is no doubt now the patron Satan of Dr. Goebbels and his kind. Dulhán distracts the mind from prayer and worship. Lakis, the lordling of fire worshippers, is a little difficult to place to-day as there are no heretics; while Dasim, the prince of mansions and dinners, is surely presiding genius of the after-dinner speaker, rather than that of gluttony.

Miss Carter, illogically enough, found this story much less difficult to believe than most of what she privately called "Joe's extravaganzas."

"Then she spoke to him and said, 'O, youth, it is our will that since you were kindly disposed to my brother in the market place to-day, that you should sup with us to-night.'

"And he replied uncouthly—'If it is thy will, then lief must I do it.'

"And so, attended by her ladies, Sitt-al-Milah and Akh-al-Jahálah supped on all manner of dishes and delicacies and snow-cooled wines and she sought to discover aught about him, but in truth he was like one bemused, slow of speech and understanding. Nor did he seem to know of what purport this meeting was or of the desire the lady had for him—until she was well-nigh distraught.

"Then after questioning and conversing with him in vain, she sent for a bowl of quicksilver, as had been told her by her nurse and setting it before him made him gaze upon it until his eyes were heavy and he fell asleep.

"Then did the nurse come and look upon the youth and examine his condition and say, 'Alas, my lady, my learning is not sufficient to undo the potent spell laid upon him by the Ifrit. Would that some power would aid us in this matter.'"

"And Sitt-al-Milah fell to weeping and crying out for help and beating her breast.

"And suddenly the Ifrit whose soul she had saved from the snare appeared before her, but swiftly following him was another Ifrit, he who had first appeared to Sitt-al-Milah in a dream and they prepared to do battle. This they did assuming various shapes and forms and sometimes the one seemed to be gaining victory and sometimes the other, and the lady sat by trembling and afraid. But finally the evil Ifrit was vanquished and fled howling from the tent. And the good Ifrit took the web of enchantment from Akh-al-Jahálah, drawing it out through his nostrils while he slept. Then he gently wakened the youth, who sat up and perceiving the lady trembled violently in every limb and fell upon his knees, for her loveliness smote him to the heart and he desired her.

"Then she raised him from his knees and sat him beside her entreating him to tell her his story. And he told her all that the old nurse had told her mother and which you already know. Adding that he had been spirited away from his father and sold as a slave to the cloth merchant and that his name was not Akh-al-Jahálah which means Brother of Ignorance, but Gharám, which means desire and love longing. And indeed he was in truth a prince of Al-Aksa.

"Then swiftly the lady and her retinue broke camp and returned to the palace of Sitt-al-Milah's father and the strange story of the ensorcelled prince was made known to him. The King entreated him honourably and gave him the lady in wedlock and they abode henceforth in all happiness and delight until death.

"And," said Joe, "this story is true and indeed resembles your case, Miss Carter, for although the Major may not be ensorcelled and so prevented from knowing himself or knowing you as you are; yet the lady did not refuse, in fact she sought the help of the good Ifrit and was not too stiff-necked in her pride to do so.

"But," said Joe, "there is another reason why I should like to be of service to you in this matter, Miss Carter, and when you have heard it you will forgive me and not gainsay me, for know that the evil Ifrit was none other than . . ." He stopped. Georgina was fast asleep and had been for the past five minutes.

Joe sighed. Then he picked her up carefully and put her to bed.

CHAPTER XV

TO SAY THAT Georgina was nervous about going to North Africa is the grossest of understatements. She was, in fact, cold with fear. She had not hesitated in making the decision to go, and she had no thought now of turning back. Richard was ill; he needed her. In his delirium he had spoken her name—actually cried out 'Georgina.' But that did not alter the fact that now, with a little leisure to think over the implications of such a journey, she was absolutely terrified. Her heart felt too big for her chest, and it jumped up and down like a jack-in-the-box. Her stomach seemed to be in a perpetual state of going down in a very fast lift, and although the weather was far from warm and she herself felt frozen to the marrow, she found herself perspiring.

As she waited for the hour of departure, pacing up and down the living room, while Joe, the picture of unconcern, sat in a corner reading 'The Boys' Wonder Book of Electricity,' she relived all that had happened in the past three days since Tuesday night, or rather, early Wednesday morning.

Joe, of course, had not obeyed her instructions about not interfering. He was a born meddler, and though he meddled from the highest motives, nevertheless it was more than a little disconcerting to have an Ifrit play the rôle of fate in one's hitherto well-organized, if dull, life.

He had, the minute she had been stowed away safely in bed, flown off to the Savoy, discovered by some unstated means that Richard was still there, had discovered—also by means unspecified—the whereabouts of his room and had spent several hours there, going through luggage and private papers, trying to find out his destination. This adventure had provided him with the information that the Major snored with the sound of small thunder, although it provided him with nothing else, excepting a forage cap which he had quite shamelessly stolen. He was, she reflected, positively psychopathic—or did she mean kleptomaniacal—about head-coverings.

After these few practically profitless hours he had returned to the flat, before she awakened, and had prepared her breakfast at the usual hour, so that she should not know that he had disobeyed her instructions. Not that she would have noticed had there been anything suspicious about his looks or his conversation; she had been far too tired and dispirited for that.

When she left for the office he returned to the Savoy, to find the Major at breakfast, and had, in fact, stood invisibly behind his chair while he ate. He reported with some delight that the Major ate a big breakfast—porridge, scrambled egg, three cups of coffee, two slices of toast with marmalade, and admonished

her, with what—had he been English—might have been called
'archness,' to remember in future the Major's tastes.

He stuck to the Major all day like an unseen burr on his
clothing, and learned with satisfaction that he was due to leave
the following day for—the place was not mentioned.

On Thursday afternoon the Major left the country, accompanied by various other people—and Joe. Once in the 'plane it
was easy to discover its final destination, and easy to hop back
and forth from 'plane to flat as the occasion, or politics, dictated.

It was not until Friday morning that she learned the whole
story, or any part of it, for that matter, and then Joe had wakened
her, incoherent, breathless, and out of a welter of words, of
maddening diversions from the real news, she had learned first
that Richard had met with an accident. His 'plane had either
crashed or been shot down—Joe didn't know which—off the
coast of Africa.

Fortunately for the occupants, Joe had been a passenger at
the time. (Many of them later attributed their lives to a miracle
or a one-in-a-million chance—both of which were true.) He had,
by what would have been prodigies of valour, had he not been
so gifted, rescued every one of the passengers and crew—laid
them tenderly on a shore, and had then, with really remarkable intelligence, swooped upon the nearest town, picked up
an ambulance and driver and had deposited them next door
to the victims, waking the driver, who, although surprised to
find himself several miles outside the town, was not surprised
to find what he mistook for an Arab pointing and gesticulat-
ing towards a row of men neatly laid out on the beach. With
Joe's help the patients were deposited rather uncomfortably in
the ambulance, and the excited driver hared back to town. Joe
tactfully disappeared—he had to get breakfast by this time. The
driver was mentioned in despatches and, humanly but regretta-
bly, claimed full credit for the exploit. It appeared that he had
actually heard the 'plane crash, but thought it a dream, but in
the dream he had driven to the spot where the injured lay, and
had single-handed brought them back, only to find the dream

was true. (This was, at any rate, the story the newspapers gave, though not till several weeks later.)

All this Georgina had extracted from Joe only that morning, and she wasn't sure now whether she'd got it in chronological order, for his story was so embellished with comments, such as those about the Major's unfortunate snoring habit and his capacity for breakfast, as well as hundreds of other details which at any other time might have been amusing or even embarrassing, but which were now, in these desperate circumstances, irrelevant, infuriating and highly confusing.

But Joe had sworn that, as Richard was put into the ambulance, he had half-opened his eyes and spoken her name, and if Joe were to be believed, he had moaned "Georgina" several times from the hospital bed where he lay (for Joe had visited him that afternoon) with his leg in a cast, his head bandaged and his face flushed with fever.

So here she was at 11 p.m., pacing up and down the living room, a pot of calves' foot jelly clutched in her hand, about to set out for North Africa, and feeling rather as if she were about to be hanged instead.

There were many things about the proposed journey which alarmed her greatly. First, the possibility of being shot down. Joe might be impervious to shrapnel, tracer bullets and the like, but she, being mortal, was not immune and was mortally afraid. Even though there was small likelihood of their being spotted by an A.A. battery or a fighter 'plane (either our own or the enemy's, it made little difference in her case, as she was sure to count as 'unknown aircraft'), they might by some horrible mischance themselves mixed up in an air-battle, or dog-fight, or whatever they were called. After all, what *had* happened to Richard's 'plane?—even Joe didn't know. Really (now that it was so intensely brought home to her) it was terribly brave of Mr. Churchill to go flying about all over the place, with the air positively charged with menace, but then, she presumed he *did* have fighter escort or something equally as good, for the government would surely run no risks with his person.

Then there was always the risk that Joe, in the excitement of an air-battle, might drop her, and she had no desire to end up a sticky mess on any foreign territory, friendly, neutral or enemy. Nor did she desire a plummet drop into the sea. If only she had a parachute her mind would be a little relieved, but parachutes were impossible, of course. Why didn't they sell civilian parachutes at the Army and Navy Stores? Really, some shops had no enterprise these days! Fear had by now made her blissfully illogical, and she wondered next if an umbrella mightn't be better than nothing. Oh, not her own black silk umbrella with the grey lizard-skin handle, but one of those great, striped canvas affairs used to create a shady patch in a garden. That might do. There was one belonging to the building somewhere about—it appeared on the lawn every summer, rain or shine. But it was so heavy—how could she travel a thousand or more miles hanging on to a giant umbrella? It was an absurd idea—none the less it might be worth it. But then again, it mightn't, for to be captured alive in any territory—enemy or otherwise—would probably mean being shot as a spy, and Miss Carter felt, with certain justification, that she was just not the Mata Hari type.

Finally, even though the journey were negotiated in safety, there was always the possibility of discovery upon arrival. Discovery, she felt, would be highly undesirable and unpleasant, not only for herself, but for Richard—while no court of law could be expected to believe her story, even supposing she were allowed a trial after her arrest, and not just clapped into a rat-infested prison to moulder away, or be nibbled to shreds. Miss Carter was extremely, but excusably, hazy about just what the set-up was in North Africa, but she presumed the government was to all intents and purposes French—and the French were *so* excitable. As for the Moroccans! One just never knew. The position of their own women was peculiar, to say the least, and what would be her position, should she fall into their hands? It was true that Lady Hester Stanhope had got along famously with the Arabs, but despite her admiration for this dictatorial and courageous character, Georgina admitted again that she was just not the type. And besides, one did hear such sinister stories of mutilations—which were the least of the indignities inflicted upon an enemy—or did that apply only to an Abyssinian meeting an Italian?

She managed to pull herself up with a jerk, realizing how fantastic and ridiculous some of her fears were. Nevertheless, the whole thing *was* very tricky, and she wished, not that she had not decided to go, but that circumstances were less difficult—less hazardous.

She realized, too, that she was tiring herself with these thoughts, and with pacing up and down the room. She must have covered miles in the last hour or so. She crossed to the mantel and picked up the pot of calves' foot jelly she had bought to take with her, for she entertained doubts as to the nourishment contained in North African food, particularly for a man who had just suffered injury and exposure (Richard probably had pneumonia by now) and he'd need more than fruit to keep up his strength. She set the pot down again—missed her aim, and it smashed to pieces on the hearth.

"Damn it," said Georgina, stopping to survey the mess. "I hope that's not an omen!"

Joe was beside her in an instant with a cloth. "Let me clean it," he commanded. "You must go and rest now, for I perceive you are nervous and agitated with excitement."

"Not excitement—fear," Georgina confessed bleakly. "How long is it before we leave, Joe?"

"Another hour, but it is foolish of you to trouble yourself with fears, Miss Carter, for most surely shall I shield and protect you from all harm."

Georgina flung herself into a chair, took a cigarette from a box on the table beside her, and lit it. It was unusual for her to smoke, but she had to do something. No wonder the troops smoked so much. She exhaled the first puff and addressed Joe. "I sometimes wonder," she said, thinking of his previous assurance that he would guarantee her safety, "if you really know what kind of world you now live in."

Joe stopped mopping up and, squatting back on his heels, looked at her thoughtfully. "You know, Miss Carter," he confided, "on many occasions I wonder that myself. For most certainly it appears to me that the world has progressed far beyond my intelligence and my magic."

Georgina laughed, but not with amusement. "Then obviously you do know," she sighed. "Well, if it's any consolation to you, I think we're all in the same boat—we've progressed beyond our own human capacity to make the best use of our progression. Oh dear, what an involved sentence, but you know what I mean, I'm sure. Of course, you'll probably live to see things differently. What an odd thought—you'll go on and on, I suppose—Ifrits don't just die or disappear, do they?"

"That question I cannot answer—for I do not know, but it neither troubles me nor makes me afraid."

"You're very fortunate," Georgina said. "We know, more or less, but we are afraid."

"This world," Joe remarked, sticking a finger in his mouth to taste the jelly, "seems to me to be ruled by fear. It is just as well that you dropped that jar, Miss Carter, for indeed it contained no delicacy, for there is no taste, no body, no texture to this stuff. People are always being afraid. They fear not only outside things, but things within themselves. You are all imprisoned by fear, just as I was imprisoned in the wood—and you, Miss Carter, are afraid now, not only of the journey, but because you have discovered that you are in love with . . ."

"Please, Joe!" Georgina stopped him.

"Oh, very well then," Joe said crossly, "but you see it is true. Now when something really important happens to you, you refuse to admit it or discuss it, or see how you can make the best out of it. You should have let me handle this affair for you. I would have . . ."

"You seem to be doing well enough with it as it is," Georgina said drily. "How long now, Joe?"

"Just time for a cup of tea," Joe said.

"I think," Georgina said, "if you could conjure up a bottle of whisky, I'd prefer it."

CHAPTER XVI

IT WAS WITH some astonishment that Miss Carter found herself lying on the ground in what appeared to be a grove of trees. It seemed only a few minutes ago that she had heard her own clock strike twelve. She remembered perfectly the drink, the setting-out on the journey, then—nothing.

"Joe," she whispered softly.

"I am here and at your service." He moved into her line of vision. "Are you quite alright now, Miss Carter?"

"Yes," she sat up, "I think so—did I faint, or did you mix some of that dreadful stuff in my drink?"

"No, I did not," Joe said flatly, "for you have forbidden me to—not but that the thought didn't occur to me when I found you were so torn with emotion, but I resisted the temptation, as I had no wish to incur your displeasure."

"Really, Joe, you should have been a professional after-dinner speaker! Well, I wonder what happened, then?"

"You just lost consciousness," he told her. "I think perhaps I flew too high, but I was nervous of flying too low because . . ."

"Quite right," she cut him short. "Lucky for me your speed is so great. I really must get an oxygen mask. I wonder how fast you can go really—do you know?"

"I can suit my speed to the occasion—I can travel with the speed of lightning if it is so desired—or as slowly as the 'plane in which the Major travelled—nay, even as slowly as the heavy-winged vulture, who rests upon the air before he strikes his prey. I can . . ."

"Oh Joe," Georgina said impatiently, "perhaps you could tell me all about it another time—but do tell me now where we are."

"Nearly at the end of our journey—we are in a grove of olive trees not ten miles distant from the town. If it meets with your approval I will now go on a reconnaissance flight over the city, enter the hospital, and make sure that all is safe for you."

"What! And leave me here in this wood alone?" Georgina's voice held the terror she felt.

"Yes, but you will be quite safe, for I have explored this grove to-day and am persuaded that it is a most secluded spot, and I shall not be more than five minutes, so that even if anything untoward should happen to you I shall still be able to rescue you. Have no fear, Miss Carter, for I have you under my protection, and no evil can befall you."

That sounded all very fine, Georgina thought, considerably agitated, but any number of highly unpleasant things could happen to one in the space of five minutes. A knife or a bullet, for example, could do one in in decidedly less time than that! Joe was sometimes just a little too cocksure, too over-confident, for her taste. She started to protest again, and perceived that she protested to the air. Joe was no longer beside her—he had vanished.

She stayed her first impulse to cry his name. That would be foolish, and, indeed, might prove fatal. She shuddered and pressed herself close to the tree-trunk, hoping for camouflage and protection, for the moon was full and soft, and the grove was stippled with light. There was nothing to do but to wait, and try not to be afraid. She looked at her watch; she could see its face quite plainly in the moonlight. It really was a wonderfully bright night—but it made her extremely nervous.

In other circumstances, she told herself, trying to observe the situation objectively, I should most certainly have enjoyed this. If I were not here by illegal methods—if I had paid for the trip—if it were peace-time—this would really seem marvellous, for I have always enjoyed travel. In fact, when I was younger my ambition was to go about the world seeing new places and meeting new people. She laughed silently, remembering prosaic holidays on the Continent. How eagerly she had looked forward to them . . . how uniformly disappointing they had been.

She looked about her . . . the grove was very beautiful and the trees were, indeed, olives—very old and silvered. They were like the olive trees she had once seen at Rocca di Papa—she had thought that one of the loveliest sights in the world. But these trees were ghostly in the moonlight, and even as she looked, their gnarled trunks seemed to be contorted into sinister faces.

I wonder what part of North Africa I'm in, she asked herself, hastily withdrawing her thoughts from their unpleasant fancy—for Joe knew only the place, not the name of it. Perhaps I'd be less fearful if I knew. It's always *such* a help to know where one is. That wretched Ifrit—he's been gone much longer than five minutes, I'm sure. She looked at her watch again, and observed that Joe had been gone just a little more than a minute. Time was purely relative! At this moment she felt that she understood the theory perfectly. One hour with Richard, for example, was but five minutes; waiting as she did now was several centuries.

If she could only believe, as Joe did, in predestination, it might be a great comfort and help in these circumstances. But really, was it possible that Sulayman—or whoever it was that predestined things—could have arranged that at this precise moment in time she, Georgina Carter, would be standing in an olive grove in North Africa, in the middle of a war, waiting to creep into a hospital to see Richard Taylor? No, that was a little too much to expect of Sulayman's foresight. Besides, there was no good in believing in predestination unless you knew how things would turn out in the end! Still, her worst fears for the journey had proven to be completely unfounded—in fact, after all that agony of worrying before the event, she hadn't even known the journey was happening after the first few seconds. Perhaps she had fainted from sheer fear or nervous exhaustion! So wasn't it really very foolish to be worrying now? She found herself murmuring "What is to be will be," and added, as a cautious afterthought, "even if it never comes to pass." It sounded all very biblical or Pearl Buck Jacobean, but was, she realized, utter nonsense. It did, however, make her feel better. She sighed with the easing of the strain. She felt less as if she had eaten a highly indigestible meal.

Then she heard footsteps.

She froze to the tree. Her spine welded to the trunk as if by ice. There was no mistaking the sound! Footsteps—soft footsteps—several of them, accompanied by faint rustling noises. Perhaps it was Joe! It couldn't be! One never heard Joe approaching—he just appeared. That was one of his accomplishments to which she had never accustomed herself. She strained her eyes, and with horror saw, approaching her through the trees, two figures clad in white.

Perhaps they wouldn't see her. Perhaps they'd pass by without noticing her. But even if they didn't see her, they'd certainly be attracted by the drum-beats booming out of her chest. What were they doing in this grove at such an hour, anyway?

Yes—they'd seen her! They stopped suddenly, a few yards away—stood motionless and stared at her. She had a quick hope that perhaps she terrified them as much as they terrified her. But it was a forlorn hope, for after a moment they moved towards her together, and she observed that one held a rifle in his hands—and furthermore, it was pointing straight at her.

She saw now that they wore heavy robes—and it flashed across her mind quite erroneously that the name for this garment was 'burnous.' They wore odd little round caps on their heads, and they both looked rather large and menacing. She was surprised at the triviality of her observations. They stopped within two feet of her—the man with the rifle held it only an inch or so from her chest.

Suddenly Miss Carter was no longer afraid. Or perhaps fear had gone so far that it had become courage. She was conscious now that she was only angry—really very angry.

"Take that dangerous thing away," she commanded, putting out her hand and plugging the bore of the rifle with her thumb. "The very idea, pointing a weapon like that at a woman!"

The men were obviously slightly nonplussed. They broke into loud, excited conversation, of which she understood not a single word.

"I know perfectly well," Georgina went on, in a firm, rather loud, voice, "that it appears odd that I should be here at this hour of the night. But my motives and intentions are altogether harmless. Indeed, I am only waiting for a friend."

Obviously the two men could not understand a word of this, although they could not mistake the tone. They conversed together again. Then one moved forward a few paces and seized her by her free arm.

Although enraged, she was not fool enough to cry out or resist, for that wretched man with the gun still held it at her chest, and furthermore, her finger was plugging up the barrel, and she had no intention of having her hand blown off as well. She removed the finger with as much dignity as she could muster, and with her now free arm removed her captor's hand from her other arm.

"You will please keep your hands off me," she said coldly. "If you wish to apprehend me, do so, but there is no need to use either violence or force."

The man was so surprised by her action that he just stood and stared at her. She could see in his face his amazement and puzzlement. He turned again to his rifle-holding companion and made some remark. The gunman nodded.

"I am an Englishwoman," Miss Carter said—not that even the most uneducated Arab or Berber could have mistaken that for a moment—"and you will please take me to the British Consul in the nearest town, *at once.* She hadn't even the remotest idea what the nearest town was, or whether such a thing as a British Consul existed there, especially in time of war. But it was a good, firm, intimidating thing to say, even though her captors couldn't understand a word. Miss Carter had always subscribed to the principle that when in difficulties in England, one always asked a policeman; when in difficulties abroad, one always asked the Consulate.

But the unarmed man had now turned his back to her and was making off rapidly through the trees, while the gunman looked quite horridly menacing. It was no good—she'd lost! Her courage ran out through her toes—was his companion going for help or a large, sharp knife? For a rifle was a noisy way of despatching a prisoner, and she had an uneasy feeling that these men were not really about any legitimate business themselves, else what would they be doing in a deserted olive grove at this hour, carrying firearms, and wearing no badge of identification or uniform of authority whatsoever?

She thought bitterly of Joe and his boast that he would save her if any trouble arose. Saving Richard and the crew and passengers of that 'plane had made him over-confident, and she was, she was afraid, about to pay for his conceit. Save her? Well, he'd better return pretty quickly, for that gun might go off at any moment, then there'd only be her body to save.

Even as these thoughts passed through her mind the gun suddenly leapt from the man's hand, sailed through the air and dropped with a clatter some distance away. The gunman himself struggled wildly, clutching at something unseen which seemed to be clamped across his mouth, and emitting short, grunting noises. Then he shot straight up off the ground, appeared for an instant beside his startled companion, who was by now about fifty yards away, then both of them, like figures in a pantomime suspended by piano wire, were jerked up and out of sight.

Miss Carter let the air out of her lungs and slumped down to the foot of the tree. She was as weak as a kitten, and her hands and knees shook. In a second Joe was there beside her.

"Presumptuous dogs," he said fiercely, flinging a bundle down beside her. "How dare they lay their unclean hands on you! Had I had the time and the necessary instruments I should have had their manhood for this affront! I trust you are not in any way hurt, Miss Carter?"

"Oh no," Georgina said, "a little occurrence like that is nothing. It is true that my heart is probably permanently dislocated, but in time my tongue and teeth will no doubt get used to their new companion, and you may have noticed that since you left my hair has gone snow-white—but that's of no importance."

"I am glad and thankful that you are alright," Joe said gravely, missing the sarcasm. "Indeed, it was a most unfortunate experience for you to undergo, but of course, you knew that I should return in time, and that must have stayed your anxiety—as for your hair, it is indeed white, but it is the moonlight which gives that effect."

"It is fortunate they didn't shoot me on sight, as they might well have done," Georgina said drily, "because then, Joe, you'd have looked an awful fool—for I should have been as dead as a doornail, despite all your boasts."

"Ah, but Miss Carter," Joe said, and his tone was one of slightly smug melancholy, "you do not understand, all this was . . ."

"Don't tell me, I can guess—predestined!"

Joe agreed, smiling broadly. "But yes," he said. "You see, it's . . ."

"Nonsense," Georgina finished the phrase for him. "You'll never make me believe—" she broke off. Really, to be arguing about such a thing, at such a time and in such a place, was right next door to insanity. Besides . . . "Perhaps in this case," she admitted grudgingly, "—you may be right. Mind you, I said may be, for I really don't know why that man didn't shoot at me when I plugged up that gun."

"They will have ample time to repent of their misdeeds," Joe said, "for they will find it difficult to get down off that high mountain, particularly without any clothes on." He bent down and picked up the parcel he had flung beside her. "And now to business," he said cheerfully. "In this parcel I have for you a disguise, Miss Carter, and I will explain all that it is necessary for you to do."

It was only then that she noticed that he was wearing on his head the tarboosh which had so recently belonged to the man with the gun.

CHAPTER XVII

GEORGINA, CATCHING SIGHT of herself in a highly-ornate Venetian glass mirror in the entrance hall, thought with a certain amount of pleasure that she really looked very well as a nursing sister. The blue and white striped dress, the crisply-starched cap and apron, barely showing where they had been folded, were really most becoming, and lent her an authoritative look which helped to increase her confidence in the role she was playing. If stopped by anyone on her journey through the hospital she was almost sure she could get away with her act successfully. A new sister . . . just detailed to the hospital . . . oh yes, she'd seen matron (always provided that the questioner didn't happen to be the matron herself, but that was unlikely at this early hour of the morning), and had been assigned to night duty in one of the wards.

It was a good story, she felt, quite plausible, and had the advantage of being more or less true. For she *was* taking the place of a sister assigned to night duty—a sister who now slept peacefully in the nurses' quarters, having imbibed with her pre-duty cup of tea a very small quantity of bhang. Further-more, she was now wearing the sleeping sister's uniform. Joe had really arranged the whole plan quite brilliantly, that, she was bound to admit. But how strange it was that she should feel no pangs of conscience about drugging a sister and borrowing her uniform! It led her to the sad conclusion that where one's heart was involved one's conscience could be given a soporific— at least for a time!

As she passed through the entrance hall, ascended a short flight of marble steps, turned left, ascended another staircase and then turned right, she thought—observing the slightly clenched, forward position of her right hand—how odd it was to be holding on to the invisible coat-tails of an invisible Ifrit, for Joe was now leading her, as he had done ever since setting her down outside the building, invisibly to her ultimate destination.

She had observed, on entering the place, that it had once been (apparently very recently) a magnificent private villa, standing in fine grounds, a beautiful new cream-washed build-ing, with wings that stretched like arms towards the sea. Inside there were still many traces of the original inhabitants, statues and pictures, mirrors and hangings, all remained as a reminder of the taste of the previous occupants. The key-hole shaped doorways fascinated her—and there were a great many of them along this corridor. She wanted to peep inside each door and see what lay behind it—how well she understood Bluebeard's wife at this moment! What a piquant mixture of over-civilized French and Moroccan design the whole place was!

She was startled out of her thoughts, and the slow, impressive step she had adopted, by a thin little voice which chirped "Good morning, sister."

A door had opened, and a small young sister had greeted her. Georgina nodded coldly, distantly, and passed on. Her heart thumped unpleasantly—what if the little sister wanted to stop and talk? But the little sister did not follow—she turned in the opposite direction and walked rapidly away. A hurdle successfully over, Georgina thought, rather pleased that she had been able to quell any attempt at conversation by her haughty demeanour. But she hoped that the small young sister hadn't been too crushed by the snub. In a way she was rather sorry that she had not been able to stop and talk to this child, and to find out—oh, all sorts of things about the hospital.

She suddenly felt herself bump into Joe. They had stopped outside a door.

"This," his voice whispered close to her ear, "is the ward you must pass through to get to Major Taylor's room. His is the door at the far end, and he is alone."

The door opened into what she judged must be one of the wings. It was a long room with heavily-curtained windows, which must give a view of the garden and the sea. Now it was full of hospital cots. A night light burned, barely illuminating the place. It was very still. She stood on the threshold a moment— frightened again, but this time not for herself. Supposing the occupants of those cots should wake and require medicine? Supposing they were in pain? What terrible thing had she done to come here masquerading as a nurse, and depriving them of the care and attention which no doubt they badly needed? This was criminally thoughtless of her. Then she saw something which both startled and relieved her. In a chair beside the door an orderly sat, and he was sound asleep. Provided that Joe, in his zeal, hadn't drugged the man, the patients were all right!

She felt the pull of the coat tails in her hand, and followed them down the room. It seemed at least a mile long. From either side came the sound of heavy breathing, and once an abrupt,

sharp snore, from a bed on the left, startled her so that she
nearly jumped out of her skin.

They stopped again at a door at the end of the room. "Joe,"
Georgina whispered, tagging at his solid but unseen coat tails,
"did you drug that man at the door too?"

"No," his voice answered, "I did not. I thought it unwise to do
so, for if anyone came and found him drugged, the consequences
for us might be, not dangerous, but unpleasant. Though, as it
turns out, there was no need to drug him. Still, should he be
awake as we go out, it may be necessary for you to address a few
words to him."

"Oh, I couldn't," she said, jerking his coat tails again to give
emphasis to her words. "I wouldn't know what to say . . . and I
should be terribly afraid."

"Fiddle-de-dee," Joe's voice replied. "Of course you know
what to say. All that is necessary is a remark which indicates
that all is well. For the man himself is new here to-day, and he
cannot possibly know that you are not the real sister—though,
Miss Carter, you do indeed look the part to perfection—it is a
great pity that . . ."

"For pity's sake don't go off into a speech now," Georgina
interrupted. She felt all the old nervousness returning in the
face of these possible complications. "Let's get this thing over
with quickly, since we've been fools enough to come this far."

The door facing her swung open silently. "He is there," Joe's
voice held all the drama of a conspirator's—really, he was cut out
for harem intrigue. "I shall stand guard outside and warn you by
knocking on the door, should anyone approach. Three knocks
will mean danger—two will mean that the danger is past."

He pushed Georgina into the room before she had time to
ask what to do anyway if 'danger' threatened. The door closed
softly behind her. She was in Richard's room at last. But what
a room! It was not large compared to the other rooms she had
seen in the villa, but for some reason it had not yet been stripped
of its furniture and ornaments. The walls were a pale cerulean
blue, the domed ceiling almost midnight blue and studded with
Venetian glass stars outlined in silver. Some were purely orna-

mental, like the Pleiades in miniature grouped over her head; others, like those nearest the walls, served to conceal the soft lighting which irradiated the room. Two vast curved and fluted wardrobes, shaped as great Corinthian pillars split in half and painted the same colour as the ceiling, stood against the right wall, and were separated by a small dressing table with a moonlike mirror. The table was bare of all ornaments save an incongruous hospital chart. The carpet, a deep yellow, was so soft that she felt she stood on moss. A thin nude, possibly masculine, possibly feminine—good gracious, it was both!— with chocolate drop eyes, had been breathed upon canvas and hung on the wall in a frame made of pale branched coral. Opposite this was a great, star-studded curtain, falling in heavy folds from ceiling to floor, possibly concealing a window or a door. Richard himself (for she presumed that hump was Richard, though his face was shielded from her and from the light by a screen painted to illustrate the various intimate incidents in the life of Aphrodite) lay in a bed that would have done credit to a Du Barry. It was shaped like a gigantic opened oyster shell, supported at the foot by two plump cupids in an obvious state of masculine unrest.

"How *very* French," Miss Carter thought, as she moved softly towards the bed and around the screen. Yes it *was* Richard lying there, though she knew him more by instinct than by eyesight, for his head was thoroughly bandaged and the light was dim. She could see that his right leg was encased in plaster, for only a light silk coverlet concealed the bulky outlines of the cast. One arm was bandaged as well, and his cheeks were stained with scarlet. Was he asleep or unconscious?

She bent down and kissed him softly on the cheek, obeying a sudden impulse. One half of her was appalled at the liberty taken with a defenceless man—the other half was glad that she had done it.

He stirred a little and moaned. She stood motionless, watching him. Slowly his eyelids opened and he looked at her with big, fever-bright eyes. "Hello, Georgina my dear," he said faintly,

"I knew you'd come—that blasted brother of yours said you wouldn't—but I knew you would—"

"Of course, Richard," she said softly, "you knew, and you were quite right. Here I am."

"Robert's a funny chap, you know," he murmured, licking his dry lips. "We're great friends, but I can never get anything out of him about you. Do you know what he said when I asked him yesterday if he thought you liked me at all?"

"No," Georgina answered faintly, "I've no idea. Tell me."

"He said," the sick man went on, "'Oh, Georgina, she doesn't give a hang for men old boy—too independent for that—the new woman, you know—needn't think you can make an impression on her—others have tried and failed. I know Georgina—she's my sister. A damn good sister she is too.'"

"That," Georgina said gently and sadly, "was very wrong of Robert really, but I daresay he didn't really know how I felt— didn't know anything about me—I gave the wrong impression. It was my fault. I was always too self-conscious—too shy . . . Poor dear Richard, feverish and lost in the last war."

"Course he didn't know anything about you," Richard went on, "That's precisely what I told him myself. 'Old boy,' I said, 'you don't know a damn thing about Georgina, and you don't really appreciate what a fine sister you've got.' That touched him—that got him on the raw—nearly had a row, both of us claiming we knew you best . . ."

"That was nice of you, Richard—to think that about me; but you know, Robert and I are really great friends. I'm devoted to Robert . . ."

"Nothing more natural," Richard said, his eyes bright. "And now let's show old Robert how wrong he was about you. We'll get married to-morrow, won't we. I've got three days' more leave— special leave—Robert can be best . . ." his voice trailed away. "I'm so thirsty," he complained fretfully, "so terribly thirsty."

She turned away—not that he would notice her tears, but to see if she could find a carafe of water anywhere in the room— and even as she turned she heard three soft knocks on the door.

It was incredible, the rapidity with which her mind worked. Almost without consciousness of thought she found herself in front of one of the great curved wardrobes; she opened the door—shelves and drawers. She flew to the other wardrobe—ah, that was better—meant for hanging clothes, but now quite empty of everything but Richard's stained and tattered tunic swinging forlornly on a coat-hanger. She got into the cupboard and pulled the door to—just in time. She heard the outer door open and a man's voice say (with a broad American accent), "Better get a handy man to fix that door, Matron—it seems to be sticking."

Joe must have delayed them a bit by hanging on to the door handle as hard as he could. They didn't know how lucky they were—they might have found themselves on a mountain top instead of in Richard's room! It was fortunate that Joe had restrained himself, she thought.

She supposed the two visitors had reached the bed by now, for she heard the screen being moved, and the man's voice say "Looks decidedly feverish . . . but that's to be expected—any congestion in the lungs? No?—good! Amazing accident, wasn't it—he's lucky to have escaped alive—Richard was always a lucky dog though."

Then she heard, very faintly, Richard's voice saying over and over again, "Georgina—water—"

"Better give him a sedative," the man said, "can't have him tossing about like this with a cracked skull—I'll certainly have a lot of fun pulling his leg when he convalesces, about this Georgina business . . ."

Georgina in the wardrobe felt slightly sick at this remark. But it was obvious that the doctor was a friend of Richard's, and it was certainly a comfort to know that he had a friend in the place.

"I'll instruct the night sister to give him a sedative," the woman's voice answered, and Georgina thought she detected more than a hint of frost in the tone. Apparently Anglo-American relations were strained between the doctor and the matron. "She should be on her rounds by now—we shall probably find her in the ward as we go out. Any further orders, Captain?"

"No, no. Sorry to have dragged you out at this hour, but Major Taylor and I come from the same neck of the woods—Michigan, Miss Gorman, and I thought I'd better take a look at him before hitting the hay."

The woman's voice thawed slightly as she said, "We've had a busy day—you must be very tired. Organizing a new hospital is a terrific strain, apart from the floods of casualties. Can I make you a cup of tea?"

"Bless your little pink heart, no. And Miss Gorman—you've done a magnificent job with this Villa—I do congratulate you."

Georgina was vastly relieved. Anglo-American relations were now obviously on the mend.

She heard their voices die away as the door closed, but she did not move from her hiding place, although she felt quite suffocated, until she heard Joe give the prearranged signal. Then she stepped out of the wardrobe.

Joe was inside the room, visible, and standing with his back to the door. "Make haste, make haste, Miss Carter," he hissed, "for we must away from this place with the swiftness of the hawk as he drops upon his prey. We cannot now leave by the way we came, for that orderly by the door is now awake, and the matron and doctor have questioned him as to if he's seen the night nurse. He is to tell her to see the matron immediately. So how can you pass him, when they have just left this room and have not seen you here? That other nurse has a determined face . . . she will search the hospital . . ."

Georgina clasped her hands in despair. "Oh dear, oh dear," she wailed in a whisper, "now I've got that other sister into trouble, and probably Richard won't get his medicine. . . . Oh, how awful! What shall I do—what shall I do?"

"There is no time for vain regrets," Joe said firmly. "We must fly, else there will be further trouble. Is there an exit from this room—for unhappily I did not ascertain this fact when here before . . ."

"I don't know," Georgina said, "but I presume that curtain conceals a door or a window." She pointed a slightly shaky hand at the wall.

Joe disappeared, and was back in an instant. "A door," he said, "into a private hammam—there is a window there, but it is barred. I can slip through the bars, but it is obvious, slender as you are, that you can't."

"But can't you break the bars?" Georgina asked.

Joe looked astonished. "But, Miss Carter," he said, "surely that is against your laws—and your teaching—it would be, what do you call it? Oh, breaking and entering . . ."

Georgina stamped her foot with sheer rage, fear, impatience and irritability. Luckily the depth of the carpet made it a soundless stamp. To have her own scruples boomerang back at her like this, when she was in peril of her life! Well, not exactly her life, but her reputation—they had now become practically synonymous . . . to be found in Richard's room . . .

"Break those bars, Joe," she commanded. "I will explain later how circumstances can alter cases—but get me out of here quickly!"

"At *your* command," Joe said, with a nice emphasis, and held back the curtain for her.

"I'll follow," she said. "You get on with the job."

She went over to the bed. "Good-bye, Richard," she said very softly, "good-bye, my dear," then made her way over to the curtain again. I am a wicked, foolish, vain, impetuous woman, she thought, as she drew back the curtain; There will be a lot of trouble over my visit to-night, and furthermore, Joe will have no faith or belief in my guidance any more. She opened the door, and found herself in a bathroom. She had just time to notice that the whole room was iridescent with mother-of-pearl, and that the shell motif was here given free rein (even that article of plumbing euphemistically called a lavatory was shaped like a giant conch shell) when Joe said, "All is now ready, Miss Carter . . ." and they were off.

Back in the olive grove again, she changed into her own clothes, silently and swiftly. "What shall I do with the uniform?" she asked. "We really must get it back to its unfortunate owner—"

"I shall take you home first," he said, "then I shall come back here and return it to her. If you can hold your breath for two minutes—or less—we shall be home without discomforting you in any way. But tell me, Miss Carter, now that it is safely over—are you not happy to have made the journey—for, despite the final slight upset, the plan worked nearly like clockwork—the whole affair was, I think, very well timed indeed."

Georgina shook her head. "No, Joe," she said, "no, the timing was wrong, but it's not your fault that I was twenty-five years late!"

CHAPTER XVIII

GEORGINA WAKENED suddenly. For a moment she did not know where she was—the olive grove—the fantastic bedroom—concealed in a wardrobe—then the insistent clamour of the telephone bell told her she was home in her own flat. That must have been what had wakened her. She jumped out of bed, seized a dressing-gown, went into the living room and answered the 'phone.

It was Margaret Mackenzie, issuing a pressing invitation to come to tea.

"Margaret dear, I'm *so* tired I just don't think I can drag myself out to-day." The minute the words were out of her mouth she realized that she'd committed a bad psychological blunder; Margaret would think that that was just a feeble excuse because she didn't want to come—that she was, in fact, avoiding her. But how on earth could she explain that she'd been up nearly all night rushing to and from North Africa? She tried, however, to repair some of the damage to Margaret's pride by saying, "Do you think you could manage to come here and have tea with me instead—or is that too much fag for you?"

"Are you *quite* sure you want me?" Margaret asked, with painful plaintiveness.

Georgina wanted to shake her. "Don't be a goose," she said. "Of course I want you to come," she hoped her voice sounded convincing, "and I do want to see you. It's only that I think I'm taking cold—that's why I'm so tired—the change in temperature, you know . . ."

"The what? But Georgina, it's been uniformly wet and cold for days . . ."

"Yes—yes dear, I know. But I got awfully hot in the night, and then awfully cold—and I've only just wakened up. Oh, I know it's after twelve o'clock but—"

"That," Margaret said, "sounds to me like a feverish chill. You go straight back to bed, Georgina, and I'll come along as soon as possible to see how you are." She rang off.

"Bother!" Georgina said vigorously, and aloud. Really, it was terribly kind of Margaret, but it was such a pity that she had to come to-day. Now, *what* had become of Joe?

She called his name, but there was no response. "Bother," Georgina said again. "I wonder where he's got to now. Of course—he was returning to North Africa with that uniform, but he should be back by this time surely. I hope nothing's happened. I *did* want to ask him about Richard."

She went into the bathroom and turned on the tap. A hot bath would liven her up a bit—perhaps make her feel less cross. She opened the medicine cupboard and noticed that Joe (who usually ran her bath for her), with his customary prodigality, had filled it to the top with bottles of various oils and unguents for the body, scents for the bath. The bottles and jars were wonderfully beautiful to look at, but there was no way of telling their contents. She sniffed at several—they seemed too sweet— too heavy. Then she found one which reminded her slightly of lemon verbena—that was better! She poured a few drops into the bath water. In an instant the room was filled with a delicate fragrance. It was quite remarkable how refreshing the scent was.

Really, she thought, as she relaxed in the bath, I haven't enough imagination to colour a postage stamp. I probably have enough rare scents and perfumes and the lord knows what in that medicine cabinet to drive many a woman quite mad with envy. And they must be worth a small fortune too. Yet I choose one simply because it smells like lemon verbena! And I've never

dared yet to anoint myself, simply because I think I should hate
it—or that it would be vulgar. I must be an awful trial to poor
Joe, who remembers only harem women with all their exotic
tastes and fancies. . . . I wonder why he makes no attempt to go
home . . . perhaps he hasn't a home any more. Or why he doesn't
attempt to find the remainder of his clan—if any. Or are they all
still tied up in trees and rocks—or perhaps they're still wicked,
and he's afraid of falling into bad habits again. I must ask him
about this some time. Even if he couldn't find his people—or
didn't want to—he'd probably be much happier pandering to
some Persian prince or Indian potentate, instead of spending
his time having his too generous nature and miraculous powers
inhibited by an elderly maiden lady of decidedly conservative
tastes and outlook. But I should certainly miss him!

Ah, if it were only peace-time, she thought, washing behind
her ears, then she'd be able to use much less restraint upon
Joe. She could have all sorts of things, go travelling to so many
places without feeling guilty about it. But during the war, being
in sole possession of an Ifrit was a little too much like having a
private black market at one's fingertips. Really, Joe ought to be
used for the good of the country. She must think that out too—
but presently.

She finished her bath, dressed quickly and returned to the
living room to undo the black-out before preparing breakfast
or more correctly at this hour, luncheon. She was, she realized,
ravenously hungry.

But the black-out was already undone and a watery spring
sunlight touched the shabby parts of the room so that they
stood out unpleasantly. The table was laid, and several steaming dishes awaited her—while Joe himself stood smiling behind
her chair, waiting to attend her.

"Hello Joe," she greeted him gladly, "when did you get back?"

"I returned just as you were running your bath. I did not like
to disturb your ablutions. You will, however, be glad to hear that
Major Taylor is vastly improved in health to-day. The fear of
pneumonia has fortunately proved groundless. May I help you

to some porridge, or would you prefer to start with fruit—for I brought some fine oranges back with me."

"I am relieved to hear about Major Taylor." Georgina settled down in her chair. "Porridge please, Joe—I'm starved. Travelling gives one such an appetite. Do you think he's out of danger?"

"Yes, I should say so. His eyes are no longer bright with fever, and he seems more calm—your visit undoubtedly did him good. But I shall visit him every day, with your permission, so that I may report his progress to you and keep your mind at rest—or perhaps you'd care to accompany me?"

Georgina shuddered, and swallowed a spoonful of porridge. The adventures of the night were still too vivid in her mind, and she wondered now where she had found the courage to go through with them. "No, thank you," she said, "I might not be so lucky next time; besides, if Major Taylor is better there's no need for me to go. He won't need me—won't even remember that . . ." she went back to her porridge.

"It's a pity that nursing isn't your profession, Miss Carter," Joe said, after a pause. "You look really very well in uniform, and furthermore it is, I believe, a well-known fact that convalescent men frequently fall in love with—nay, marry, their nurses. It no doubt has something to do with an infantile desire for mother-love, but nevertheless, the object is achieved. Why I was reading in a book by a Viennese doctor only the other day that . . ."

"Joe," Georgina said, "you are simply incorrigible. And you read too many books. You just never learn what can and can't be said. Still—it's very odd, but I don't seem to mind now. In fact, you might even tell me why you are so anxious to see me married?"

"You would be happier," he said. "Besides, you are such a good, kind woman, it would be pleasant for you to have someone to be good and kind to."

"Oh dear!" Georgina pushed her porridge plate away. "I more or less asked for that. . . . How awful it sounds—as bad as being called well-meaning. A good, kind woman—how frightful—or isn't it? Never mind, Joe, you meant it well, I know. Now, what's in that?" She indicated a silver entree dish.

"Grilled kidneys," he told her. "I learned, as you shall see, quite a lot about the English breakfast when I was at the Savoy . . . to be truthful, I fetched these from there."

"Oh dear—oh dear," Georgina said again, and realized that she sounded alarmingly like the White Rabbit. "You shouldn't have done that, Joe. Goodness! I can't lecture you now. Perhaps I can send the Savoy an anonymous half-crown. Don't do it again, please."

"Certainly not," Joe was indignant at the suggestion. "For now I know how to do them myself—and please believe that I am fully aware that you are a woman of many screw-pless."

"Of what?"

"Screw-pless."

"Oh!" She pronounced it correctly for him.

"Thank you," he said gravely.

"I haven't as many as I used to have," she told him, a trifle defiantly, for somehow she felt as if he had referred to them as if they were a bad habit or a disability of some kind. "In fact, I believe I lost a number of them last night, and shall probably never be quite the same again."

"That," said Joe, "will probably be beneficial."

She looked at him sharply, and saw that he had not meant to be rude.

"That is as it may be," she said, a trifle sententiously, "but Joe—I haven't wanted to mention this before, because I always seem to be telling you what not to do—but you just don't wear a solar topee indoors." She pointed rather rudely at his headgear. "It is worn purely to protect the head from the sun; and for that reason is never worn in England at all. Where did you get it?"

"Off a man's head," he confessed. "It was wrong, I know . . . he was walking in the road outside the hospital, and I pretended I was the wind and snatched it away . . . it was too hot for him to chase after me—and indeed, I am glad he did not try . . . but I did pay for it. I slipped a little bag of gold into his pocket. He was a soldier. . ."

"I think," Georgina smiled, "I can forgive you this time. He probably is very grateful for the gold."

CHAPTER XIX

BREAKFAST OR LUNCH finished and swiftly cleared away, Georgina was just settling down to the papers and a cigarette whilst Joe busied himself in the kitchen, when the doorbell rang. Oh lord, Georgina jumped to her feet—that's Margaret Mackenzie—I'd forgotten she was coming so soon. "Joe—Joe," she called, and he literally sailed into the room. "That's Miss Mackenzie at the door. I forgot to tell you she was coming, I'm sorry. Do disappear quickly . . ."

Then she went to the door. "Hello, my dear," she greeted Margaret, kissing her lightly on the cheek. "How nice of you to come. Do come in—will you put your things in my bedroom? I'm afraid it's not done yet—I'm feeling lazy—but you won't mind that."

Margaret followed her into the bedroom. "I expected to find you in your bed—not airing it," she remarked reproachfully, as she removed her hat and coat. "Really, Georgina, you don't take proper care of yourself." She looked at herself in the mirror and jabbed at her hair with a comb. "We're neither of us as young as we used to be, you know, and it just isn't wise to let one's health go to rack and ruin."

"But my health is excellent," Georgina said, astonished at this sudden attempt to classify her, not only as ageing, but ailing. "I'm just a trifle over-tired like everyone else—there's nothing to be in the least alarmed about."

"Oh yes there is," Margaret insisted sagely, "and I've made up my mind to speak to you about it, even if it means"—she paused—"even if it means losing your friendship." She finished in a little rush.

"Goodness gracious!" Georgina said, "this sounds dreadful. Come into the living room. An unmade bedroom is too sordid for words, and quite the wrong atmosphere for breaking friendships in." Now really, all this was going to be just too tiresome. Margaret had come on a mission—she had suspected that all along. Margaret was obviously well-intentioned, but she was, equally obviously, going to ask a number of very awkward questions which would demand answers which she, Georgina, was not prepared to give. How on earth could she stave her off? Perhaps by treating everything as a joke—either that, or pretending to be an imbecile . . .

She led the way into the living room and patted Margaret into an easy chair by the fire. "Do sit there, dear, and get yourself thawed out. And would you like a cup of tea to warm you—or a drop of whisky?"—remembering the bottle Joe had produced out of thin air prior to the journey of the night before.

Margaret gave a forced little laugh. "No thank you—no tea—and certainly not whisky at this hour." This was indeed worse than ever she had thought it to be—if Georgina started drinking so early in the day! . . .

"It's very good for warding off a chill," Georgina said, fully conscious of Margaret's disapproval. "I think I'll have a drop myself," she added perversely, though she didn't want it a bit, particularly on top of a large meal—but really, Margaret sat there looking so unbearably smug that it practically drove one into a course of action quite foreign to one's nature. Besides, whisky *was* good for a chill, and it had been Margaret who had inflicted the chill on her in the first place.

She excused herself, went into the kitchen and mixed herself a minute drink. Joe appeared suddenly out of the broom cupboard. "How long will she stay?" he asked, in a low voice.

"I wish I knew," Georgina answered gloomily. "Probably all afternoon. Very dull for you."

"Shall I snatch her away?" he enquired helpfully.

"Good Heavens, NO! She'd die of fright!"

"Very well then—I shall prepare tea for you. You can pretend you've done it yourself."

"All right—but do it very quietly, and remember, *nothing* fancy or exotic—just plain sandwiches and ordinary cake, and remember *no* soporifics in the tea."

He nodded, and she left the kitchen and returned to Margaret. Margaret, she thought, looked a trifle flushed and uneasy. Of course, if she hadn't known Margaret so well she might have suspected!—but that was a horrid thought and unworthy too—Margaret's look was undoubtedly caused by a too-close proximity to the fire—she certainly would never stoop to listening at doors!

The plain fact was that Margaret had listened, and had just missed being caught in the act by a matter of inches. She'd stood at the living room door, which was slightly ajar, and had heard Georgina's voice and a man's voice emanate from the kitchen. Though unable to distinguish a word they said, her fears, had they needed further confirmation, were certainly confirmed then. So it was not drink alone which was shattering Georgina mentally, physically and—yes—morally! . . . Morally first of all! Margaret repressed a shudder. How could she ever tackle such a problem? How even begin to broach such an indelicate subject?

Georgina sipped her whisky and thought how utterly revolting the taste was.

Margaret pretended to be engrossed in the newspaper.

The silence between them began to be overcharged with significance.

Georgina thought, it's plain as plain that Margaret just doesn't approve of me any longer. True, I've been a bit offhand about her lately—but have I changed so much in the past two months? I wonder. She plunged into the 'silence.' "It's such a long time since we've spent an afternoon together, isn't it?" she said. "One's life seems to get so filled up with things. . . . It *was* nice of you to come."

Margaret put down the newspaper and took a deep breath before replying. Then she said: "It *is* a long time—and you know, Georgina, I've felt lately that your attitude—oh, not only towards me, but towards everything—has changed, and that in consequence you were—er—avoiding me."

Georgina attempted a not very successful look of surprise. "But Margaret dear . . . how very silly—what put such an idea into your head?"

Margaret answered, not looking at Georgina, "Well, you can't deny that things haven't been the same between us lately. I hope, Georgina—indeed, I'm sure—that I am not unduly sensitive, but it has seemed to me that recently something—or someone—has come between us."

Margaret's frequent use of the word 'between' made Georgina think of a personal relationship which had much in common with a limpet stuck to a rock. Still, Margaret didn't seem to be accusing her of anything very definite, at least not yet! That was a relief! "Really, dear," she said, setting down her glass, "that's utter nonsense." She was terribly sorry about Margaret; she felt a worm about the way she was having to lie to her even now. Margaret, after all, had been her friend for a long time—was it perhaps true that one outgrew one's friends as one developed oneself—she'd really never been very enterprising about making friends, anyway. "We've known each other for such ages," she continued, hoping to soothe Margaret's wounded pride, "and if I've seemed . . . what shall I say . . . a trifle distant—a little strained and unco-operative lately, it's only because I've been—well, perhaps worried—and over-tired . . . the war, you know, I think it affects all of us . . ."

"But *what* is it that's worrying you?" Margaret persisted. "Can't you tell me? Perhaps I can help."

"No," Georgina said hastily, and shook her head. "No dear, I'm afraid you can't—though it's terribly kind of you to offer, and I *do* appreciate it . . . but it's nothing really very serious, and I shall just have to manage it by myself." She hoped that would satisfy Margaret, but was afraid that it might merely rouse her helpful nature further—and what could she pretend to be worried about?

"I believe there's quite a good concert on this afternoon," she added. "Wouldn't you like to listen to it?" and without waiting for a reply, she crossed the room and switched on the wireless.

The 'Egmont' overture was just in its initial phrases. "How lucky—just in time," Georgina said with false enthusiasm. "I'm so fond of the Egmont, aren't you? I always feel it does me good." She felt that the transition from an involved personal conversation to one that dwelt on the dear delights of music had been abrupt, to say the least—perhaps crude, and even rude, were better words—but in the circumstances it just couldn't be helped.

She resumed her seat and pulled her knitting out of the work-bag. "Socks for Henry," she commented brightly.

"Is that the same pair you were working on when I was last here?" Margaret asked, rather tactlessly Georgina thought.

"Yes—isn't it shocking? I've been so busy I haven't had a chance to finish them."

"What *have* you been up to?" Margaret's attempt to keep her voice light and correctly disinterested was a complete failure. But Georgina appeared not to notice this.

"Oh, dashing about a bit . . . and, of course, teaching Joe takes up a great deal of my spare time," she answered absently, for her mind was off again in North Africa.

It wasn't until Margaret repeated "teaching Joe?" in a most peculiar tone of voice that Georgina realized what a colossal slip she'd made. . . .

"Oh yes," she said, in what she hoped was a natural voice, "a—er—refugee—from the Middle East—a sort of Persian person—a friend of his lives in this building. I help him with his English," she finished triumphantly—for the story was quite true, not counting the bits she'd left out.

So that was who HE was! That, Margaret thought, explained a great many things—if not everything. And, of course, Georgina, poor deluded woman, was hopelessly enamoured of the fellow. A Persian! That made it much worse! Women to the Easterner, as everyone knew, were little more than chattels—they were all so terribly polygamous or worse. How horrible—how sordid— how tragic the whole thing was. Georgina was, of course, at the Dangerous Age—she, Margaret, was broadminded enough to realize that, for she'd read about it in novels—but she must be saved from herself, or at least from making a fool of herself, poor dear—but how?

"Oh, good!" Georgina said, relieved that her story had gone down so well—at least, Margaret hadn't queried it yet. "Myra Hess and the Emperor."

"The Emperor! Who . . . ?" Margaret was startled out of her unhappy thoughts.

"Yes—the concerto, it's just been announced—didn't you hear? Isn't it wonderful?"

Margaret was rather glad of the concerto. It would give her time to think things out, give her time to plan what to say—how to cope with the situation. For say and cope she must—it was her moral duty as Georgina's oldest friend to do so.

And so they listened to the concerto in comparative silence—occasional little nods in time to the music . . . slight humming of the theme in the second movement . . . "ahs" of appreciation at the finale, were the only conversational gestures made.

At the end she left Margaret to the applause and went out and turned the gas on under the tea kettle—observing that Joe had left the tea tray all ready. She removed a small, deep dish, which looked as if it were made of solid gold and was filled with all manner of salted nuts, and hid it in the china cupboard. It would never do for Margaret to see that—it would simply bring on another flux of questions! She wondered where Joe was now—she didn't dare call him. Perhaps he had just slipped over to North Africa to see how Richard was. Richard would never know—could never know—how well he was being looked after.

She returned to Margaret with the tea things—the concert had finished and a semi-religious programme was getting under way. She switched it off.

"Now," she said, pouring out the tea, "do help yourself to sandwiches. These are—" How perfectly silly—she hadn't the vaguest notion what they were. She really ought to be more careful. "These are—quite nice," she finished, "while those"—pointing to another plate, "are even nicer!"

Margaret took a quite nice sandwich and bit into it abstract-edly. She had hardly heard Georgina's remark—she was wondering how to start on the subject uppermost in her mind. Should she lead up to it gently—or plunge boldly in? The latter course, although more difficult, was probably preferable, for Georgina, she had noticed, had an unhappy habit of changing the subject quite shamelessly, and she mustn't be given that chance. No, she'd better give up the idea of a tactful preamble and go directly to the heart of the matter. And she must just remember all the time that she was doing it, not because she liked or wanted to, far from it, for nothing could be more disagreeable or distasteful, but for poor Georgina's OWN GOOD.

She put down her teacup so firmly that she nearly knocked the bottom out of it. "Georgina," she said, "there is something I want to ask you."

Georgina hoped that she didn't look as alarmed or as guilty as she felt. "Is there?" she asked, smiling faintly. "Well, do have another cup of tea first."

But Margaret was not to be put off. "I realize that what I have to say may damage our friendship irreparably—" (that's twice she'd told me that, Georgina thought—I believe she enjoys the idea), "but," Margaret went on, "it must be said. No matter how hard it is for me—no matter how you take it, Georgina, I must say it, and I hope you know in your heart that I mean it for the best." She looked towards Georgina for encouragement, but found none. Oh dear, she thought, I hope I'm not mistaken—but the memory of the voices overheard in the kitchen—the whisky drinking—the admission about the refugee—no, no, there could be no mistake.

"Georgina," she plodded on, "you *are* in trouble . . . no, don't deny it," she added swiftly, as she saw the attempt at protest, "for I *know* you are—you can't hide it from me, Many little things have told me that you are—and I am here to help you. You can tell me *everything*. You need have no fear—for you know I am not narrow—and I shall neither blame nor condemn you. Human nature is, alas, frail . . . we all realize that—and even the strongest amongst us are tempted, and I quite . . . ."

"Just what are you driving at, Margaret?" Georgina said, icily.

"There, there," Margaret said, as if she spoke to a fretful child, "you don't need to pretend with me."

Georgina felt like biting her. What a tone—Really! It brought out her worst nature—but poor Margaret—no wonder she was suspicious. She, Georgina, had certainly given her cause to be. But of just *what* was she suspicious? She couldn't possibly have *seen* Joe—and if she had—well, of course, that might look a little odd to some people—but surely—surely Margaret knew her too well . . .

"Margaret Mackenzie," she said firmly, "tell me what is in your mind."

Margaret flinched. She wished she hadn't started the conversation. She wished she were home. She wished Georgina weren't so difficult. How could she say what was in her mind—it would sound simply too awful. She hedged—"You must know what's in my mind, Georgina, without my telling you." How terrible it was to have to think of dear Georgina as a fallen woman!

"I haven't the remotest idea what's in your mind, so you'd better enlighten me." There was no mistaking the tone of Georgina's voice. It was firm and implacable.

"I don't think you're very well," Margaret said, lamely.

"Stuff and nonsense! That's not it." Georgina brushed the statement aside. "Besides, we've been over all that before."

"Well then, I think . . . I think you are making yourself ill."

"I'm what?"

"Making yourself ill—by doing things you—er—shouldn't do."

"Please be more explicit, Margaret."

Margaret closed her eyes and gripped the arms of the chair just as if she were at the dentist's. "Oh Georgina," she wailed, "that I should be forced to say this out loud to you!"

"Better say it to me than think it about me," Georgina remarked, a trifle grimly. "It can't be so dreadful, Margaret; I'm conscious of no crime. Come now, tell me—you'll feel better once you've got it over."

"Well," Margaret made a great effort, "it's only this . . . don't you think perhaps you are possibly—er—taking too much?"

"Taking too much? What on earth do you mean? You make me sound like a kleptomaniac!"

"I mean too much . . ." Margaret whispered the dreadful word, and added that it was easy to understand how such a thing could happen almost without a person's being aware of it themselves, what with war, worry and strain.

"So that's it!" Georgina said, quite calmly. "I'm a secret drinker, am I—or perhaps a public one—well, well, is that all, Margaret?"

Margaret was totally unprepared for this reaction. She had rather expected Georgina to fly into a rage, to heap abuse on her. The anger of a person discovered—the rage that attempts to conceal a weakness. Or alternatively—and this was the picture Margaret had seen more vividly—a completely collapsed Georgina—a Georgina dissolved into pitiful tears, asking for help, while she, Margaret, a veritable rock, consoled and cajoled her out of the dreadful habit into which she had so unfortunately and unhappily fallen. But this Georgina, calm, collected—even a little amused—Margaret certainly hadn't bargained for—was this, just pure brazenness on Georgina's part—she had neither admitted nor denied the charge. Was it just the attitude of one so sunk in the mire of alcoholism that she no longer cared what her best friend—or the world—thought? And what of this revolting Persian protégé—there was certainly a mystery about that—teaching him English, indeed! He was undoubtedly at the bottom of this. She must find out! She owed it to Georgina. She had gone so far, there could be no turning back now. If friendship were lost—it was already lost—

"I know," Margaret said, attempting to choose her words carefully, "that what I have just said must have come as a very great shock to you, Georgina dear, but there was no use in my beating about the bush, was there? And such a statement was surely better coming from me than from anyone else. And you know, dear, you must take courage—it's not too late. We must first find the *cause*—and then we are well on the way to a cure. That's only common sense, isn't it?"

"Yes, yes," Georgina agreed. "And what do you think is—er—causing it, Margaret?" It was as well to humour her, she felt, for after her first desire to laugh had worn off it was abundantly clear that poor dear Margaret was decidedly touched—if not actually quite insane. Of course, there was a bad hereditary factor there; the whole family was a trifle, well—odd. There was that queer brother who was always inventing quite ridiculous things, and a sister (never mentioned) who had run off years ago with a Portuguese trapeze artist and was presumably living in sin in South America. No, Margaret must be humoured and then got quietly home somehow—perhaps Joe could be pressed into service—for if Margaret were potty she'd never know anyway.

So she said "Well, dear, and what about the Cause?" which made it sound exactly like votes for women, but she couldn't help that. "Or perhaps you'd like to go and lie down for a bit before telling me—you must be very tired."

This was undoubtedly a trap! To be asked to lie down in the middle of an afternoon and a conversation! Why, there was no telling what Georgina, in her highly nervous state, would do—probably lock her in the bedroom and sit at the door, a naked breadknife in her hand, raving like a maniac. She would not fall into it. "No dear, I am not tired," she said weakly, "I'm just very worried about you."

"That's very sweet of you—but there's really no need for you to worry."

"But I worry about the cause," Margaret continued bravely "You see, I think I know what it is."

"Splendid!" Georgina said, enthusiastically. "Do tell me, for I'm at a loss to know what it is myself."

Margaret was pleased to see how calm, yet interested, Georgina appeared to be. That was a good sign. Her fear of being done a mischief evaporated. Now was the time to make it clear that she knew all. "The cause," she said, "is, I think, unrequited love."

Aha! The thrust had hit home, and hit hard. She could see the colour flood into Georgina's face. Of course, she'd only put the unrequited in to be polite—the qualifying adjective should have been 'illicit'—she had just saved herself from using that word.

But she certainly had her answer in the most positive form. That compromising blush. She was right! How awful! Women made such pitiful fools of themselves when caught in the throes of a late passion!

"Margaret!" Georgina exclaimed. "You don't know what you're saying." It was the only comment she could think of in the circumstances. Margaret might be mentally overwrought, but how on earth had she guessed? Of course, that bit about drinking was just plain crazy, and served to show the unhappy unbalance of the mind. But where, or how, had she learned of her feeling for Richard? His name had never so much as been mentioned between them, of that she was sure—

"I *do* know what I'm saying," Margaret assured her, "and really, there's no good pretending with me, Georgina—for I've seen you with him."

"You've what?"

"Yes," Margaret said, in an irritatingly patient tone, "remember the day you came to the office in your new clothes?" She did not think it necessary to add her suspicions as to how those clothes had been obtained, for that would really be too coarse.

"Of course I remember." Georgina hoped to heaven that she didn't look too guilty.

"It was that evening—I was coming away from the lecture and I saw you in a car with a man. Oh, I'd suspected what was wrong before, but—"

"That man," Georgina put in coldly, "since you're asking for information, was an old friend of my brother's and of mine. He's been out of England for years—I can surely go to the theatre with a man without being accused of being infatuated with him—or worse." That tone and explanation should certainly put Margaret off.

But Margaret merely thought 'a likely story.' And would Robert have an old Persian friend? Not Robert . . . or would he? After all, India was full of various nationalities. As for Georgina's indignant attitude and tone—that was to be expected—again she hadn't absolutely denied the charge!

"Dear Georgina," Margaret said, "I'm sure all this must be very painful for you—it's painful to me too. But I do understand—I think—how easily one can be swept away by emotions which in stabler times have other—er—outlets. The papers are full of such things. Then, of course, all of us want to help the unfortunate refugees in this country as much as we can, but!—well, surely my dear, I needn't say any more—" She was rather proud of the tolerant tone of this little speech.

"No, you needn't say another word," Georgina assured her, having at last fathomed what Margaret was driving at—she didn't know whether she was angry or amused by it, it was all so incredible. "You've said quite enough as it is. Now just let me get this straight—you think that, A, I am drinking like a fish, and B, that I am living in—er—sin . . . for I suppose that's what you mean . . . with a refugee. That's it, isn't it?"

"Georgina!" Margaret was quite genuinely shocked by such outspoken language. "There's no need, dear, to put it quite so bluntly." Of course, once a woman forgot herself morally she was bound to forget herself verbally as well. It was all a part of the dreadful process of deterioration.

"Blunt or not, it's what you thought, isn't it?" Margaret's mental aberration obviously took the form of a vicarious sex enjoyment, an obsession which she could not admit to herself and had therefore subconsciously transferred to her, Georgina. What a very great pity. Margaret, she was afraid, would have to be analysed.

Margaret herself had an uneasy feeling that something had gone wrong somewhere with her diagnosis of Georgina's 'trouble.' Georgina seemed so calm, so composed now, yet she certainly had been upset by that remark about unrequited love not five minutes ago. "I don't know quite *what* I thought," she defended herself, "but I didn't *say* it the way you put it."

Georgina laughed. Poor Margaret—she was sorry for her—she must try to rid her of this curious complex. "I don't suppose you'll believe me, but I hope you will, when I tell you that neither of those two accusations is true," she said gently, "and that this whole affair exists only in your imagination. Surely, Margaret, you have known me long enough to realize that my nature is incapable of both those—er—things."

"I'd be only too happy to believe it, Georgina," Margaret answered, but the answer didn't ring quite true, because her mind told her that it was cunning the way Georgina had twisted the facts so that she, Margaret, would look both mischief-making and foolish. There was, she realized, nothing she could do for Georgina now, except to stand by her. She had given Georgina the opportunity to break down and confide in her, but Georgina was obviously bent on pursuing her own doom in her own unhappy way.

"You can be happy then," Georgina assured her, "and we'll forget all about this discussion this afternoon. That's the best thing to do." Poor, poor Margaret—couldn't something be done for her, or would she only get worse. Who would be the next victim of her tortured imagination? Perhaps it wasn't psychological—perhaps something had gone wrong with her glands—glands seemed responsible for practically everything these days—and she needed treatment to put her right. But how was she to suggest such a thing to Margaret? What could she do to help? Nothing at the moment; she would just have to stand by and watch Margaret until the deterioration became more obvious—then she would firmly insist on her seeing a doctor.

Margaret said feebly, "I feel as if I'd bungled things rather badly, Georgina."

"Not at all, dear," comforted Georgina, "it was kind of you to worry about me, very kind and I appreciate the thoughtfulness of your motives . . . but your imagination just got the better of you—goodness knows, that happens to all of us at times. But now you're quite satisfied that I'm still the same person I used to be and that I'm not leading an—er—immoral life!" As a matter of fact, she *was* leading a double life, but had she said so . . . !

"Yes," Margaret answered and was convinced for the moment that what Georgina had said was true. Now that her whole theory had collapsed she felt horribly weak and embarrassed. "And now, Georgina, if you don't mind, I think I'd better be going home."

Georgina did not urge her to stay. It was better for Margaret to go home and be quiet . . . besides, she was really feeling pretty tired herself. She murmured how nice it had been to see Margaret, and how wise it was to have had a 'frank talk,' and led the way into the bedroom for Margaret's coat and hat.

Margaret picked up her things and put them on. "Does your charwoman come on Sunday, Georgina?" she asked.

"Goodness no—she hardly comes at all these days." That was more or less the truth, for Joe did all the housework.

"Oh," Margaret said in an odd little voice.

Only then did Georgina notice that the bed had been made and the room was spotlessly tidy. Joe had, as usual, been a little over-zealous. But what explanation could she give? What could she say that Margaret, in her state, would or could believe? It was impossible for her now to summon Joe—to confront Margaret with him . . . for even if he just appeared from thin air, Margaret wouldn't believe it. She'd think he'd been hiding under the bed or in the wardrobe, and it would merely confirm her suspicions about the silly story of the Persian refugee. What an idiot she had been. No, there was no untruth that would get her out of this—no truth either, for that matter. The only way to treat the situation was to ignore it. She did—or rather tried, by saying "Well, dear, I shall see you at the office to-morrow morning. Shall we lunch together?"

"Yes . . . no . . . I don't know," Margaret wailed unhappily.

Georgina ignored her agitation as best she could and led her to the door. "Well, we can decide that to-morrow," she said. "Goodbye, Margaret."

Outside, Margaret clutched the stair-rail for support. Her brain whirled like a roulette wheel. Suddenly it stopped. She hadn't been wrong after all. It was even worse than she had suspected. That dreadful refugee who had seduced poor Georgina was living in the flat! Even if the bedroom so mysteriously tidy hadn't made her think it, that ostentatious pink turban carelessly tossed on the top of the wardrobe would have told her the truth. Even Georgina, abandoned as she was, would not wear that kind of hat. Alas, Georgina—lost—lost—. Margaret staggered out into the wet, darkening street.

CHAPTER XX

THE POWER of suggestion, Georgina thought, was certainly a power to be reckoned with, for the chill which Margaret had suggested she was suffering with on Sunday, had by Tuesday morning become a most alarming fact. She had already been two days in bed with it, a temperature of 101° and a splitting headache. And now, to-day, Thursday, with a normal temperature she lay in bed feeling quite weak and rather sorry for herself. The truth was that Georgina had hardly had a day's illness in the whole of her adult life—very fortunate considering the difficulties of being ill and living alone at the same time—and she took her chill in the nature of a personal insult. She had been through a lot these past few days!

Joe had looked after her with the most tender and embarrassing solicitude, plus a knowledge of medicine which came straight from the year 2,000 B.C. Miss Carter was hot? The cure for this overheating was the direct opposite—she should be laid in a cool mountain stream really, but failing that ice or snow packed about the body would do. Miss Carter was cold? Then Miss Carter must be practically roasted over a fire. There were so-called aromatic herbs, which when applied to the nose made it cease its excess of fluids. There were evil-smelling salves and incantations to ease the chest. A dried and powdered toad dissolved in wine was a superb draught for strengthening the heart, whilst there was nothing like a prodigious noise for driving the evil ache out of the head. It was only by dint of repeating the word "No" firmly and constantly that Georgina had saved herself from double pneumonia, complicated by acute chilblains and severe burns. Small wonder, she thought, if she felt thoroughly exhausted—and really Joe must be found something useful to do. Looking after her and keeping an eye on Richard's convalescence was hardly the right kind of job for an adult Ifrit.

So she lay and thought about the problem. It seemed to her that to own, or apparently own, an Ifrit with certain supernatural powers, one who could get about so easily, so rapidly, unseen and unheard, was a great personal responsibility and also a great gift which should be put to its best use. Should be made to serve some larger purpose; should, in fact, be used to benefit mankind.

Having arrived at this conclusion Georgina fell asleep and awakened much refreshed. Joe was in North Africa at the moment so she could continue her thinking undisturbed.

Certainly, she told herself, Joe had genius of a peculiar sort and Joe was also her peculiar responsibility; therefore, it was up to her to see that this genius was used properly. But what was so confusing was to try to discover in just what capacity Joe would be most useful. She considered first the censorship. By reason of Joe's knowledge of Eastern languages—archaic as it might be— he would be of some use there. But that really did not seem to be the best place for him, for it made use of a perfectly ordinary ability, one which was possessed by a great many human beings.

Then there was the Ministry of Information; he might be useful there as a sort of cultural representative of various Middle Eastern countries—or as an adviser on customs and habits, for Miss Carter had reason to believe that manners and modes in the East hadn't really changed much in thousands of years—even if they had, the Ministry could hardly be expected to know that. But even so, she was not sure what kind of adviser Joe would make, for he was inclined to be impetuous and not even an Ifrit could cut through ministerial red tape.

But the Intelligence Service! Ah! there Joe could and would be invaluable, a real secret weapon, a master-spy who could never be bought or caught! Miss Carter grew quite excited about this prospect. She pictured Joe invisible at Berchtesgarten—or hidden in a bowl of fruit on Hitler's sideboard. She saw him concealed behind Goering's medals, lurking in Goebbels' portfolio, or wandering and listening—a wisp of smoke—in the chancelleries of Hitler's Europe. To learn the required languages would be, she felt, quite simple for anyone as gifted as Joe, and he already knew a smattering of German picked up on a Dutch ship several centuries ago. Yes, this was a truly excellent idea. Fever had undoubtedly sharpened her imagination. She relaxed, having decided on the Intelligence Service as a career for Joe; all that remained to do was to think out the best way of presenting him to the correct department. Georgina knew no one whom she could consult as to the correct procedure in a matter such as this, and she somehow could not see herself with Joe in tow, waiting endlessly in a succession of anterooms which led to some under-official—she just didn't have time for that. Besides on entering all government buildings identity cards had to be produced and business stated—and Joe was without an identity card. She could, of course, smuggle him into the building in her handbag and produce him only at the right moments—but how would she herself get in? Whom should she ask to see? If only Richard were here to advise her and to take Joe in hand! For she had determined—after the unfortunate business with Margaret last Sunday—that she would take Richard into her full confidence—tell him all about Joe—introduce them to each other (no matter what Richard thought), all this, of course, if she ever saw Richard again—

Well, the best thing to do was probably to write to the War Office. Write cautiously explaining that she had an . . . an . . . well, not an invention—no, a matter of importance to communicate to the proper authorities and ask for an interview. At that interview she would produce Joe; after the interviewer had recovered from his very natural shock, she would explain Joe's powers, put him through a few tricks and dear Joe would be immediately recognized, regularized, and pressed forthwith into service of incalculable value.

She had just decided all this when Joe returned from North Africa with a basket of oranges and lemons garnished by a bunch of bananas.

"I trust you are feeling much better after your sleep," he said, setting the basket down beside the bed. "Indeed, I can see by your eyes that you are much refreshed. This surprises me, for quite frankly I despaired of your life when you refused my treatment."

"I despaired of my life at the very thought of it," she told him. "Joe, what lovely fruit. Can I have a banana . . . how is Major Taylor?"

"He progresses marvellously," Joe answered, selecting a banana and handing it to her. "The Major has a wonderful constitution really for a man of his age."

"Goodness, he's only fifty," she said, nibbling the banana. "You should talk about age, Joe; I am surprised!"

Joe chuckled. "The human race is not the same as my race," he said, a trifle obviously.

"And very fortunate, too," Georgina said, but wasn't quite sure whether or not she meant it. "Is the Major able to sit up and read now?" What she wanted to find out was if he were writing any letters, but she couldn't be quite so blatant as to ask that.

"Oh, yes," Joe answered her, "and furthermore, Miss Carter, you remember the room Major Taylor is in?"

"I'm hardly likely to forget it," Georgina chewed the banana slowly.

"Well, did it not strike you as odd that in that room there was apparently no window?"

"Odd," Georgina said, "is not the word."

"The reason for that, I have discovered," Joe said. "It is quite marvellous . . . the roof opens, so that one is in a room with the sky for a ceiling . . . is not that truly wonderful . . . Sulayman's palace, had nothing to equal that."

Georgina did not tell him that such a device was not in the least remarkable. She thought it pathetic in a way that he should think such mechanical inventions the height of magic. "My goodness," she said, "what a good idea and how pleasant for Major Taylor."

"All he does is press a button by the bed and the dome splits in half and slides back," Joe said excitedly. "You will not be angry when I tell you that I pressed the button several times.

Major Taylor was astonished—he thought that something had gone wrong and reported it . . ."

Georgina smiled. "I should have been tempted to press the button myself," she said. She hoped, privately, however, that Joe would not be side-tracked by such trifles when on government service. Berchtesgarten, she was sure, was simply full of gadgets. "Joe," she said, changing the subject. "I want to write a letter; will you get me my notepaper from the next room? It's in the second drawer of the tallboy."

"Certainly," Joe beamed, "I will be able to take the letter immediately to Major Taylor."

"It isn't to Major Taylor," Georgina said, "and even if it were you wouldn't be able to take it. We're not supposed to know where he is . . ."

"But we do," Joe said, "he's in the hospital near Rabat . . ."

"Shush," she said sharply. So Rabat was the name of the place. "Do get me the paper, Joe, and then leave me for a bit. I've a most important letter to write." She had decided not to tell Joe what she had planned for him until she heard from the War Office and the interview was safely arranged. He would only make her life hideous with questions if he were told beforehand.

Joe brought her the notepaper and left her. "You'd better get on with Trevelyan's History of England," she told him, "we've been neglecting your education lately."

"Yes, Miss Carter," he answered with a lugubrious sigh, and closed the door.

Miss Carter spent a full hour over the composition of that letter, She wasted a great deal of good notepaper, consoling herself that it was in an important cause—before she got it exactly to her satisfaction. She recalled to the mind of the individual or department addressed that her brother was Colonel Robert Carter, missing at Singapore (this gave her a certain military standing, she felt). She explained that she had an important communication to make, a communication which would undoubtedly shorten the war and be of material (a curious word to use in this connection, she thought) advantage to the Intelligence Branch of the War Office. She begged for an early interview and remained faithfully theirs, Georgina Carter.

The fatal letter finally finished, she called Joe and asked him to slip down to the post-box with it. If he asked any questions she could tell him she was writing to the War Office about her brother.

But for once Joe did not enquire—he was probably so thankful to get away from British history that he would have gone to the ends of the earth gratefully and without asking why.

The minute he had disappeared, Georgina regretted her rashness. She should have waited until she was well before making such a decision (or had she been afraid that if she waited she might change her mind!). And really wasn't it wicked of her to dispose of Joe so airily without even consulting his wishes in the matter. She, who had been so firm about his not being her slave, was certainly treating him as if she owned him body and soul! Furthermore, she realized, with regret superimposed upon remorse, that she was going to hate parting with Joe. She'd miss him terribly, but after all, he'd be doing a great service and that was all that mattered, personal considerations couldn't and shouldn't interfere.

CHAPTER XXI

GEORGINA WAS recovered from her cold by the week-end, which with Joe's assistance she spent in Penzance, where the weather was kind and really did her good. She expected a reply to her letter any day now but as time passed no letter came. Nor did she have any word from Richard.

She went to the office each day and was quite miserable and relieved. Miserable about Richard. Relieved in a way that the War Office was taking its time. Sometimes she felt sure that it was a good sign—they were ignoring it. Other times she was equally certain that it was a bad sign—they were considering it seriously and might (horrid thought) even be watching her movements. When this latter mood hit her she felt absurdly guilty and developed a little habit of looking quickly behind her at intervals as she hurried to and from the office.

Relations with Margaret continued friendly but strained. The studious avoidance of the subject between them, plus their watchful awareness of each other, made friendship slip into the superficialities of acquaintanceship. Georgina, for her part, was relieved to observe no further apparent symptoms of poor Margaret's obsession—and Margaret was gratified to feel that so far as she could judge, Georgina had given up drinking. Perhaps her talk had done some good after all.

So several weeks passed and Georgina's uneasiness and unhappiness increased. Joe, whose daily visits to Richard had been stopped by Georgina, for he was practically well now, was distressed at her condition, attributing it solely to a burning and bootless love for Major Taylor. He did his best to cheer her up, sometimes with a bunch of flowers, strange, beautiful and exotic; sometimes with a bejewelled box of nard, sometimes with great boxes of wonderful sweetmeats, sugared violets and rose petals, great black brandied cherries, candied oranges stuffed with raisins and chopped blanched almonds; and he would suggest from time to time that she needed rest and recreation in some warm climate, adding with his inimitable brand of subtlety that obviously the North African climate was just what she needed.

On a Thursday in the middle of March Georgina came home from the office to find Joe awaiting her with two letters.

"From Major Taylor at last," he cried, handing her an airgraph.

"Probably from Henry," Georgina answered, snatching it from him and tearing it open. It was from Richard.

Joe smiled. Had Georgina questioned the smile she would have discovered that ten days earlier Joe had read the letter over Richard's shoulder, and that for days before the letter was written Joe had, every night as Major Taylor slept, whispered in his ear, "write Georgina . . . write Georgina . . ." and that it had been a great temptation (which he had successfully resisted) to snatch the letter away and play postman himself. Only then, of course, Miss Carter would know that he had been visiting Major Taylor against her instructions.

Georgina, however, was absorbed in Richard's message. He told her the weather was good, that he had been ill but was now recovered (no statement of what had really happened); he was now going on somewhere else . . . didn't know when he'd return to England . . . might in fact not return but go straight to the States . . . was there any news of Robert? If he could he'd get someone to bring her a few oranges. Admonished her to take care of herself and prefixed his signature with the word 'Sincerely.'

It was a disappointing and exasperating letter. Just what she had expected she didn't quite know. The only sentence with any human feeling was the one which said, 'Take care of yourself,' but that was only a well-meaning form of politeness.

She handed the letter to Joe whose face had changed with hers, so that he now wore an expression of gloom. "Perhaps you'd like to read the Major's letter," she said, "he doesn't say much. Now what about the other letter . . ."

Joe handed her an official-looking envelope. She tore it open and read that she was thanked for her letter but that *full* particulars of the nature of her business would have to be stated *in writing* before an interview could be granted.

She was both relieved and angry at this. Relieved that for the moment she didn't have to part with Joe. Angry that it should have taken nearly a month for the War Office to send her what was obviously a form letter. They probably thought her some harmless lunatic with delusions of grandeur—or worse.

She went into the living room, Joe following, and grew more and more indignant at the thought of such treatment. She was angry . . . yes . . . she had a right to be angry at such stupidity (she would never admit to herself that this anger was not purely a result of the War Office letter, but was also a result of her disappointment in Richard's letter). Stating the nature of her business indeed! As if she were a pedlar—how would this look on paper? Dear Sirs, I have in my possession one (1)

Ifrit, whom I think should be of supreme service to the Intelligence Department as a spy, as he can travel by his own power anywhere at any time, at any speed, becomes completely invisible if so desired, and can conveniently fit himself into a nutshell and be carried about in the waistcoat pocket. How I came by this Ifrit is neither here nor there, but I will inform you of the chance which brought this about at the interview, which, I trust, you will now arrange.

No! such a letter simply would not do. Whatever doubts they'd entertained as to her sanity would certainly be confirmed. She would then have to pester them with letters—chain herself to the railings of the House of Commons, do all sorts of things, for which she had neither taste nor aptitude, to get a hearing—if ever. She could see herself eventually, if she persisted, being visited by some official army psychiatrist and whisked off to some equally official 'home' to be reconditioned and taught weaving and bead work. But this thought had its humorous side—if the psychiatrist fantasy did happen in reality, she could produce Joe in the so-called flesh and then what would happen? What did happen to a psychiatrist when confronted by the 'visual hallucination' of his patient—would he try to rationalize it—or would he know when he was licked, retire gracefully and certify himself?

"I see no reason for being disappointed in Major Taylor's letter," Joe broke in upon her thoughts. "When one considers, as I have often considered, that the English have no language of love with which to express their innermost feelings."

"Who said I was disappointed," Georgina interrupted, hoping the question would serve as a denial.

"You did not need to voice your feelings," Joe explained, "for your face expressed what was in your heart. But look you, Miss Carter, here is even a further reason for hope. Major Taylor would not want to express his free feelings by a letter which would be seen by the crass eye of the censor. Now if you would allow me to act as private courier."

"No," Georgina said. "It simply wouldn't do, Joe . . . besides I may have other plans for you."

"Plans," Joe said eagerly. "How splendid. Am I permitted to know what they are . . . ?"

"No," Georgina said, "if you don't mind I'd rather not tell you yet. I hardly know what they are myself, but what about some dinner, Joe?"

Joe clapped his hand to his head. "Fool, fool," he said, "forgive my carelessness. I am unworthy to be your servant—that I should permit you to starve . . ."

"It's hardly as bad as that," Georgina laughed.

"You shall have a wonderful dinner," Joe promised as he left the room.

Miss Carter's thoughts reverted to the War Office. So Joe would now never become a member of the Intelligence Department. Well, it was England's loss, not offset by her personal gain. Quite illogical!y she found herself feeling hurt on Joe's account that he should be so churlishly ignored, that his gifts should be so spumed—it was preposterous and stupid.

Georgina's good common-sense was not so apparent these days. When an Ifrit suddenly comes into your life and turns it very nearly upside down, common-sense is a commodity which appears to have little market value. As it cannot accept the fantastic without attempting to rationalize it, thus causing intense inner conflict, it is better to toss common-sense gently overboard right at the first, and take instead the motto, "I believe it because it is impossible."

Georgina had certainly found this to be true . . . and where, just where, she asked herself, had common-sense ever got her anyway.

The idea now struck her that if Joe couldn't be an accredited spy with the necessary credentials, he might at least be a private spy. For having been foolish enough to tell him she had 'plans' for him, she must now try to work out something for him to do. Otherwise his questions would make life unbearable. Supposing then that Joe became a private spy—her private spy, in fact. It would be interesting to be the only person in England who knew with whom Hitler's patience was exhausted. To know what was going on in that pseudo Valhalla of his on the mountain top;

to find out if possible, what his next moves would be, if any. Even if Joe couldn't understand the language perfectly, he could at least observe what happened. Georgina began to feel quite excited about this prospect. It combined rashness and daring with perfect security. Of course, what she'd do with the priceless information when she got it she didn't know—perhaps badger the War Office with it—not that *they'd* pay any attention—or turn herself into a super Madame Tabouis (of course, under an assumed name), and make a fortune. Georgina was quite carried away by this scheme and was only brought to earth by Joe and a truly magnificent dinner.

As she ate her way through tortue clair—sole veronique—Coq au vin—crêpes Suzettes (Joe had been learning a lot unbeknown to Georgina by nightly visits to the great hotels in New York), she outlined, very roughly, her plan. He was enchanted; such a scheme had all the elements of intrigue and danger which he had so sadly missed in the past three thousand years. He promised her—and she believed him—that given a chance he could pick up the German language in a fortnight or so.

She determined that the very next day would see the beginning; she would invest in a 'Teach Yourself German' book and a whole set of Linguaphone records; she would even let him go invisibly to night classes!

CHAPTER XXII

FOR THE NEXT fortnight Joe trained with the singleness of purpose of a Japanese athlete about to enter the Olympic games. He had once boasted (when Georgina was explaining the workings of the Censorship to him) that he could learn any language in two weeks. She naturally enough had not believed him. Now she found that this had not been a wild statement— it was perfectly true. How he had managed to do it she did not know—but he proved his ability by listening to the B.B.C. news in German and translating it for her with ease and rapidity. Her own German—inept as it was—was just sufficiently useful to prove that he had really mastered the language.

What an asset he'd be to the diplomatic service after the war! For she had heard it rumoured that diplomats were going to have to learn the languages of the countries to which they were accredited. What a gift to possess! A gift amounting to sheer genius as inexplicable, as wonderful and as frightening to contemplate as infant prodigies or child chess wizards.

Apart from providing him at first with the necessary text-books and giving him information on what classes to attend at the Polytechnic, she had not assisted this aspect of his education in any way. Nor did he tell her that he had spent many invisible hours with von Arnim and his staff, listening and learning from them in preference to night classes.

Georgina did, however, attempt to teach him the rough geography of the country he was about to enter as a highly unde-sirable alien, and by means of photographs collected with some difficulty from old newspapers and magazines, tried to give him a picture of the man he was to shadow.

She sent him off on his mission one evening in early spring—feeling absurdly near to tears and urging him to take all possible precautions and to return speedily. He left in a puff of smoke and a drizzle of rain, very sensible of the importance of his mission, for on his head he wore his British policeman's helmet.

Georgina did not sleep that night; she did not even try to. She attempted to knit, to read, to mend clothes, to write to Henry, but she could not keep her mind on any of these things. She drank innumerable cups of tea. She tried to follow Joe with her mind, but found that completely impossible. She attempted to think out a letter to Richard, but this too failed for all the time her brain, her eyes, her ears, were waiting for Joe's return. It was, of course, foolish to expect him back within six or seven hours, but after that . . . It was reasonable to assume that as it would take him less than five minutes for the return journey, he need not be away very long . . . she had told him merely to contact his man, pick up whatever information was available and return—there was no need for anything more elaborate on this first journey; it was merely to pave the way for subsequent journeys.

But by morning Joe had not returned, nor did he return the following evening, nor the next day, nor the next. Georgina passed through all the stages of worry, fear and frantic anxiety, ending with colossal self-accusation and remorse. She had no doubt sent poor Joe to his death—if Ifrits could die. Or perhaps he had deliberately decided not to return. Perhaps he was tired of her (and she couldn't blame him for that—for life with her must be insufferably dull). Perhaps he had broken the spell of Sulayman and gone back to his evil ways or his people. But that was impossible! She felt she knew Joe pretty well and that there wasn't a kinder, gentler spirit alive. Joe, she was sure, wouldn't willingly hurt a fly (of course, he had been pretty rough with those Arab gangsters in the olive grove, but that was different— and he hadn't really hurt them—merely inconvenienced them, slightly). No, she found it very difficult to believe that Joe had ever been as wicked as he claimed to have been. It was impossible to visualize him as the evil genius he said he had been once. She had come to the conclusion long ago that any story he told of the bad old days was a form of exhibitionism—a boastful make-believe, like children playing at being bandits—for there was a definite child-like quality about Joe. No, Joe would never willingly desert her, she was almost sure of that. That's what made the whole affair so awful; she had played upon his trust, his childish love of excitement, merely to gratify her own curiosity, to satisfy a whim, to humble the War Office. To set herself up as a potential source of information, she had just casually sent poor Joe to his doom, without even bothering to enquire whether or not he really wanted to play this dangerous game; without even troubling to ascertain whether or not an Ifrit had any vulnerable spots. A sordid story. She hated herself. How could she, Georgina Carter, have been so criminally thoughtless? . . . why she was little better than a murderer.

But the night of the third day, as Georgina brooded supperless in front of her fire, Joe was suddenly there beside her. The relief at seeing him, plus the suddenness of his appearance which never failed to startle her, jerked her from remorse to anger.

"Joe," she snapped, "where on earth have you been all this time? I told you to come straight home. I've been worried absolutely sick about you."

"I, too, have been worried, Miss Carter," Joe answered gently.

"Oh, my poor Joe," Georgina cried, realizing suddenly how ungracious she must have sounded. "Can you forgive me for sending you on that dreadful journey? I've been hating myself for doing it ever since you left. And you were gone so long that I thought . . . I thought . . ."

"Some harm had befallen me," he supplied and she was grateful that she did not have to explain that at one stage in her vigil she had been tempted to think of him as a deserter. "No, you need not have feared for me on that score," he continued, "though great explosions surrounded me. Look," he held out his policeman's helmet so that she could see the hole torn in the side of it.

"Oh, Joe!" she exclaimed. "I wonder you escaped . . . how awful . . . and your helmet damaged too. . . . what a pity . . ."

He fished a shell splinter out of his pocket and handed it to her. "A souvenir," he said. "I caught it as it went through the helmet, for it nearly knocked it off my head. I could have brought you several camel loads of those bits of metal," he told her, "for I joined up with a squadron of planes as we approached the capital. It was perhaps foolish of me to expose myself to quite so much anti-aircraft fire, but you know how interested I am in flying and in the way poor man has taught himself the secret known only at first to us and to the birds . . ."

"Yes . . . yes . . . Joe . . . indeed," she interrupted, for it was obvious that Joe was embarked on his story and would as usual approach it by devious routes and embellish it by hundreds of little touches so that it would take hours before he got to the main facts. "But you must be terribly tired, so before I hear your story let me go and make you some coffee."

"Indeed no, you must not, Miss Carter," Joe said, putting his treasured helmet down on the table and looking at it sadly, "for I am not tired in the least . . . we Ifrits do not tire . . . but I am bewildered, in a puzzle is, I suppose, the correct phrase . . . and to be truthful, worried."

"All those things add up to tiredness, Joe, so *I* shall make the coffee," she said firmly. "Please let me," she went on not at all firmly, "for it would make me feel less guilty about you. You don't know how I've sat here reproaching myself for sending you on that insane journey, whilst you've been away."

Joe looked vastly pleased by this remark, and with very slightly calculated shyness, dropped his head and started a protest. But Miss Carter took none of this in for she had already left the room.

She returned to him ten minutes later, carrying a large pot of coffee and two of her best cups on a tray. She was by this time quite eaten away with curiosity to know all about his trip, but she restrained herself admirably as a sort of penance. She set the tray down deliberately and poured out the coffee. "Here you are, Joe," she handed him his cup, "Drink it up—it will do you good."

"Thank you, Miss Carter," he accepted the cup, "it is indeed kind of you, and although as you may or may not have guessed, we Ifrits have no real need of food and drink, yet we like the pleasures of the table and this coffee will be trebly delicious because you have made it."

"Thank you," she said, thinking how perfectly outrageous such a remark would be from anyone else, "and certainly you yourself produce food as if you enjoyed it . . . I'm glad to hear that you're able to eat, even if you don't need to. I approve of all appetites, provided they're properly cultivated and not allowed to run wild, of course . . ." She was slightly surprised at herself for making such a statement, but it had just seemed to say itself without her realizing the implications. "Now tell me, Joe . . ." she went on a trifle embarrassed, "all about your trip . . . that is if you feel like it. You said you were puzzled and worried. Why?"

Joe settled down cross-legged on the carpet. "I am unhappy," he said, shaking his head, "very unhappy, for I have on this journey been in the presence of a most powerful evil. An evil which I had once known and immediately recognized, even though so many centuries have passed since last I saw and knew it."

"I don't quite follow you, Joe," Miss Carter put down her cup. "Didn't you see Hitler?"

"That man! Oh yes, I saw him. That is, in a way, what I mean. He calls himself by another name this time. But no matter how often he changes his name or his form I should always know him."

"Do you mean . . . I don't know quite how to explain it . . . but is his a case of daemonic possession?"

"If that means does his body house a demon, the answer is NO. For if that were the case one could be sorry for him, one might even forgive him, for he could not be responsible for his actions, save for the weak moment when he allowed the demon entry."

"I ought to warn you again, Joe," Georgina said, for she saw which way the conversation was going, "that I definitely do not hold with these occult or supernatural theories. I am by nature purely practical and unimaginative, as you know, and I believe that to explain things away by er—supernatural agencies, is really an easy way out . . . if you understand what I mean by that. And yet . . . and yet wasn't it Goethe, himself a German, who had held and propounded the curious theory of the German love for the daemonic!"

Joe smiled. "I do understand," he said softly, "yet you do not question me?"

"Oh you!" Georgina stopped. She realized suddenly that she had become so accustomed to Joe and his powers that she now accepted him as almost natural . . . that she lumped him in with wireless, aeroplanes, submarines, sulphanilamide and penicillin—all miracles in their way, but easy to explain and understand if you had that kind of mind (which, she admitted, she hadn't). For they were based on certain principles, followed certain laws . . . no, she simply couldn't pursue that line of thought—it was too confusing. Joe was a sort of scientific discovery which she had made, quite by accident . . . that was the best definition of

Joe. "Oh you," she repeated quite confused by this time, "there is some quite simple explanation to account for you, of that I'm sure . . . though I admit I don't know what it is . . . so let's call you the exception that proves the rule." She felt all this was a pretty lame explanation and indeed might even be insulting, but she was loath, at this stage, to go back on her claim to being purely practical. For—horrid thought—the practicality lately was being whittled away until very soon there'd be only the claim left with nothing to back it up. Besides, and here she squared her mental shoulders, besides if one ever did admit that there were such things as supernatural agencies—other than God and the angels—goodness knew where it might lead to. She might end like a friend of Margaret Mackenzie's who began with spiritualism and ended in a private asylum.

Joe was smiling and she felt uneasily that he might be reading her thoughts.

"I've never understood that curious saying about the exception proving the rule," he said blandly, "but no matter, yet if the . . . shall I call it theory . . . which I am about to propound disturbs you, then I will refrain from telling you the story, for I would not agitate your sensibilities nor disturb your peace of mind for all the worlds in the universe."

"Oh no, Joe," Georgina cried, feeling for a moment that she would gladly toss aside all scruples for the sake of the story (which in any case one wasn't bound to believe). "Do go on, I'm really terribly interested in hearing everything. Whether I believe it or not . . . your theory I mean, not the story . . . doesn't lessen my interest in the least. I only warned you that I might be sceptical so that you wouldn't be disappointed if I disagreed with you."

"You are such a strange person," Joe said, "yet, you know, Miss Carter, I like you."

"And I like and trust you, Joe dear," Georgina said impulsively, more moved than embarrassed by his compliment. "Now do go on . . . you were saying . . . ," she recalled to him, "that although Hitler was not possessed by a demon, yet he seemed to you to be evil incarnate."

Joe nodded his agreement. "But I believe he is the master of a demon," he said slowly, "or rather master of an Ifrit."

Georgina nearly jumped out of her skin. "An Ifrit," she exclaimed in horror, for hadn't she just admitted that Ifrits were possible. "Oh Joe! you don't think . . . no . . . I can't believe it. . . . It's absurd . . . fantastic . . . what makes you think so?"

"Because I have seen him," Joe told her calmly. "I saw him whilst I was there . . ."

"You saw whom?"

"Hitler and his Ifrit," Joe said patiently, "don't you understand how simple it all is, Miss Carter?"

"It's about as simple as Einstein's theory," Georgina said crossly for she was a little frightened. "I do wish you'd begin at the beginning and explain everything," which was unfair of her, she realized, as she had delayed his telling in the first place.

"Listen then, Miss Carter," Joe poured himself another cup of coffee. "I cannot begin at the real beginning for that must have been when Hitler released the Ifrit. So I can only tell you what I saw while there and draw certain conclusions from that."

"That will do beautifully, Joe," Georgina said with mild sarcasm, "and I'm glad to know that even an Ifrit isn't infallible," she hated herself for the remark the minute it was made. She supposed it was reaction—she had expected so much from his visit to Hitler and was about to get so little. So little that could be of any material use to anyone, for it would rank with the other legends about the man . . . the other theories from the Oedipus complex—through glandular deficiencies to cancer of the throat. The War Office had been wise, she concluded, a trifle bitterly, wise in their stupidity.

But Joe had not noticed her irritation. "I had a most difficult time finding that man," he told her, almost as if he had stood on a street corner surveying a crowd. "That is why I was so long away. He wasn't in Berlin and I don't blame him, for I myself arrived there in the middle of a hell of an air raid—if you will forgive my language. Nor was he at the Russian front—and I don't blame him for that either, but to be brief I could not find him until I went to that house of his on the mountain, and there

I found he was expected to arrive the next night. I thought it foolish to return and tell you, for in my absence the plans might be changed and I would lose track of him. So I stayed there and waited for him."

It flashed across Georgina's mind at this point in Joe's narrative, how absolutely fantastic the whole thing was. A reformed Ifrit—a British Ifrit at that (for she supposed that his long residence in this country had given him a nationality, even though it mightn't allow him, for purely snob reasons, to rank with the oldest families) pledged to harm no man, no matter how evil, was the only outside person able to get near enough to Hitler to shoot him.

"It was nearly nightfall when he arrived," Joe continued. "I was waiting for him—invisibly, of course—in the big room with the view over the mountains. He was accompanied by men I did not know, whose pictures you have not shown me. I had the impression that they all hated and mistrusted each other, but dared not show it. They spoke amongst themselves in German, spoke of the defences of the new Europe, of consolidating gains by cutting losses. To be quite truthful, Miss Carter, I hardly understood what they were saying although I knew the words they used—for it did not seem to me to make sense at all. It was as if they were constantly reassuring themselves that certain things of which they were afraid would not happen. Hitler did not speak at all during this—he sat loosely in a chair with his strange eyes half closed. His face is curious when he is in this mood, it has the blurred outline, the unhealthy pallor of the hashish addict—the face of the assassin under the influence of his drug—for as you know that descriptive word is derived from hashish."

"Yes, I do know," Georgina interrupted, "yet you astonish me for we have been led to believe that Hitler neither smokes nor drinks, and also has an aversion to—er—flesh of any kind. Therefore, I don't see quite why he should remind you of a dope fiend."

"Drugs," the Ifrit pointed out, "are not always chemical compounds and you know that perfectly well, Miss Carter."

"If you tell me religion is the opium of the people, Joe," Georgina parried, "I shall scream—or hide your helmet," she smiled. "Not that I don't agree that I am both stupid and obvious to-night—my trouble is—and I admitted it only ten minutes ago—I lack imagination, and I *know* it—so you must forgive me."

"Whilst I tend to adopt the attitude of the pedant," Joe said gracefully, "nevertheless we understand each other quite sufficiently, I think. And presently you will understand why I say that Hitler looks like an addict. For know you that all the time these other people were with him and spoke together I was uneasy. I felt that there was something missing, or something about to happen—or even that there was something in that room—an influence, a shadow perhaps, of which I was unaware, just as they were unaware of me. After a time Hitler rose and dismissed them all, saying he wished to be alone. He wanted to think, he wanted to open his mind to his . . . . he used the word 'Intuition,' Miss Carter, as if it were a person. The men who were with him were, I sensed, not pleased by this; they looked at him with something akin to contempt—none the less, they went. After they had gone Hitler dismissed his bodyguards—then he too left the room, I following. Together we went to the top of the house in a cage-like thing that moved of itself, and which deposited us finally in a small, sparely furnished room. I think no one has ever been in that room save Hitler or perhaps a servant. Against the wall was a cot, and on this he threw himself. He lay there silent a few minutes, then he said, 'Come.'"

Joe paused for a moment and fixed his eyes on Georgina. She noticed for the first time that his eyes were not dark brown, almost black, as she had thought, but were strangely flecked with colour that seemed to move and change . . . they were like great black opals. She wondered uneasily for a moment whether he had not really hypnotized her with those eyes into believing all the strange things that had happened . . . it was all very strange, yet she was for some reason not afraid.

"On the pronouncement of this word 'Come'," Joe continued, "to my amazement, nay my horror, an Ifrit appeared. He was dressed in the most absurd manner—even more absurd than the clothing men in this country wear—for he wore a body-covering made of shining metal and fur, shoes which were laced up the legs with thongs, and he carried a spear. On his head he wore a helmet, and this I envied him, for it was made of metal and had curious horns on either side. His hair was the colour of pale gold, Miss Carter, the colour of yours—and his eyes were falsely blue. For a moment I hardly recognized him in this garb—but there was no mistaking him really—it was he who had tried to usurp Sulayman—to set himself in his place as ruler of the world."

"Joe," Miss Carter said, not knowing whether to laugh or cry at such a tale. "If I didn't know you so well I should disbelieve every word of your story. As it is I can barely credit it with any reason. Good heavens, has that man no sense of humour whatsoever . . . but of course he hasn't; An Ifrit costumed as Siegfried—or his kind—it's simply too preposterous. And how can he reconcile that with his famous racial theory, I wonder." She spoke more to herself than to Joe about this. Then she turned to him, "Joe dear," she said, "you'll understand that I do find all this rather hard to believe . . . are you *quite* sure you weren't mistaken? . . ."

"I could not mistake the presence of my old master, no matter how he disguised himself. And make no mistake, Miss Carter, he is still as evil as he ever was, perhaps more so, for he has more scope for his talent."

"I don't doubt that for a moment," Georgina cried, "it's the absurdity of those Wagnerian opera trappings which makes me think the whole thing impossible. . . . But I interrupt you, Joe . . . do go on for it is an enthralling story anyway."

"I was, as you may well imagine, greatly afraid," Joe continued. "Afraid that my erstwhile leader might see me, for although I was invisible to mortal eyes, my invisibility does not, or at least did not extend to the eyes of the members of my tribe. Yet I was not observed by him—and that is something I did not understand at the time. Though I think I understand it now."

"Perhaps evil can never see good," Georgina put in softly, but Joe was too engrossed with his story to hear the remark.

"You must try to understand my feeling, Miss Carter," he went on, "a feeling which was of great pain to me, and made me forget my mission—for there I was at last in the presence of one of my own kind . . . the first member of my family I had seen for 3,000 years—and I knew him to be evil. I knew too that I could not vanquish him—for I no longer believed myself to have any of that kind of power and indeed he was always more powerful than I. Furthermore, I was no longer allowed to harm Hitler or any man, for that would break my vow and cast me back at once into my old master's power. Had I become known to my former master, he would have charged me to join him, to become again his lieutenant in wickedness, and had I refused to obey this order, then he would have destroyed me, for only an Ifrit can encompass the total destruction of an Ifrit. . . . Perhaps it was weak of me not to disclose myself, to allow myself then to be destroyed . . . not to make a stand," he said passionately, "but I could not see what purpose it would serve, yet at the same time and mixed up with my fears, I was tempted to do just that—so strongly tempted by the love to fight . . . and because it was so strong a temptation, I knew I must resist it. It would have meant too that all your life, Miss Carter, you would never have known what happened and would have reproached yourself—or thought ill of me. Besides, I could not leave you—with my office to you as yet unfinished. So I prayed for the return of Sulayman—he whom I had once attempted to overthrow! For know that it is written that he will return one day and his power will be mighty—but my prayer remained unanswered. So I was compelled to stand by helpless and watch those two, whispering together and in doing so I expiated all my past."

"Oh my poor, poor Joe," Georgina cried, and she was very moved by his story, for even if it weren't true, he obviously believed it and it caused him pain. "How awful it must have been for you—and if it's any consolation to you, I think you made the right decision . . . but not because of me," she interposed hastily. "In fact I blame myself for this whole affair, my pride and vanity sent you, and I am most truly sorry I ever sent you on such a mission. I swear I will never ask you to do such a thing again. Do you think you can ever forgive me?"

"But there is nothing to forgive, dear Miss Carter," Joe told her, "for it is obvious to me now that all this was foreordained for me, and one does not question wisdom, no matter how inscrutable it appears to be."

"And indeed I am grateful to you for having sent me on this mission, for although perhaps I failed you—and if that is so I am truly sorry—yet it taught me something which I had not known before . . ."

"And what is that?" Georgina asked, wondering what mechanical contrivance had caught his eye.

"You will forgive me when I say that I cannot tell you. It is a personal thing—something which I have learned about myself . . . it may be true of everyone—who knows."

Georgina was startled by this—and even possibly a little hurt at Joe's refusal to tell her for she said rather stiffly, "I'm sorry—of course I didn't mean to pry."

"But dear Miss Carter," Joe cried, "this I must tell you apart from the private thing—for it will please you. That I should make the journey—or that the chance of the journey was offered to me was certainly predestined—yet I had a choice—that is something I, in my ignorance, had never realized. Circumstances may be foreordained yet of free will one is allowed to choose the path of action within those circumstances. And so I made my choice when I met the other Ifrit—yet only time will show me if I made the right one."

Georgina was silent for a moment. She, refusing to believe in predestination, yet envied him. It must be a comfort. Yet in a way she felt she ought to protest, as this belief so obviously excused her of all responsibility—a dangerous doctrine and one which should really not be tolerated. But she couldn't argue with poor Joe about it now. He'd been through too much already. She had expected from him some world-shattering secret . . . some invaluable piece of information . . . something hard and material that could be turned into a weapon, and used to shatter this man Hitler. But what had she learned? Something which might shake the world—if the world believed it—but the world wouldn't—any more than she did—and she only half believed it. "Joe," she said, "just tell me one more thing before we close this discussion for ever. How did Hitler contact the Ifrit—do you know?"

He shook his head. "No," he said, "I don't . . . I can only conjecture that he released him by accident just as you released me, but when that was I do not know . . . it may have been years ago, and that during his imprisonment the master Ifrit had occupied his time in thoughts of revenge. . . . But perhaps I do him an injustice."

"What on earth do you mean by that?" Georgina was genuinely surprised, "if that Ifrit were evil, how can you do him an injustice?"

"If he were evil I couldn't. But supposing he had really repented during his imprisonment, repented and resolved to do good, and then the man who discovered him, whose slave he became, used him for evil purposes because he himself was evil . . ."

"But he should have been strong enough to resist," Georgina cried.

"It is not easy to resist," Joe answered gently, "particularly when one is in bondage. I tell you, Miss Carter, had it been I instead of that other Ifrit, I too should have returned to wickedness. It is fortunate for me and probably for the world that you were the one to release me. For few people would have used me as unselfishly as you have done, or would have cared for me and tried to teach me the rights of things with no other purpose than for my own good and advancement."

Georgina gulped—this was awful and so untrue really, for Joe had become one of the comforts of her life, and if that weren't purely selfish!—besides, how very nearly had she erred in sending him on that journey despite his protestations that the journey had taught him something of value . . . the thought made her feel quite ill . . . she had, by the skin of her teeth, avoided the gravest consequences. It was, however, a relief to know that all her nagging at Joe, her prohibitions had been accepted in the spirit in which they were given. She said, "If I have been able to help you in any way, Joe, I am glad, for you see I am very fond of you. You are, I know, my friend." This speech embarrassed her a little—she felt she was getting into an emotional state and might easily burst into tears at any moment. Goodness, she thought, what a sentimental pair we are.

"But I think I see what you mean," she went on, getting safely back to the subject without disaster. "You mean that this Siegfried Ifrit became a source of power to Hitler and he used that power for evil . . ."

"Exactly so," Joe nodded. "And the tragedy is, although you may find this odd coming from me—that Hitler had he so chosen could have used that power for good, for understand this and make no mistake about it, my old master was in bondage to him. And it is the truth that my old master was head and shoulders above the rest of our tribe—no matter how big we made ourselves. He was brilliant and his power was great—greater by far than mine. Such a misuse of his talent," he finished sadly.

All power corrupts, Georgina thought—absolute power absolutely. And remembered how she had descended to lies and evasions and had practically lost Margaret Mackenzie because of Joe. This on a larger scale. . . . She chased off her thoughts abruptly . . . could she really believe the story of Hitler and his Ifrit . . . and if one did believe it . . . where did it get one? What purpose did it serve?

"How will it all end?" she asked him, feeling suddenly very tired. "Do you know, Joe? Can you tell me?"

"No," Joe answered, "I don't know and I can't tell you. I only know how it ended in Sulayman's time. But things are so different nowadays. Nothing seems to be sharp and defined. Colours are less clear . . . so are consciences. . . . It is difficult for mortals to say to-day . . . 'this is white' . . . 'that is black.' . . . People aren't sure any more. It is all very puzzling for you, and I am very sorry," he sighed, "for I understand that to speak with authority is deemed intolerance and to be too tolerant is considered laziness or apathy. But as for that Hitler," his voice rose, "and his Ifrit, I can tell you this. In the end, although Hitler still thinks he is the master, his slave will destroy him. For there is only one thing of which I am sure in myself, and that is that evil and hatred destroy not only those against whom they are directed, but him who directs them as well. That is the law, unaltered and unalterable."

Georgina stood up and Joe uncoiled himself from the floor. "Joe," she said, putting her hand on his arm. "It seems to me that men to-day have gained for themselves most of the power you Ifrits had, and have used it no better. It makes me quite sick to think of it . . . don't we ever learn!"

"In time, Miss Carter," Joe said soothingly. "In time one learns, as I in my small way have learned, or one is destroyed."

CHAPTER XXIII

FOR SEVERAL WEEKS after the German episode life settled back into its old routine—not the pre-Joe routine but the pre-Richard way of living, and Georgina was thankful for it. She answered Richard's letter after a decent interval, and said nothing but that she hoped he was well again and that the daffodils seemed to be coming up in Regent's Park. That episode was ended, too, and as she looked back on it from her present becalmed state, it seemed to her that she had been possessed of a sort of madness which was in complete contrast to her normal personality. It made her a little ashamed to think now of the thoughts she had entertained then. Her behaviour was, she thought, excusable, however, if one thought of it as a flare up, a last desperate attempt to grasp life before it slipped forever. The expression of a deep, long sublimated need to attach oneself to someone as a sort of insurance policy against old age and loneliness. All this was, of course, slightly revolting to think about . . . and the only thing to be thankful for was that she could have made such an awful fool of herself—and hadn't.

As for the Hitler episode, she thought she saw that in its true colours, too! A desire for importance; a wish to be regarded as a person, not just a cypher, a number on an identity card; a subconscious expression of "if no one will have me for myself then they must be forced to envy, admire, respect me for something I can do." That, too, was mixed up with Richard. Oh, folly, folly . . . avoided by a hair's breadth.

She did her best to patch up her difference with Margaret Mackenzie. Life was indeed too short to lose your oldest friend, because of a stupid misunderstanding. And although she avoided any further explanation of her previous conduct, yet by little ways and means, by small confidences and genuine affection, by going to the theatre, by lunching together, Margaret was gradually won back. It is true that she credited herself privately with having saved Georgina—of having snatched a brand from the burning, but she had sense enough and was genuinely fond enough of Georgina not to be superior and patronizing about it. They were both still a little strained, a little suspicious in each other's company. But this, too, with time and patience would dissolve away and all would be as it had been before, Georgina thought, and was honest enough not to dislike the idea itself, but merely to regret rather sadly the dullness implicit in it.

Of course, there was always Joe, but even he presented now an increasing problem. Longer, lighter evenings with double summertime in the offing, would almost make Joe a prisoner again. At least it would make it impossible for him to go about with her visibly in the evenings. And somehow, she couldn't see herself walking down the street with an invisible Joe and looking harmlessly potty because she apparently carried on a conversation with herself. There'd be no more sneaking into cinemas protected by darkness—at least not until next autumn—and Joe was so passionately attached to the movies. He thought them the most wonderful thing in the world and was particularly addicted to Western films. He was especially envious of the hat worn by the cowboys. And so Georgina had once bought him a sombrero with a metal-studded hatband at a theatrical costumier's in St. Martin's Lane. His delight and gratitude at this small gift were almost pathetic. The only trouble was that she had great difficulty in persuading him not to wear it when they went to the cinema. She wondered if his reason for wanting to was that it would make him feel a part of the picture before him, a part of those wild, exciting scenes—and of course, if he felt that way, heaven alone knew what might happen.

Yes, Joe was even more of a problem now. And there was his future to consider, too. But when she thought of his future which, by all appearances, seemed to embrace eternity, her mind boggled and refused to comprehend the fact, other than to point out that in the face of this, it was ridiculous to worry about Joe's being kept in hiding until autumn.

Nevertheless, being human, she did worry. . . . Perhaps he should be sent back to his people—for it was obvious now that some of them must still be floating around—but Georgina could hardly bear to think of this—it was too much like sending a trusting child out into a terrifying world alone. Still, she must really speak to him about it—one day. For lately she had observed that Joe himself seemed a little touched with melancholy, a little less his gay, impulsive child-like self. Had the meeting with that other Ifrit aged him . . . made him unhappy . . . unsettled? Certainly something had changed him. Was it the private thing he had learned on that trip to Germany? Often she caught him, as they sat together in the evenings, with his book in his lap, not reading but staring into the darkness, as if his strange colour-flecked eyes penetrated the walls that hemmed him in, and saw far beyond into some strange country or period of time in which she had no part.

One evening as they sat thus, he said to her apropos of nothing, for they had not been conversing: "Miss Carter, if it is not rude of me to ask—for you English have curious notions about such questions—tell me, are you wealthy?"

"No, Joe, I'm not," she told him, surprised that he hadn't noticed that she wasn't, but then, she supposed, standards in the East or during his previous sojourn in that part of the world, were considerably lower than in England. "I am, however," she continued, "a lot more fortunate than most people, for I have a small private income, and for the war at least I have a salary. I live carefully, you know, and I've managed so far to live fairly comfortably. But, of course, that may not continue to be so, for money has a way of decreasing in value as time goes on. Or rather, I should say my income remains fairly stationary, but the cost of living increases. It comes to the same thing in the end. Of course, if taxes go up any more I shall be sunk . . ."

"Would you like to be wealthy?" he asked, putting aside his book. (It was 'The Outline of Wireless' which she had got for him from the Marylebone public library the day before.)

Georgina laughed. "I really don't know," she answered, "it seems to me that no one is wealthy these days, what with super-tax and all wealth is probably nothing but trouble to those who possess it. But I confess I wouldn't mind being a trifle more secure financially—I'll be dead before Beveridge does me any good. . . . Why do you ask, Joe?"

"Because I can produce bags of gold for you if you wish," Joe said, waving his hand to encompass the room, "enough gold to fill this room and more . . ."

"Bags of gold!" Georgina said, startled, for it sounded too absurd and unreal . . . then she remembered the 'gold' with which Joe 'paid' for things. "Good heavens, of course you can. You're a sort of private gold mine . . . I'd entirely forgotten . . . where do you get it, Joe?"

"The lost treasures of the earth," Joe said, "caves and buried treasure houses. Gold laid up by kings and princes long dead . . . the hiding places forgotten . . . I shall fetch you some."

"No!" Georgina cried. "Don't, don't do it, Joe." Of course she was a fool but the idea terrified her. There was some unnamed dread about it . . . besides what was it Joe had said about her? . . . that she had never used him for selfish purposes. She didn't quite understand why, but she knew she must not accept this offer. No, not accept . . . she must refuse now while the determination to refuse was still strong . . . otherwise . . . But couldn't she accept just an ounce or two! . . . No, she couldn't because there was fundamentally no difference between accepting an ounce or a ton! Besides, wasn't there a law about hoarding gold nowadays. But there was so much she could do with it, though. Make Henry independent for instance . . . give Marga-ret Mackenzie a private income and free her from the tyranny of her ancient parents . . . donate large sums to charity. Surely if she used it only for good . . . but surely, too, all this would be in the nature of a sop to her conscience. . . . "Not even a little bag," Joe persisted with the voice of a serpent.

"No, not even a little bag," she said wildly, feeling her resolution failing. "Oh Joe, why did you ever start this subject? You've put me in a dreadful state . . . really you have, please, please don't ever mention it again." She was really most distressed. What was the difference in taking gold from Joe and inheriting a fortune? For the life of her she couldn't answer that. She began to feel that her whole sense of values was slipping and as it slipped disclosed her as either a hypocrite or a colossal fool.

But she was suddenly snapped out of this wrestling bout with her conscience by the fact that Joe had vanished. His book lay open on the floor but he was no longer beside it.

"Joe," she called . . . but there was no reply. She was stung into action and a sense of disquiet. Had she finally driven him away with what must seem to him her totally irrational moods? Or had he just taken himself and his melancholy out for a walk? She got up and searched the flat for him—not that she really expected to find him, but because it gave her something to do.

After a fruitless search, complicated by further conscience searchings, she returned to the living room to find him there again, just as if nothing had happened. But something had happened, for beside him on the floor was a small chest—a chest so old that she wondered it did not fall away from its metal bindings. The wood was discoloured with age and flaked and split, while on the floor the outline of the box was traced by a thin line of dust.

"Do not be in the least alarmed, Miss Carter," Joe said, raising a protesting forefinger. "There is no hated gold in this box. But its contents, which are mine to give, and which at the time of my trouble with Sulayman—all honour to his name—were safely stored away, are yours."

"Nor must you gainsay me in this matter," he added hurriedly as she started a protesting sentence with the words, "Now, Joe"—"for I will not have it otherwise, and if you refuse my small gift I will place this box and its contents forever in a cavern at the bottom of the sea. So you need not be troubled in that curious conscience of yours, for I understand your way of thinking now—and I will never give you cause to be troubled again."

. "Joe dear," Georgina said, "what have you been up to now! And how can I accept whatever it is?" She felt the remark to be totally inadequate in the circumstances, but she was, she felt, very inept at answering pretty speeches in kind.

"You can accept and I know that you will," Joe said firmly, "for have I not already told you that it is mine to give, and so you would not wound me by refusing. Look!" he commanded and opened the lid of the chest, or rather it came away in his hands for the wood had rotted from the hinges.

Georgina bent down and looked within. Then she quite suddenly sat down. Dust tickled her nostrils and made her nose itch. But what she saw had nearly seared her eyeballs. For the box seemed full of strange gems and jewellery that glittered and sparkled with a thousand lights. She looked up at Joe doubtfully. "But," she started unbelievingly—and he cut her short with a laugh and a wave of the hand.

"No, do not speak," he said in a delighted voice, "for I see that you are almost overawed by these poor baubles—" (she was glad he had mistaken doubt of their genuineness for awe). "Come, sit beside me," he continued, "and we will look at them together for they are yours. Yours to keep or sell as you desire. For although you said money decreases in value, these trinkets never will—they will, I hope, increase so your whole future is secure in this box." Georgina, almost too dazed by what she had seen and various contradictory emotions, obeyed him. She sat down on the floor by the chest and he squatted happily on his haunches beside her. "This," he said, pulling a stone the size of his two fists from the box, "is of not much value but it is, I think, pleasant to look upon." If was a lump of malachite whorled with darker green. She had seen an altar made of it once in some church in Italy.

He put it on one side. "That," he commented, "and this," fishing another lump from the box, "will do as paper weights."

The second chunk proved to be a six-sided sapphire crystal, the size of a cucumber and banded wonderfully with colour—blue, pink, brown, grey, white, yellow.

"What a lovely thing," she cried, "like a bit of solid rainbow."

"Of little value," Joe said, putting it aside, "still it delights the eye. And here is a curious thing—a smargadas still caught in its original limestone."

He handed it to her and she saw it was an oblong emerald embedded in rock. Before she could remark on it he had put a pile of emeralds, some cut, some uncut, into her lap.

"These," he remarked, "benefit the eyes. As you know, I am something of a physician."

Georgina nodded, not daring to remark on how well and bitterly she knew this talent of his—or what she thought of it.

". . . and I assure you there is nothing to compare with a smargadas for drawing out inflammation or clarifying the vision. People will be glad to pay you vast sums for those jewels if they have defective eyesight."

Miss Carter did not say that this last remark made the emeralds sound as if they were false. She was, in fact, still almost too numb to say anything at all. There she sat with a small fortune in emeralds in her lap, while Joe bubbled happily that their real value lay in curing styes, conjunctivitis and cataracts.

"Now these," Joe piled handfuls of amethysts of every size and ranging in colour from white to deepest violet, "are equally serviceable stones—though possibly not for you, my dear Miss Carter, for the virtue of the amethyst is in that it prevents drunkenness. A person who wears an amethyst can drink and drink—yes rivers of wine—and yet never lose himself or fall insensible to the floor."

Georgina giggled a little hysterically, remembering Margaret Mackenzie's first accusation. "Joe," she said, "they are simply wonderful, even apart from their virtues—I just don't know what to say . . . how to express . . ."

"Then say nothing," Joe said reasonably, "for this is, as yet, nothing," and as he spoke he piled diamonds on the floor beside her.

"Good lord," Georgina exclaimed, startled out of her bemused state of fondling semi-precious stones. "Are these real?"

"Yes," Joe said, "and very fine too, though these greasy-looking round ones look so because they are not cut. . . . But look at this." He pulled a cut stone nearly the size of an almond from the pile. It was a lovely apple green colour. "Very rare," Joe said, "and these too are unusual." He handed her several more stones—some were rosy pink, some a wonderful yellow and some were black.

"Oh!" Georgina exclaimed, and "Oh!" again. "I don't know . . . I can't think, I mean. Joe, these must be priceless. I could never rest with them in the house. I should be terrified out of my wits. What shall I do with them?"

"No one is likely to suspect that you are possessed of such things," Joe said calmly, "and in any case I am here. But you could store them in some vault or another and sell them carefully one by one as need arises."

Georgina recovered a little. "I'd like to see what the Goldsmiths and Silversmiths would say if I walked into their shop in Regent Street in broad daylight and flung a sackful of diamonds at them—they'd probably call the police immediately and they'd think I was a . . . oh, what is it called . . . one always finds the word in mystery stories . . . I know . . . a fence . . ."

Joe looked puzzled. "But you most certainly are not a fence, Miss Carter," he said politely, "a fence is surely a thing which . . ."

"I know, I know," Georgina interrupted. "Never mind about it, Joe—it's a silly word. Anyway, I shan't trouble myself about that now. I'll think of something to do even if it means establishing another Hatton Garden in St. John's Wood. You mustn't mind what I say, Joe," she apologized, "because at the moment I'm too stunned to know what I'm saying anyway."

"I am glad you are pleased," Joe replied, handing her a chrysoberyl she size of a hen's egg and the colour of amontillado, and informing her that it was a stone greatly prized in the East. This was followed by about a half a pint of what appeared to be, and indeed were, rubies, poured out as if they were no more than cherries. "And here," Joe said, "are little things which you can have made into ornaments," . . . and he handed her a half dozen or so of conical and dome-shaped seals, which should have been in a case at the British Museum, as well as several dozen incised and intaglioed gems. "But now we come to the ornaments to deck your person," he continued, "though I daresay to your eyes, accustomed to the marvels of this world, they will look but poor things, quaint and old-fashioned."

He sorted through the box and brought out a pair of great ear-rings.

She took them from him carefully. They were dome-shaped, of gold, finely enamelled and fringed with small pearls; a cluster of minute gold leaves half-hiding a pink pearl, was suspended from the centre of each dome. They were superb—but for her quite unwearable. Could she bear to part with them, at Christie's? She could and she would. She mentally determined that they should be sold and the money given to the Red Cross—museum pieces though they were—and laughed at herself, for the thought. It, too, was a sop—or wasn't it?

And now Joe had put a wealth of jewellery and ornaments into her already over-burdened lap. There were curious and vivid miniature feathers, some of enamelled gold, others gold set solidly with jewels. These, Joe explained, were turban ornaments, worthy of the most exotic head coverings. There were dozens of brooches, of gold and silver, set with various stones. One which caught her bewildered eye was of granulated gold, from which depended four pigeon-blood rubies, set in frames of granulated gold. There were numbers of small boxes and cases—one shaped like a thimble with a candle-snuffer top—for scented ointments. There were earplugs of white, red and green gold, set with jewels or wonderfully worked with coloured enamels; innumerable rings of strange design and shape. A minute dragon with his tail in his mouth circled the finger and was finely carved out of solid silver. A sapphire, intricately incised to resemble a bunch of grapes and shanked with tiny emerald leaves, also caught her eye. There were innumerable anklets of beaten gold. One pair were in the shape of a winged ram. And there were all manner of chains, bracelets, girdles and toe rings of superb workmanship.

Georgina sat and looked, unable to take everything in and still hardly able to speak. Absurdly she thought of the Jewel Song and wondered if the whole scene in which she was now involved weren't a trifle theatrical or operatic. No doubt at some time her mind would grasp what all these glittering and wonderful things meant—or could mean. But at the moment she felt as if she had been struck on the head with a meat axe. Even her conscience was silenced.

She roused herself sufficiently from her stupor to attempt to thank Joe, apologizing again for her seeming indifference by saying she was completely at a loss for words. But Joe would hear of no thanks. It was far less than his dear, good Miss Carter deserved, and he burst into flowery ecstasy, which she could not check and which, when stripped of its embellishments, seemed to indicate that she was the most priceless jewel of the lot and which ended cryptically with the remark that, although there might be another who was not aware of her worth, he (Joe) was highly sensible of it and of his own unworthiness.

Georgina tottered off to bed to dream not of the jewel-encrusted tree in the cave of Aladdin—but of her brother, Robert.

CHAPTER XXIV

AND IT WAS Robert who wakened her next morning. Not Robert himself, but a message from the Red Cross saying he had been wounded, but was alive and in a Japanese prison camp. Georgina sat down and wept, trying to explain to a very distressed Joe, between sobs, what had happened.

"Then your tears are really shed for joy, not sorrow," he said, much relieved, as he sprinkled a little rose-water over her; for as he explained, rose-water not only brought a person out of a death-like swoon, but also was of great efficacy in calming the nerves. "Shall I take you to your brother, Miss Carter?" he asked, looking a little worried again, for she had become quite damp with tears and rose-water.

"Oh no," Georgina gasped, "it might be dangerous—not for me, but for him and the rest of the unfortunate prisoners, if I were discovered . . . and remember how nearly we were discovered in North Africa, and that was a much simpler proposition. Why, anything just even slightly suspicious might cause them all to be shot—or—or worse." She broke down again at this thought.

"Then tell me where he is, and I will bring him to you." Joe, alarmed by this fresh outburst, sprayed more rose-water at her. It had the desired effect—like a cold, wet cloth used in hysterics—it brought Georgina round.

"Stop," she said, "I'm all right now, and I'm drenched. Look at the carpet—it's soaked. Really, Joe!"

"I will fetch your brother while you change," he said eagerly.

Georgina shook her head. "It's no good, Joe . . . I don't know where he is. I shall probably never know. If only Major—" she stopped. "I was going to say, if I ever do find out I will tell you, and I will ask you then to find him and bring him, not here—for he could never explain how he escaped to England, but to some hospital in India. He could then say—and it would be quite true—that he couldn't remember how he escaped—they'd think he suffered with amnesia."

"I live only for your commands," Joe said, making a salaam, and Georgina thought how very much more Eastern he was getting lately.

"And now I must cable Henry," she said brightly, mopping her eyes and going to the telephone.

Having cabled Henry, she bathed her swollen eyelids, dressed, attempted unsuccessfully to eat her breakfast, took the ear-rings, a splendid ruby, a yellow diamond and a pear-shaped emerald, put them in her handbag and went to her office. At lunch time they should be given to Christie's as anonymously as possible, to be sold for the Red Cross, and as she was wearing the clothes Joe had brought her, she would hardly be suspected of being in unlawful possession of such treasures. Besides, *mightn't* she have inherited them?

A cable from Henry was waiting for her when she returned home that night, telling her he was 'frightfully bucked' about the news, and that he was writing. And high time too, Georgina thought, for I haven't heard from that wretched boy for nearly three months.

She forgave him, though, because he was young, and because he must be busy, and because he was Henry, Robert's son. It was just thoughtlessness on his part, not want of affection, she told herself. How dearly she would love to see the boy again.

And why shouldn't she see him? The thought came into Georgina's mind and would not be dislodged. She had, of course, vaguely toyed with the idea before this, and had rejected it as frivolous and unnecessary, adopting the spartan attitude of one who refuses to indulge in a pleasure because the rest of the world cannot do likewise. Whether the rest of the world was as interested in its nephew as she was in hers did not enter into the argument. For Georgina had been brought up in the school that believed in self-denial for the sake of self-denial—a school which also held that unless a medicine tasted perfectly beastly it did you no good, and although Joe had certainly undermined these ingrained characteristics to a certain extent, she must still find good and proper reason for going to see Henry, other than the purely emotional one of wanting to.

There were, of course, the socks, now finished at last. But that was nonsense—they could be posted. Then there was a desire to talk about the wonderful news of Robert—that could wait. Besides, hadn't she been advocating for herself, ever since the frightening Hitler episode, a return to normal life? She had. Hadn't she practically sworn never to use Joe's supernatural powers again, except in a case of life and death? Hadn't she planned to talk to Joe almost immediately about his future— now that hers, like Mr. Wemmick's, was secure in portable property? Wasn't this desire—a desire that was almost an ache— to see Henry purely selfish?

She admitted that it was—wondering briefly and almost objectively if Richard's son Simon were as nice as her nephew. She admitted every argument against going to see Henry, and it was with relief that she lost the battle against what she had for so long considered to be her better self—and decided to go anyway. One last journey with Joe before she settled back into the normal pre-Joe groove. One last flight before she spoke to Joe about the future . . . and in speaking might, for all she knew, lose him for ever.

Joe, when she spoke to him about it, was delighted with the prospect. The idea of a journey, specially one that was to take his dear Miss Carter to see her beloved nephew, cheered him immensely. Besides, he hadn't been in Canada for thousands of years, he told her, as they looked at the large red blob on the map. Of course, Canada had not been its name then. If his memory served him, it was a beautiful, a magnificent country. "A country of splendour and loneliness," he said.

It astonished Georgina to think that Joe had set foot (though perhaps that was hardly accurate) in Canada long before the Vikings or Cabot. And she warned him that to-day the country was populated, that cities had been built there, and that Cabot had first sighted the country for England while he, Joe, was a beam in a country house.

"And so the Manitou is gone forever from the country," was his only comment. But when she asked him to explain he refused, quite flatly and without apology, for the first time since she had known him.

On the following Sunday morning Joe and Georgina stood in the living room of the flat, ready to set out for Canada. It was very early—seven o'clock—for Georgina still did not care to be seen shooting through the air at great speed by any of the AA. units. Joe, she knew, led a charmed life, and although she had done the journey to North Africa quite safely, she still didn't like the idea of shrapnel. Friendly or enemy, it came to the same thing if you were hit by it.

She wore for the occasion a warm coat, a hat tied on with a scarf, and fur gloves, for although Spring had officially arrived, it had not yet made a public appearance. Besides, Canada and the North Pole were practically the same place, in Georgina's mind. In her right coat pocket was a thermos flask and a few sandwiches. Henry's socks lay on the table, ready to be thrust into her left pocket. She knew exactly where Henry was stationed— not far north of Toronto; knew, too, the house in which he was billeted—159, Wyandotte Street—though how you pronounced it was another matter. She and Joe had checked every detail of the flight together, had plotted the course carefully. It had given her quite a feeling of importance to do this, and had made her wonder with amusement if now, with her practical and unusual knowledge of flying, she might not be of more use in the Air Ministry than in the Censor's office.

"Are you ready, Miss Carter?" Joe asked.

"Quite ready, Joe," she replied, switching out the light and groping her way over to the window.

He undid the blackout, opened the window and floated through it horizontally. Outside he did a quick turn, so that he faced the window, and assumed an upright position, as if he were treading water.

By this time she was cautiously perched on the window sill. She was always slightly nervous about this part of the procedure, despite the fact that she knew she was perfectly safe, for once, when setting out on a week-end trip, she *had* overbalanced and fallen out of the window. Joe had, of course, snatched her up to safety seconds before she was due to hit the ground. Still, the experience had left its mark upon her nervous system.

He pulled her up from the window sill as if she were a child, and they were off, shooting skywards so swiftly that her breath was rammed back into her lungs and nearly choked her. She turned her head to Joe's chest for protection, and then she found that she could breathe. And suddenly she realized that Joe must have assumed gigantic proportions, for it was as if she rested against the slope of a hill. She stretched her hands up to feel his face, but her fingers felt nothing but the smoothness of his jacket. His jacket—his jacket—the idiot! He was wearing his own clothes—the clothes she had discovered him in, instead of his lounge suit—she could tell by the feel of the silk—and she could have sworn he was properly clad in Western dress when they had stood together in the living room a minute or so ago.

As she looked up, far above her she saw a great coral cloud emerge from the darkness—the darkness, too, slipped away, and from the centre of the cloud great rays of iridescent light fanned upwards. She realized suddenly that this was no cloud, but Joe's famous turban, with its pearl ornament caught by the sun, and beneath it she could now see his face, huge and impassive, like the faces of the Presidents of the United States sculptured in a mountainside. She herself, she saw, as the sun illuminated the upper air, was no longer carried in the crook of his arm, but sat in the palm of his hand, which he held against his breast, while his fingers made a palisade against the wind. Oddly enough, she felt no fear; it was almost as if she stood apart from herself and saw the whole thing as a picture illustrating a fairy tale. She peeked out of the crack made by the thumb and index finger; below the world was still dark. Only up here was the sunlight, and she was safe and warm, rushing through space like a comet.

She looked upward again, seeing Joe's face from underneath— the great sweeping curve of the chin, the jutting promontory of the nose, gilded by the sunlight. And quite suddenly her two selves fused—it was no longer a picture. She was a part of something strange and wonderful, and she was over-awed by it. His words about Canada rang in her ears—the splendour and the loneliness. What was she doing with this strange, magnificent yet gentle creature? Harnessing him to her personal whims and trivial desires. How had she ever had the presumption to restrict and constrain him—to treat him as a child? He held her in the hollow of his hand. Who was Joe? What was he? Abu Shiháb— father of the shooting star. . . .

The light disappeared as suddenly as if it had been turned out. She felt the darkness as a physical shock—then suddenly, across the sky the stars were flung, like a handful of silver coins. Was it her imagination, or did she hear music—very faintly, as if it came from a great distance across quiet waters?

She closed her eyes and listened. . . .

CHAPTER XXV

THE MUSIC faded away. She opened her eyes. It was still dark and cold—very cold. No longer was there music and no longer was she cupped in his hand. He held her under the armpits and they gently descended into a snow-covered, fenced-in garden. It had all been a dream, then, this vision of a gigantic, sublime Joe, curving like a figurehead on a ship through the sparkling upper air. The colour, the brightness, the music, the wonderful sense of being free yet secure—lifted out of oneself—a dream, perhaps, but unforgettable, and an experience nevertheless.

"We have arrived," Joe's voice said softly in her ear, as he set her down beside the house in a small snowdrift.

"But it's so dark—so cold . . ." she said, shivering. "And oh, Joe, I'm frightened. Really, Joe, I'm the worst sort of coward—so brave in my imagination, so weak in action. . . ."

"Nonsense, Miss Carter," Joe reassured her, "there's nothing to make you afraid while I am here. You must know that by now."

At least there wouldn't be any vicious-looking Arabs to torment her, Miss Carter thought, but she'd certainly have a fine time explaining herself to the local police. Besides—fool that she was—she'd forgotten until this moment the difference in time. Ten minutes ago it had been seven o'clock in London—here it was only one a.m. She hoped Henry was sound asleep—she'd just look at him, leave the socks and silently steal away. She would not waken him or speak to him. A look should suffice—indeed, she hadn't decided what on earth she'd say—how she'd explain if . . .

"Now I will go and find what room it is in which your nephew sleeps," Joe continued softly, raising the window beside which they stood. "Did you bring a torch?"

"Yes," she answered, and pulled it out of her pocket.

"Well, do not use it as yet—for you know that I can see in the dark. Now I shall leave you here a moment. Do you not make a sound unless you need my help—then signal your position with the torch so that I may find you quickly. I shall go through the house, invisibly, of course, until I find your nephew's room. I shall know him, never fear, then I shall return to you."

Georgina found herself alone, with her teeth chattering so that they sounded like castanets. As usual, she started to reproach herself for her recklessness—her foolhardiness. Really, at her age, to give in suddenly to whims and fancies, with never a thought of their real consequences. Really, she deserved any trouble such indulgence might bring her. It was all very well to feel smugly that she was a good influence on Joe—but certainly she seemed to be allowing Joe to have a bad influence on her in some respects, and all this nonsense must stop. That wasn't fair to Joe! It was she who was having a bad influence on him. Well, it would stop—this was her last journey with Joe. Of course, she'd probably get pneumonia, standing as she did ankle-deep in snow, and it would be her last journey anywhere in this world. But really, she was as irresponsible as a schoolgirl, coming on a journey like this without deciding first what she'd say to Henry, in case she did speak to him—for Henry would not be delirious as Richard had been. Actually this wasn't strictly true—she had thought, but being unable to arrive at any definite decision, she had, with a complete lack of that common sense upon which she had once prided herself, decided to let events dictate her course of action. Here, then, were the events—or very nearly—and as soon as Joe came back she'd call off the whole thing and return straight home!

"I have found him, Miss Carter." Joe was beside her again. "His room is just above us. I've opened the window so that we can get in quietly."

"Are you quite sure, Joe?" she asked, looking up at Henry's window regretfully and affectionately. "Well, that's that. Joe, I'm sorry, but I've decided that we must . . ."

"Quite sure," Joe said, paying not a particle of attention to her last sentence, "for if I needed further proof that it was the room of your nephew I had it in the fact that there is a snapshot of you, Miss Carter—which indeed does not do you justice—stuck in the mirror on the dressing table."

"Oh Joe," Georgina wailed, "why did you tell me that?" for her resolve to return to London immediately melted away. That Henry had thought enough of her to keep her snapshot on his dressing table! The dear child—this small sign of his affection completely undid her resolution.

Joe, however, waiting for no further comment or argument, picked her up and floated through the upper window, and set her down gently on the floor.

The room was ill-lit by moonlight, but her eyes, accustomed to the dark, saw the bed in the corner and the outline of a head on the pillow. Henry dear, her heart cried so loudly and her hand shook so that she dropped her torch. It clattered to the floor.

The young man stirred, reached out a sleep-slow hand and automatically switched on the lamp which stood on his bedside table. He blinked sleepily for a moment. Then he saw Georgina, motionless in the middle of the room. "Good Heavens!" he exclaimed, and sat bolt upright.

"Hello, Henry dear," Georgina said feebly, not knowing what else to say. "This must be quite a surprise to you, I know, and I can't explain how I got here, or rather, I can, but you wouldn't believe me." What a fatuous conversation—but what else could she say? How Henry resembled his father at the same age. Robert in the last war—Henry in this. Georgina wanted to weep. Really, she'd gone frightfully emotional and sentimental lately!

Henry groaned, and covered his eyes for a moment with his hands, as if to blot or wipe away the vision. "Go away," he said. "Oh please, please go away."

"But Henry dear!" She moved closer to the bed, and Henry clutched the bedclothes in terror. "Henry, aren't—aren't you pleased to see me?" She caught sight of herself in the mirror and realized how shattering she looked—her head tied up in a scarf—the rest of her muffled up like an arctic explorer. She undid the collar of her coat and removed her scarf and hat. "There. That's better!" she said. "I'm not surprised that you failed to recognize me."

The young man looked wildly about him. "I'll never touch another drop in my life," he said fervently. "So help me, I swear I won't."

"Oh, Henry!" Georgina sat down on the end of the bed; really, this was too distressing for words. "My dear boy—you haven't been—er—drinking more than is good for you, I hope? Still, it's easy to understand how such things happen—particularly when one is in a strange country, and *such* a cold one, too." Georgina felt very broad-minded. She wouldn't fall into the unfortunate error into which Margaret Mackenzie had fallen. For a moment, sitting there with Henry, she forgot the strange circumstances of her visit (Joe, with his usual tact, was quite invisible); it all seemed so comfortable, so natural. She had often sat on Henry's bed when he was a boy—reading to him—telling him a story.

"But I didn't think I'd had too much," the unfortunate Henry said desperately, "but this Canadian rye whisky is potent stuff, one forgets that—oh, do go away. Please go away. Perhaps I'd better go and make myself some coffee." He didn't seem to be addressing her at all; it was as if he thought out loud.

"Coffee!" Georgina exclaimed, pulling the thermos flask out of her pocket, unscrewing the top and filling it with steaming brown liquid. "Here you are." She handed the cup to Henry, delighted to be able to be of such practical assistance. "I made it myself not an hour ago."

Henry took the cup as though he were hypnotized, and sipped the coffee without taking his eyes off Georgina, as if he expected her to disappear as soon as the coffee could have the desired sobering effect.

"There now," Georgina said comfortably, as he finished and landed her the cup, "that's better, isn't it?"

"No," replied Henry hoarsely, "it isn't."

"Of course," Georgina said, brightly determined not to let Henry's strange behaviour upset her, "I quite realize that this must be rather a shock to you, finding me in your bedroom at this hour, when you naturally thought me several thousands of miles away. Though really I had no intention of waking you—I dropped my torch. Of course, I'm really delighted that you are awake and that we can chat together—strange as it may seem to you. Still, stranger things have happened," she ended, remembering Richard and Africa.

"I doubt it," Henry said unhappily, "and if they have, they haven't happened to me. Of course, I was an absolute fool to have that last drink—but a chap has to break out occasionally."

"Yes, yes," Georgina interposed hastily, "and though you may not credit it, Henry, I *do* understand that point of view. Provided the occasions don't become too frequent and a habit, it's probably good for you. Your work is, I know, a great strain—"

". . . and anyway," Henry brooded, "how was I to know that it would take this form with me . . . instead of pink elephants, red spiders and purple snakes?"

"Henry, dear!"

". . . Of course, you always were a sort of private conscience to me; and I suppose alcohol has just taken this feeling, externalized it and made it a visual image. Oh, I suppose it's no more than I deserve, but—" his voice trailed away. He shook his head bitterly.

Georgina was much too distressed to reply. She had slightly resented being classed with various highly-coloured animals as a figment of a drunken imagination. But she was definitely hurt by the implication that she was Henry's inhibiting conscience. How dreadful—did Joe feel that way about her, too?

"It may be," Henry began again in a low, hopeless tone, "that I have died and gone to—perhaps my 'plane *did* crash this morning when I went into that spin—but I thought I'd pulled out of it by the skin of my teeth."

This was the last straw! Henry was not intoxicated—of that she was certain. And she couldn't just go on sitting there, driving the boy slowly crazy. It had been a dreadful mistake, her coming at all; now she must repair the damage as best she could, and as speedily as possible. She must not let Henry's reason become unhinged. All this talk of spins, and not knowing if he were dead or alive!

"Henry George Alexander Carter," she said in a low but firm voice, "listen to me—"

"Yes, Aunt Georgina." His phrase was obedient, his tone somnambulistic.

"You are *not* drunk. You are *not* dead—thank the Lord. And I *am* here. And I only came over to bring you the socks I'd knitted for you. See, here they are." She fumbled in her pocket.

"All this way to deliver a pair of socks, Aunt Georgina?" he murmured. "That was terribly kind, but surely an unnecessary trouble—"

"Damn and blast!" Georgina surprised herself with the exclamation. "I haven't brought them after all. What a fool I am. I was sure they were here—I must have left them on the table at home. Henry, I apologize—"

"All this distance and to no purpose," Henry said politely. "What a pity! Never mind—had you brought them and had I wakened in the morning to find them vanished with the dream, think of my disappointment! Of course, had they not been gone it would have been even worse."

"But Henry!" Georgina cried in despair. "I *forgot* the socks. They really *do* exist. So do I. I'm *not* a dream. I really am here in the flesh—aren't you even glad to see me?"

"Why, yes, very glad, Aunt Georgina." There wasn't a trace of pleasure in his voice. "I'm always delighted to see you, but you must admit that your visit, so unexpected as it is, is a little bewildering—unnerving even."

"Of course it is!" Georgina said impatiently. "I've said that to you myself half a dozen times. But Henry, it was quite impossible for me to let you know I was coming; you—you might have given me away." Her voice sank to barely audible whisper level. "You see . . . I left England *illegally*—without permission or permit. I know this must shock you—it shocks me a little—but no one will know—not that I consider that an excuse. But had I cabled or written you I was coming, well, you know what censors are, or rather, I do. Besides, I didn't make up my mind to come until two or three days ago. It was hearing about your father that decided me—quite against my better judgment, I confess. Still, as you say, one must break out occasionally."

Henry, who had listened to all this quite quietly, remarked: "But naturally, I agree with everything you say, although I don't understand a word of it. It all sounds logical but doesn't make sense—there's a key piece missing somewhere."

"Of course it's difficult at first," Georgina told him. "Why, I remember when I first . . ." She stopped. She had been about to say "When I first discovered Joe."

"Oh, quite, quite," Henry muttered.

But surely, Georgina said to herself, I can tell Henry about Joe. After all, he is a blood relation and twenty-one years old. And it would make it easier for him to understand if I told him, instead of beating about the bush—for he most certainly thinks now that he's mad, a victim of hallucinations or having a nightmare—just as I did at first. Besides, it would be such a blessed relief to me to tell someone about Joe—to ask advice about him.

Still, she must not spring Joe on him too suddenly, or he might, in his nervous, overwrought condition, rush out of the room or fling himself from the window. She must lead up to the final revelation by easy stages. They could then all settle down to a real talk—Joe could be quite charming and interesting, and his manners were pleasant.

"Henry, can you keep a secret?" she asked the staring young man. "But of course you can—you're a Carter," she answered herself, wishing Henry didn't wear quite such a trance-like expression. "Well, how do you account for my presence here?" she went on. "How do you think I got here? I'll tell you, but you must never tell a soul."

"No—no, dear Aunt Georgina," Henry protested, a trifle sarcastically, "pray don't tell me—let me guess."

"You never will," she told him happily, for absurdly this remark carried her back to Henry's childhood. The small boy recovering from holiday measles—the favourite guessing game—what have I got in my hand—Three guesses—if you're right you can have it. (He had always had it anyway, whether or not he guessed correctly.)

"Well," Henry said, thawing out a trifle, "you fell in with a witch and came along on her broomstick."

Georgina laughed. "Not quite, but very nearly right."

"Then you had yourself transmitted by short-wave."

"You're getting warm—put the two together."

"I give up—before the third guess," Henry said, closing his eyes as if in pain.

"Oh Henry," Georgina said. "Never mind—I'll tell you— you've read the Arabian Nights? How silly, of course you have; I read them to you years ago—"

"Only the children's edition, not the Burton translation," Henry carped.

"That doesn't matter in the least," Georgina assured him. "The thing is, you remember, don't you, the genii in those stories?"

"I've got it!" Henry cried, and there was warmth and amusement in his voice at last. "You were brought here by one of that lot! Oh, Aunt Georgina, how perfectly lovely. My dear old Aunt Georgina and a genie—how wonderful! What on earth has made me dream that? It's superb. I must write and tell you about it when I wake up. How perfectly absurd—you of all people. My dear, conservative spinster aunt and a genie—"

"It's not in the least absurd," Georgina countered, a little stiffly, for she was a trifle wounded by the fact that Henry found it so divertingly incongruous that she should be associated with a genie, and 'conservative spinster aunt' wasn't very pleasant either, even if it were true, and even though he had tossed in 'dear old' as well. "And Joe isn't a genie, he's an Ifrit."

"A what?" Henry exclaimed, good-humouredly.

"An Ifrit. As far as I can make out it's nearly the same thing. I've never liked to enquire about the differences between a genie and an Ifrit, because I felt it might be delicate ground and Joe might be touchy about it."

"Did you say his name was Joe?" Henry asked. "How marvellous. We've a French-Canadian here whose name is Joe—Joe Janisse. I had a drink—several drinks—with him this evening. Why, of course! That's it! That's probably what started this train of thought in my subconscious. You were already in my mind,

Aunt Georgina. I was going to write you about the old man—and then this fellow Joe Janisse—Joe Genie—"

"I only call him Joe," Georgina said—really, her explanation hadn't helped a bit, he still thought he was dreaming and didn't believe a word of it. She wanted to shake him. "I named him in honour of Stalin. His real name is Abu Shiháb. Would you like to see him? For I know that unless you do you won't believe I'm telling the truth."

"I'm dying to see him," Henry said.

"You shall," Georgina promised. She stood up. "Joe," she called softly to the empty air.

And Joe appeared. Not instantly and complete as he usually did, but slowly. First a faint mist gathered beside her—this spun round, gathering speed until it whirled like a small tornado, and as it revolved it took form and colour and shape. As a performance it was unsurpassed. Dear Joe—he was playing up beautifully, having no doubt heard the whole conversation. He stood beside her now in all the magnificence of his Oriental dress. He made an obeisance to her.

"Your commands, O mistress, more beautiful than the harvest moon," he said.

"Bravo!" Henry cried. "It's just as I pictured it."

Georgina was delighted. Joe was certainly giving the situation the authentic flavour. "There," she said to Henry, "you see, it's quite true. There he is. That will do, Joe—you can forget your Eastern manners, Western ones will do now. This is my nephew Henry, as you know. And Henry, this is my—my very dear, kind friend, Joe."

Henry held out his hand. Joe, at a look and a nod from Georgina, took it. But instead of a Western handshake he raised it to his lips and—bit it.

Henry let out a horrified and horrifying yell. Doors slammed throughout the house—footsteps rushed along passages, and in the noise and confusion Joe snatched Georgina up and out the window away—away back to the flat.

"What possessed you, Joe, to do such a dreadful thing?" she asked, stamping her foot in rage, as he set her down in her own living room (yes, the wretched socks were reproaching her from the table). "You bit Henry—yes, you did; I saw you do it—and after I'd said you were so kind. That was a barbarous thing to do—I'm surprised at you, Joe."

Joe looked a trifle abashed. "Forgive me," he apologized, "but it was necessary."

"Necessary to bite my nephew Henry? Poor boy!"

"Miss Carter," Joe said, "your Henry is not like you, nor is it necessary that he should be so—but it *is* necessary that the young respect their mothers or those who have brought them up tenderly and kindly. Henry, I regret to say, did not believe you, did not believe even when he saw me with his own eyes. Therefore, I thought to remind him sharply and physically that, although he did not believe, that was no proof that you were untruthful or that I did not exist. I am sorry if I have angered you, but this is a lesson the young—and old too—must learn."

"Oh!" Georgina said, mollified and a little touched by his explanation. "But Joe, he won't believe now. He'll still think he had a nightmare."

"None the less, he will never forget," Joe said, "and he will be less sceptical in the future. Furthermore, Miss Carter, you will agree that it was high time to get you away, for already here it is daylight."

"Yes," Georgina agreed wearily. "You're quite right—it's after eight." She looked at him sharply. "Joe," she said, "I thought I had a dream about you when we were making the voyage out . . . I thought I saw you—saw myself—"

"Ah-h." Joe stopped her with a long sigh. "At last—" He broke off. Then he said: "Will you not speak of what you thought you dreamed, Miss Carter, and will you go now and have a hot bath, for you are chilled—and I will get your breakfast." There was a new note of authority in his voice, gentle but unmistakable.

"I will, Joe," Georgina answered sadly, for she was suddenly aware that he was no longer the Joe she had first known. The child-like quality was still there, but he was no longer a child—eager, a trifle irresponsible and under-developed. He was wearing his own costume—his own turban—it seemed in some way symbolical that he had not brought a new hat back with him from Canada. "I will," she repeated, looking at him intently and observing too that his face had in some subtle way changed—it was the same, but different—more clearly defined, and it was beautiful. Calm and compassionate . . . "and afterwards I must talk to you about—about—"

"I know," said Joe, quietly.

CHAPTER XXVI

SHE FINISHED her bath . . . dressed with care . . . for perhaps the talk with Joe would be . . . and she wanted him to remember. . . . She went in and had her breakfast; she would wait until after— wait until things were cleared away and straightened round before speaking to Joe. They could then settle down together in front of the fire and talk. She still felt tired and melancholy. The trip to see Henry had been such a fiasco—all her own silly fault, of course—that made it all the worse. Perhaps that was the reason for her depression. Superficially, yes—fundamentally, no.

Joe waited upon her attentively but silently. She felt that he probably guessed her thoughts—or was it because he, too, like everything else, had become remote and unrelated to her?

While he cleared away and washed up, she sat by the fire looking at the paper but not reading a word. She thought over what she would say to him. She would explain first . . . but what would she explain? Whatever she said, no matter how she phrased it, mightn't it sound as if it were merely an excuse to get rid of him? He was certainly aware of something of the sort—perhaps that accounted for his aloofness. And it wasn't true that she wanted to—she hated the thought that she might lose him—the flat would be empty and forlorn without him. So would she for that matter, for there was no use denying it, she had grown terribly fond of Joe—and because she was fond of him she must let him go if necessary. She'd done what little she could for him—and how paltry it seemed beside what he'd done for her. But in an odd way, that had nothing to do with thinking or feeling, she sensed that there were other events, other people who waited for him somewhere. Bigger events—bigger people— waiting and able to do more. Perhaps there would be someone with more intelligence, more imagination, for she realized quite clearly now that no matter what power, supernatural or otherwise, was given to one, the use of it was completely conditioned by the intelligence and imagination of the possessor.

She herself was deficient in both those qualities, she admitted regretfully—still she had taught Joe what she could—and perhaps that counted a little, although to be quite candid he had taught her a great deal too. In any event, she could say quite truthfully that no matter where Joe went no one could be more genuinely attached to him than she was—if that were any consolation.

She was startled out of these thoughts and the chair by the door bell ringing. Margaret! she thought—how awful—as she went to the door—but it wouldn't be Margaret this early, and unexpected.

She opened the front door. There stood Richard Taylor.

"Georgina dear!" he cried.

"Richard," Georgina said.

"I just chanced finding you in—how wonderful. . . ."

"Where on earth did you come from?"

"Straight from the airport."

It is doubtful if either of them really heard what the other said, for they spoke simultaneously.

"For goodness sake come in," Georgina said. "The surprise has bowled me over. Have you had any breakfast?" She led him into the living room, noting that he walked with a worse limp than before, and now used a stick.

"Yes, thank you, I have—but I could do with a cup of coffee if it's not too much trouble."

She sat him down in a chair and flew into the kitchen. Joe was there. "It's Major Taylor," she hissed at him. "Have we any coffee left over from breakfast?"

Joe smiled and nodded, his aloofness gone. "I knew he'd come," he hissed back. "Dear Miss Carter, I am indeed overjoyed."

"Don't be absurd," she admonished, and then added: "So am I . . . I think . . ."

He handed her a tray—on it were cups and the coffee pot. "I shall go away," he said.

"But not far," she urged. "Oh, Joe, don't go away, please . . . Just stay invisible . . . in the kitchen."

She went back into the living room. "Richard," she said, "this is one of the nicest surprises I've ever had. I was feeling quite gloomy before you turned up." She handed him a cup of coffee.

"Georgina," he said, taking the cup and setting it down on the table beside him. "What I'm going to say will probably surprise you even more, and there's no good my trying to dress it up. Perhaps I should have written you about it—but, well, I thought really it would be better if I saw you in person." He drew a deep breath. "Georgina," he said, "will you marry me?"

Georgina put her own cup down so suddenly that she cracked the saucer. Really this was very odd. There, sitting across from her, was Richard Taylor asking her to marry him at ten-thirty on a Sunday morning. The most extraordinary things seemed to happen in this ordinary living room. And a month, six weeks ago, if he'd asked her, she'd have answered: 'Yes, Richard'—just like that. Now—well, perhaps he was still a little delirious—perhaps that crack on the head! She asked him: "Richard dear, did you say what I thought you said?"

"I don't know what you thought, but I said, will you please marry me, Georgina," Richard answered firmly.

"Am I mad, or are you?" Georgina enquired, and realized that this was no thing to say in such circumstances.

"I'm not in the least mad," Richard told her. "In fact, I've never been saner—but if you accept me I think it may mean that you are."

"It will mean no such thing!" Georgina retorted indignantly.

Richard smiled broadly. "Then you will! Oh, Georgina, you're a darling. That's wonderful."

"But I haven't said I would!" Georgina spoke a little wildly. "Oh, Richard, I'm not hedging for the purpose of appearing coy— God forbid that I should be coy at my age—or any age for that matter—but I honestly don't know what to say. It's all so sudden."

"Sudden for you," he said, "but not for me. Georgina, this has been in my mind for a long time. From the evening we went to the theatre, in fact. I very nearly asked you then, but I thought I didn't stand a chance—you hardly knew me. . . ."

That's the second time he's hesitated, Georgina said to herself—the big idiot.

". . . Then when I went away," he continued, "I was ill. I was in an accident, but I'll tell you all about that later. It isn't important, it made my stiff leg stiffer, that's all—but what *is* important, Georgina, is that I was absolutely obsessed by the thought of you. I heard your name repeated and repeated out of the thin air—the very walls seemed to speak it . . . and once even—in my delirium—it seemed as if you stood beside my bed. . . ."

Georgina hoped that the blushing would be taken as a sign of embarrassment, not of guilt, for she was thinking: 'how awful of me—false pretences—I must tell him—I can't—yet in his delirium he *did* tell me . . . that he once . . .'

"I am not going to pretend, Georgina," Richard went on firmly, and she was grateful that he did not yet expect her to speak, "that I am passionately in love with you. Indeed, if that were the case, knowing myself as I do now, I should regard it as the worst possible sign. . . ."

Well, really, Georgina thought. Richard in his desire for an exact definition of his feelings was not displaying much thought for hers—what he wanted, obviously, was not a wife but a housekeeper. But she said noting, and in finishing his remarks he redeemed himself.

". . . it would be," he went on, "but a transient phase and so, suspect. But I am," and his voice took on a new note of intensity, "most deeply attached to you, Georgina . . . all these years, though you don't believe it, I've preserved a fidelity of memory which is really quite astonishing, when I think back on it. . . ."

Dear Richard, she thought, he was nothing if not honest and sincere, even though he appeared to be the most tactless man alive—it was really most endearing, this trait.

". . . but I love you, Georgina, quite quietly and dearly. More than that, I like you and admire you . . . I should have told you that right at the first," he smiled wryly. "I put the cart before the horse by just asking you to marry me out of a blue sky. But I do think and believe that I could make you happy—that—that we could be happy together. There isn't any more I can say," he finished pathetically.

Georgina gulped and was silent. Now she would have to answer him, and what would she say? No longer possessed by that strange and brief (thank God) madness which had made her believe that she was in love with him, she could see the situation quite clearly, Richard was a dear, and she was, she knew, extremely fond of him; they had certain things in common, certain memories fashioned a long time ago, but possibly stronger for that very fact. They were both lonely—it was true Richard had his work and his friends, and she the censorship and Margaret Mackenzie, but this wasn't enough. They both needed affection, a sense of belonging—the stability and continuity of a quiet emotional relationship. They were both 'getting on.' She did not need to marry him for economic reasons, so that fact wouldn't colour her decision.

On the negative side there was the enormous change this would make in her way of life—but hadn't that already started with the coming of Joe! There was the adjusting to be done to the external as well as the inner aspects of living. And more than this, was it enough to marry a man, to change one's whole life out of affection, respect and a need for being needed? No, she said, it was not enough, certainly not enough at the age of twenty-one—but at forty-seven! Surely those were the best and perhaps the only sensible reasons for marriage. She thought for a moment that all this careful weighing was desperately cold-blooded, or might be called cold-blooded and calculating by anyone who could read her thoughts. Yet she didn't in the least feel cold-blooded. She felt quite warm and happy. She knew her answer—had known it all along really—but long-formed habits of mind, common sense in fact, made her seek adequate reasons for this answer.

She looked at Richard; he was observing her very steadily.

"Well," he said.

"Well," she answered. "I will, Richard. I think . . . I think it will be very—er—nice being married to you."

Richard stood up and came limping over to her chair. He took both her hands in his. "Georgina dear," he said. "Thank you. Life is going to be very pleasant for both of us from now on. I wish I could tell you how happy I am that you've said yes—but I can't—I could probably write a leader about it for the *Tuskalee Gazette*— but I'd rather spend the rest of my life proving it to you."

"Dear Richard," Georgina said, standing up. "I do feel very awkward about this—I never was any good at explaining the way I feel about things."

"I understand," Richard said, dropping a kiss on her fore-head, "and you don't need to try. For we've such lots to talk about anyway. For example, when shall we get married? Frankly I think the sooner the better, though I don't want to rush you, for I have to return to America very shortly, possibly within a week—and I must arrange to get you there, too. Do you think you'll like America, Georgina?" he asked anxiously.

"I shall certainly try to . . . and I shall succeed," she said, "though quite truthfully, Richard, the idea terrifies me. What is more likely is that America won't like me—that's what worries me. I'm quiet, you know—I don't make friends very easily—I'm not the type of visiting Englishman or woman that America's got used to. I'm not in any way remarkable—in fact I'm just rather old-fashioned and conservative. And, oh Richard, what about Simon, won't he hate your marrying again?"

"America and you will get along famously together," Rich-ard assured her. "The real America isn't written in headlines you know—it's written in the everyday human activities as reported by the small town newspapers. America isn't New York, Boston, Chicago, San Francisco—any more than England is London, Birmingham, Manchester, Liverpool. These are only the facial features by which you recognize a country—a photograph in which you see eyes, nose, mouth and ears—and even these may be distorted by the camera angle. But the colour, the personality, the bones, the blood, the heart are found in the people, the good common, the 'not in any way remarkable' man or woman, to use your phrase, Georgina. Yes, you and America will like each other, despite your differences—and listen, Georgina, it's almost more important, in fact it is more important in the long run than that Churchill and Roosevelt should be blood brothers. . . ."

"Goodness," Georgina said, a trifle alarmed, "you make me sound like an ambassador."

"You are!" Richard said, a little pompously. "Everyone of us out of our own country is an ambassador, or should be. . . ."

"But Simon—" Georgina said.

"Oh, Simon!" Richard answered. "I'm sorry I forgot to answer that. I was too busy making a speech. You must curb that tendency in me, Georgina—it's so tiresome for everyone. But as for Simon . . . you needn't worry about him—he'll be delighted— he'll be even more delighted and I daresay relieved when he finds I've married you. Simon is a perfectly healthy, extroverted young man—you won't find any neurotic jealousy there, if that's what's worrying you. Though, poor Simon, he won't be there to welcome us home . . ."

"Poor Richard," Georgina said quietly—and thought of Robert. She must tell Richard the news of Robert—but that could wait.

"Do you think you could marry me on Thursday?" Richard asked suddenly. "I've wanted to say that before, but I didn't have the nerve."

"This Thursday?"

"Yes, I know it's an awful rush, but chances are that I have to leave by next Sunday, and it takes three days to get a licence—and don't laugh, Georgina, but like every member of the American Army I shall have to get permission to marry—of course, it won't take a minute in my case."

Georgina hardly heard this at all—all she was conscious of was the word 'Thursday.' "But—but—" she said, "my job . . . my clothes . . . the flat . . ." and to herself—Joe—yes, Joe—that was the most important consideration of all—the very thought of him made her feel guilty and responsible. She really must tell Richard about Joe—she'd often wanted to; in fact, at one time she'd determined to, given the chance!—and he wouldn't be so absurd about it as Henry. Yes, she must confess about Joe—she'd feel better about it, and although such a confession would include her visit to Africa, that didn't matter now. In fact, it would only serve to show Richard that she *did* care for him. And Richard would be able to give her some *very* useful advice on Joe.

She disengaged her hand from his, sat down and drew a deep breath. "Richard," she said, "there's something I want to tell you first."

"Well, fire away, my dear."

"It's about—about—" Now that she had started it all sounded simply ridiculous. "I don't know how to explain it," she said helplessly. "How or where to begin—"

"My dear, don't bother if it troubles you," Richard told her kindly.

"Oh, it doesn't trouble me particularly . . . it's the beginning that's going to sound so odd . . . but I do want you to know about it . . . I do want to tell you about Joe . . . and ask your advice."

"Joe!" he exclaimed, sitting down heavily on the settee.

"Yes, Joe . . . my—"

"Don't," he interrupted. "No, Georgina dear, don't tell me. I don't want to pry into your affairs—they are your business—they belong to you—"

"But," she cried desperately. "You don't understand. It's not private . . . I mean I've kept it quiet deliberately . . . because I had to . . . but if it hadn't been for Joe I'd never have met you again."

"Nonsense, Georgina," Richard said warmly. "I should have looked you up. You can depend on that."

That, Georgina thought privately, was not strictly true. Feeling the way he did now about her he might have. But feeling the way he had then . . . he might not have done so.

"You see," Georgina went on pursuing her line of thought, "Joe took me to Brighton that week-end, or I'd never have been

there." The minute the words were out of her mouth she realized how they must sound to Richard—sheer innocence had
given them a most equivocal meaning. She blushed; really she
was a hopeless idiot. No matter how she tried to explain Joe she
managed to give the wrong impression. "I mean that—"

What she had been going to say was interrupted by Richard. "Georgina," he broke in gently, "I don't want to know about
your past, my dear—no matter how—er—recent it may be. All
I'm concerned about is your future—our future. God knows
there are pages in my past which I . . . well, I can't honestly
say I regret them—but the point is they're finished—done. You
wouldn't want to question me about them—and I wouldn't
want you to. The same applies to you, Georgina—the past is
personal—and private."

She said nothing. What could she say? If she persisted—if
she finally explained, he might feel he had to offer some frag-
ment of his own past in return. And obviously he wanted to
avoid that. Furthermore, and this was far more important, when
he realized how he had misunderstood and misjudged her and
how, because of this, he had been led into making a small speech
on understanding and tolerance, he really would feel a most
awful fool. Even though she disliked being put in an equivocal
position, it didn't really matter. In a way Georgina was a little
surprised that Richard should think what he obviously did think
about her. Yet she wasn't in the least indignant about it—yet
she felt it was terribly unfair to Joe. Poor old Joe—what *was* to
become of him?

Some day, perhaps, when they'd settled down, she'd be able
to tell Richard the whole story. But not now. Even summoning Joe from wherever he was hiding—probably in the broom
cupboard—would do no good. Richard would find it all too difficult to believe. Might even think it some rather horrid trick—a
sort of Pepper's ghost brought up-to-date. And anyway she
didn't want him to think he was marrying either a mad woman
or a practical joker—far, far better that he should think her—
well, 'light' was hardly the word. No, he had so obviously and
generously forgiven her her unperformed sin that she'd better

leave it at that for the moment anyway. And honestly, now that she thought his attitude over, it really was tolerant of him—showed a magnanimous nature. A nature often expected but seldom found in men of his generation and age.

Richard broke the rather awkward silence that had fallen upon them. "You silly creature," he said, "you needn't think you can escape me now. Even if you confessed to being a veritable Messalina, I shouldn't believe it—and it wouldn't make any difference."

This, Georgina thought, was carrying tolerance too far! But it was obviously only a rather unfortunate figure of speech, and was meant most kindly. She smiled. "It's not as bad as that," she assured him, "and what you've been thinking is, well—a little wide of the mark. But, Richard, to go back. . . . About marrying you on Thursday . . . there are some things—one thing in particular I must settle before I can answer you—"

"There must be any number of things," he said. "If I can be of any help."

"Oh, you can help about a lot of things, but not about—"

He raised his eyebrows. "I quite understand," he said.

Georgina laughed. "No you don't," she said. "You don't understand in the least. I'm sorry to make such a mystery about it, but one day I shall explain fully and in detail."

He stood up. "Listen," he said, ignoring the subject. "Will you dine with me to-night at my hotel? I'll leave you now, because I'm quite sure you'd like to be alone—to—er—to get used to the idea of marrying me."

Dear Richard was so kind—and so obvious. She stood up too and walked to the door with him. "I'd love to dine with you," she said—and added impulsively: "Richard, you are a dear, good, silly thing."

He picked up his hat and coat and turned and kissed her. "I'll ring you later on," he promised. "Good-bye, my dear."

When he was safely gone she summoned Joe.

He came immediately. "Dear Joe," she began, "sit down. There's something I want to tell you." Really, what a confessional morning she was having.

Joe smiled. "There is no need to tell me—for I know. You and Major Taylor will be married at last! And I am glad and happy that this is so. Yet did I not tell you it would come to pass?"

"You did," she laughed, "and you did your best to implement it, though I restricted you there. But how did you know? You didn't—" She was ashamed of this thought and stopped short.

"No, I did not listen," Joe said. "But I know it to be so. Your face, dear Miss Carter, speaks to me of what is in your heart. It is curious, but lately I find I know things without knowing how I know them. It is as if I were being given some strange new power—an insight, perhaps—hitherto denied me."

"Oh, Joe," Georgina said. "I *am* glad—in a way. I can't explain how, I know it means that your past is . . . well, it's a sign of development I think. And that's really what I want to talk to you about. Please don't think that what I'm going to say has anything to do with the fact that I'm going to marry Richard, because it hasn't. Indeed, I've been trying to find the courage to speak about it for weeks."

"Dear Miss Carter," Joe said, "of that, too, I am aware."

"Then," Georgina said, with tears in her eyes. "Then you know that—I think—I feel—"

"That I have outgrown your usefulness. Yes, I know," Joe said, "and because of this you are worried as to my future. But, Miss Carter, before we go on, may I tell you something?"

"Yes Joe, of course."

"I have lived," Joe said, "not even I know how long. And in all that time no one has ever been so kind, so really good to me as you have. Not, I admit, in those early days before disaster befell me, that I gave anyone an opportunity to treat me well. But you, Miss Carter, have treated me as a friend, with affection and understanding. Even in the first days of our acquaintance-ship you let me bear your name, and I know that in those days I was to you a worry, a nuisance, nay, even a danger. Yet you never once were harsh to me. All this indeed I understand now and appreciate."

"Joe," Georgina answered, and a perfect little cascade of tears bounced down her cheeks—for to-day, so far, had been one packed with emotional disturbances of one kind and another. "That isn't true at all. I often scolded you, and didn't understand you, and was impatient and irritable. In fact, many times I've reproached myself with not being more—more—"

"Not a word," Joe interrupted, "will I hear you say against yourself, Miss Carter, for no matter what you did you did out of kindness and affection and a desire that I should learn how to live in this strange world—all the more remarkable, too, when I consider that in those early days you feared me—feared yourself. To go on being kind when one is afraid! That is indeed a test—a—"

"Don't, Joe," Georgina stopped him, "it embarrasses me. Besides, you have been more than good to me—and quite unsuspecting you taught me many things—you—you freed me—just as I freed you."

But Joe did not heed her remark. "I was still unreformed," he went on, "when you released me. It is true I had repented, but had I fallen into other hands it would have been easy for me to sink back—you have given me my future, for it was you who gave me the strength and knowledge to meet my test on that strange journey to—"

"Nonsense, Joe!" Georgina said firmly. "You told me yourself that you'd resolved to be good . . . besides, what about predestination?"

"You were undoubtedly predestined to find me," he told her, "but not necessarily to treat me kindly. No, you of your own free will helped me to develop and strengthen my resolution. And now—"

"And now," Georgina said, "you have outgrown me, Joe. You see, I know that as well as you do."

An unchecked tear rolled down Joe's cheek. "I can never outgrow your kindness," he said, "but—"

"The dream!" she cried. "Oh, Joe—I know it wasn't a dream, though I am forced to call it that. Up there in the sunlight—up there close to the stars. . . . Oh no, I know, Joe, the time has come. I've felt it coming for many weeks now. If I had anything to teach you, whatever it was, you have learned it. The time has come for you to learn something else—something better."

Joe bowed his head. "I am still your slave," he said.

"You have never been my slave, Joe—never! You have been my companion and my friend. It is true that you have waited on me and done everything for me—but not as a slave or a servant. Don't you see, Joe, don't you understand? I hold you in no bonds. You are free—free as air!"

"Ah! Miss Carter," he cried, "you release me—and I do not in my heart want to go. Yet it is written that I must."

"I don't want you to go either," Georgina's voice broke. "I shall miss you terribly, Joe."

"And I you—though you will have Major Taylor," Joe answered, his calm quite shattered so that he had to dry his eyes. "But as I must go, it is better to go quickly. So I will tell you the words which are needful for you to say to release me."

Georgina stopped crying. "Do you mean to say I've been holding you here in some sort of spell, because you didn't tell me how to free you? Oh, Joe—it's too absurd! You know I'd have let you go at once."

"I do know that, Miss Carter," he said, "but it was part of my punishment that I should know and not be able to tell you until the right time came. So do you not reproach yourself."

"Tell me them, now. Tell me them quickly," she urged, "for I can't bear it that you should be my slave. I didn't really realize that you were, you know. I thought it was just your exaggerated way of speaking."

Joe smiled. "It was as well that that should be so," he said. "But before I tell you, there is another thing I want you to know. I want you to know that should you ever need me, I will come to you instantly. All you must do is to say this word"—he bent over and whispered something in her ear.

She listened intently.

"You know it?" he said.

She nodded.

"And you will not forget?"

"I shall never forget, dear Joe, any more than I shall ever forget you."

"And you will use it if you are ever in desperate case and need me?"

"I promise—and I am glad and comforted," she told him. "And now, Joe, you must tell me what it is I have to say to you to release you."

He spoke to her very quietly. He repeated several times the words, so that she should know them and not hesitate. Then he took her hands and said: "Farewell, my friend. You may release me now from my bondage."

She hesitated a moment. Then she stood on tiptoe and kissed his cheek. "Good-bye, my very dear friend," she said.

Then she stood a little apart from him and repeated what he had told her. "Abu Shiháb," she said. "Go in peace. By the lesson you have learned in your captivity you are released now and forever from all bondage to mankind, for it was your hatred which made you a slave. And only by hatred can you be enslaved again."

And before her eyes he dissolved away into a mist. In a breath he was gone.

"Joe!" she cried, unable to believe it or bear it.

But there was no answer, and she was conscious that the room had a new, empty feeling.

The emptiness was shattered by the shrilling of the telephone.

"Hello," she said bleakly into the mouthpiece.

"Richard here, Georgina," his voice was warm and human. "I just wanted to make sure I wasn't dreaming. You *did* say you'd marry me?"

"I did," she assured him.

"Oh, Georgina, you angel—why darling—what's the matter? You're crying."

"Of course I am," Georgina said. "I don't see why that should surprise you. After all, I've never been married before—particularly on a Thursday."

THE END

FURROWED MIDDLEBROW

Printed in Great Britain
by Amazon

46192284R00126